Virtue and Vanity

The continuing story of *Desire and Duty*

By: Ted and Marilyn Bader

©Copyright 2000 by Revive Publishing
1790 Dudley Street
Denver, Colorado USA 80215
Voice/Fax: 800-541-0558 (US/Canada)
From outside USA: 303-462-0558

Authors: Ted and Marilyn Bader

Library of Congress Card Number: 00-192347

ISBN: 0-9654299-4-6

First Edition
10 9 8 7 6 5 4 3 2 1

No part of this book may be reproduced, stored in a retrieval system,
or transmitted, in any form or means, electronic, mechanical,
photocopying, microfilming, recording or otherwise, without
written permission from the publisher.

About the Authors:

Dr.. Ted Bader specializes in liver and digestive disease. His medical textbook on viral hepatitis has entered its third edition. His wife, Marilyn, is a freelance writer and computer consultant. They are both members of the Jane Austen Society of North America.

About the Cover:

"La lecture" by Pierre Auguste Renoir. This nineteenth century painting is on display at the Louvre, Paris, France. The picture suggests the Bingley sisters, Laura on the left and Sarah on the right.

Foreword

Virtue and Vanity is written as a self-contained story. However, readers may also enjoy its predecessor, *Desire and Duty* which tells an earlier story about the main characters.

We have endeavored to present historical possibilities. Readers of our last book enjoyed historical notes and we have appended another set at the end of this volume.

All keywords were checked against the unabridged *Oxford English Dictionary* to verify their use in 1830.

We endeavor to answer all comments about this book. Please write to us in care of the publisher.

Related books of interest by Revive Publishing are listed on the last page.

Enjoy!

Ted and Marilyn Bader

Chapter One

Georgiana grasped her husband's arm more tightly than usual as they slowly descended the carpeted staircase of the British Embassy in Paris. Thomas paused for a moment and placed his hand over hers, "What can I do to make this reception easier for you?" he asked with concern.

She looked up at her beloved, the newly appointed British Ambassador. "Since I became comfortable welcoming visitors to Staley Hall, I hoped I had out grown my fears." She drew in a deep breath, "We talked about this before you accepted the position of ambassador, and I still feel this is what we were meant to do. Just knowing that you understand my shyness is a comfort." With a shaky breath she raised her chin a bit, "I shall be fine, dear husband."

"I am so proud to have you as my wife. I pray that you will soon feel as secure and confident here as you did at home in Derbyshire." He leaned to whisper in her ear, "If you feel the need to escape the crowd, just signal me and I will escort you to the garden."

Georgiana smiled. "I believe I shall always feel secure if you are nearby."

Thomas kissed her briefly and they continued their descent.

"Thomas, dear, I hope the Algerian matter has not strained your relationship with General D'arbley."

"I do not know. The French are obstinate about making Algiers into a colony after punishing the pirates and releasing the Christian slaves. . . . This despite their initial promise to evacuate after achieving their goals."

At the bottom of the stairs, they moved to the front door to help start a reception line. Soon others joined them to form the reception line. As Georgiana greeted guests, she concentrated on making them feel welcome and worried less about what they thought of her.

"Lady Staley, it is good to finally meet you," said a portly, yet elegantly dressed French woman as Georgiana greeted her. "Your husband told us so much about you when he lived here as a young man. It is a delight to see he did not exaggerate your beauty, nor your tall and elegant splendor."

Georgiana felt her cheeks blush, but kept her voice steady, "Thank you, Madame Duval. I am afraid Thomas has said little about his prior stay in France."

"Pshaw, why should he think of his friends here when he has such a lovely wife. Most of his friends were soldiers or old folks like myself." Her eyes darted to the front entry where Madame Lamballe was being announced. Arching her eyebrows she whispered, "I am surprised to see she was invited. You are indeed gracious to include her after the coquetry she used on Sir Thomas."

Seeing a quick flash of confusion on Georgiana's face, Madame Duval rushed on, "Oh my, I see you did not know about that either." Patting Georgiana's shoulder sympathetically, she whispered, "I will tell you all about the affair later."

"Indeed, I look forward to getting acquainted with all of our guests," Georgiana carefully replied as she turned to direct the matron through the reception line. "Madame Duval, this is my niece, Miss Sarah Bingley. She is staying with us at the embassy."

Sarah curtsied. After a few words of advice about the highlights of Paris, Madame Duval moved on.

Turning toward her aunt, Sarah saw Madame Lamballe progressing down the line to Lady Staley. With a worried look, Georgiana squeezed Sarah's arm and whispered, "Such beauty. I wonder why Sir Thomas never mentioned her?"

Sarah thought it best to feign a smile, to imitate her aunt's expression, as Madame Lamballe neared.

Madame Lamballe curtsied to Lady Staley and said, *"Bon jour, Madame*. It is easy to see your attractive charm which I have heard so much about. My defeat can now be accepted gracefully."

Lady Staley curtsied and tried to act as though she knew to what her Parisian visitor was referring.

Sarah's attention was interrupted by General D'arbley, the Minister of Foreign Affairs for France, who moved to the head of line next to Sir Thomas and Lady Staley.

Virtue and Vanity

General D'arbley leaned over and whispered in Sir Thomas' ear for an extended time. The English ambassador looked chagrined and said out loud, "I am glad the escapade can finally be revealed."

Sarah intervened to greet the next guest as Georgiana's attention was abruptly turned to Sir Thomas. This was the first time she had seen her aunt lose composure. It was difficult for Sarah to imagine Georgiana as extremely shy, but her mother, Jane Bingley, told her it had been so in years past.

Sarah doubted that any unfavorable exposé would ever happen to the Staleys since they were so devoted to each other. Nonetheless, Lady Staley's curiosity was beginning to affect her.

The grand room was filled with elegant ladies and gentlemen. A sharply dressed British soldier moved to the end of the line and announced that dinner was ready. The two dozen guests filed into the embassy dining room. All five of the three tiered chandeliers were aglow. Sarah had never seen so much light. The reflections off the numerous polished brass fixtures and white walls trimmed in gold dazzled Sarah.

The guests stood before their chairs at the long rectangular table. General D'arbley stood at one end and Sir Thomas at the other with Georgiana and Sarah next to the English Ambassador. The party was seated.

Sarah could rarely make it through the seven courses offered. Early on, she watched Lady Staley take small portions so as to stay involved with each course. The pheasant, the assorted cheese, and the cake were impressive to her palate.

Finally, the wine was brought and General D'arbley stood and spoke in excellent English, "Tonight, I wish to toast not only the English Ambassador, but my good friend, Sir Thomas Staley. This dedication may be long, so hold your glasses, but it can now be told of his service to me."

"Fifteen years ago, during his exile in France, Sir Thomas volunteered to travel through the territory of our political enemies with documents for our comrades in Normandy."

"Unfortunately, he was discovered and arrested. A--how do you say--kangaroo court sentenced him to the guillotine. For reasons still unclear to me, he was released and allowed to return to

Lyon. For such gallantry I shall always be indebted. I tell you this story so you can all understand why I hold him in such high esteem."

The assembled group toasted Sir Thomas, put their glasses down, and clapped their hands while some raised their voices and cried, "Speech."

As Sir Thomas stood, Sarah saw Lady Staley gaze at her husband with glistening eyes. He then spoke in perfect French, "Our admiration is mutual. General D'arbley has done much to restore Anglo-French relations since Waterloo." Sir Thomas paused for a moment and continued, "The only part about my capture that greatly concerned me, besides the guillotine, was the detection of my disguise. I asked my captors how my French had given me away and they assured me it had nothing to do with my use of the language. Rather, I suffered discovery because one of the partisans recognized me from the time of my convalescence in the local hospital."

Finishing his response, Sir Thomas moved to pull Lady Staley's seat away from the table. He took her hand and announced, "Now, it is time for the ball."

The Staleys moved to form the head of the line as several other couples joined behind them in the smooth, rhythmic dance. Sarah stood and moved towards the ballroom. Madame Duval brought her plump frame over to Sarah and smiled, "I see no unattached men here to dance with a pretty girl such as you."

"No, madam."

"I suppose it is impolite, but an old busybody such as myself is curious. . . why is it that you brush your hair so far forward on the left side of your face? Are you trying to start a new fashion trend?"

"Not at all." Sarah paused and studied the older woman for a moment. "If you will keep this to yourself. . . ."

"I promise," Madame Duval quickly rejoined.

Sarah was not sure the lady would be able to keep any kind of secret. . . but, it mattered little. Keeping her voice steady, trying to sound as if it were of no real consequence to her, Sarah answered, "It is merely to cover the scar on my left temple from a childhood illness."

Virtue and Vanity

"I daresay that makes perfect sense." Smiling and patting Sarah's hand she continued, "I find you most unaffected. We must become better acquainted. Please visit me in my lodgings sometime. If there is anything I can do while you are in Paris, let me know." Glancing beyond Sarah's shoulder, she added, "Here comes your aunt." She curtsied, "Lady Staley."

"Madame."

Quickly glancing about, she rushed on, "Let me tell both of you now what I so clumsily mentioned earlier." She lowered her voice, "Do you see Madame Lamballe sitting across the way?"

Georgiana and Sarah glanced in the direction.

"She was, and perhaps still is, one of the most beautiful women in Southern France. Fifteen years ago she set her sights on Mr. Thomas Staley." Chuckling she added, "She tried every type of refined coquetry known to Parisian debutantes without an inch of success in fixing Mr. Staley upon her. Rumor had it his heart was centered on a beautiful woman in England. Now that I have met you, it is easy to understand his loyalty."

Sarah observed Lady Staley's face blush slightly and soften as she finished looking at her formerly unknown rival and turned her attention to Sir Thomas talking with a group of men.

She said softly, "He never told me his faithfulness to me was so sorely tried."

Sarah left the ball early and retired upstairs to the Staley's private quarters. She sat reading in the small anteroom off the parlor. She heard Sir Thomas and Lady Staley come into the parlor and dismiss their servants. After a quiet moment, she heard them kiss.

Then Georgiana softly said, "I never knew you were so tempted in your loyalty while my family slandered you."

"You forget, I knew I was innocent and, therefore, had hope of one day returning to claim you. Besides, I have always loved only you." A few moments of quiet followed.

An atmosphere of tenderness floated into the anteroom. Sarah began to feel guilty about eavesdropping and thought she should make her presence known. She closed her book with more noise than necessary and stood, moving to enter the parlor. There she saw Sir Thomas and Lady Staley sitting and embracing each other.

Their embrace loosened and Sir Thomas turned to say, "Come in Miss Sarah. We knew you were there all the time, so you should not feel guilty."

"I hope to inspire the same kind of loyalty in my future husband. If you will excuse me, I will retire."

Sir Thomas stood, "You need not go yet. Please, be seated."

After Sarah sat down, Georgiana said, "Thomas, I never knew your life was in danger. I do recall having a heavy burden for you after we heard you might have been lost at sea. I do not believe I ever prayed so hard for you as I did at that time."

"When was that?"

"If, I can remember correctly, it was in mid-spring, fifteen years ago."

Sir Thomas sprang to his feet and began pacing in the room. . ."Indeed, that was the time I was imprisoned in Normandy. When the guard released me, he said it was providential, since he had never seen a prisoner like myself released. . . Undoubtedly, my lovely Georgiana, your prayers helped to save my life." Sir Thomas sat down by his wife and took her hand. After a few moments, he turned back to Sarah and inquired, "I see you were talking with Madame Duval. What do you know about her?"

"Only what she tells me, sir."

"She happens to be the cousin of General D'arbley. She is a humorous old woman and good to have around. You can trust her, but watch out. . . ."

"For what?" Sarah gasped.

"She is a matchmaker. Why, in no time, she will have you fixed up with some French count and you will fly away from us."

"I doubt that will happen," Sarah replied with feigned indignity.

Chapter Two

"Is Miss Sarah our governess?" asked the dark haired, six year old Anna Staley during breakfast the next morning.

"Why do you ask?" replied her mother, Georgiana.

Anna's twelve year old brother, Edgar, replied in big brother fashion, "Of course she is our governess, silly. She gives us our lessons and watches over us."

Georgiana silenced Edgar with a glance and then explained, "The reason we prefer to call her our niece, or for you to refer to her as cousin, is that it gives her the higher social status she deserves. For example, we could not have brought our governess to the ball last night, but we could easily bring our niece. Of course, she is actually the niece of my brother, but we give her that appellation to help her feel a part of our family."

They continued eating in pleasant silence for awhile. Edgar broke the quietness by asking the three adults, "Tell me about the ball. Did the officers wear their swords? Did you hear any exciting war stories?"

Sarah smiled at her young charge, "General D'arbley did tell us about your father's heroism during the war."

The young man's eyes grew large as his gaze turned to his father, "Why did you never tell me about it, Father?"

"Your father is quite reluctant to talk of himself as the hero."

Sir Thomas, with a serious expression, said, "I think now that you are almost a man, perhaps we can discuss what war is really like." With a wink he added, "In my office, when the ladies are not present."

Sarah said, "And I shall tell you all that the General related last night, lest your father downplays his role too much."

Anna bounced on her seat, "Miss Sarah, will you tell me about the fine gowns everyone wore last night? And, did you dance with any handsome gentlemen?"

"I shall be delighted to describe it all to you. . . perhaps before our rest time this afternoon?"

The little girl clapped her hands softly, "Mother, when Sarah tells me a story. . . it seems so real."

"You are very fortunate to have a cousin who is so gifted with words," Georgiana replied. "Now, you and Edgar need to settle down a bit. The servants will be wondering what kind of raucous activity we are up to. While I have never liked the custom of children eating separately from the family, and I enjoy your enthusiasm, we must all remember that it is impolite and not good for digestion to be too boisterous at mealtime."

"Yes, Mother," the twosome replied in unison. While both children were quiet for the remainder of the meal, their eyes reflected their eager anticipation of the secrets to be shared with them later in the day.

Near the end of the meal, a servant entered with envelopes on a tray and said, "Letters for Miss Bingley and Lady Staley."

As Sarah opened her letter, she mumbled, "It has been forwarded from Staley Hall from a publisher in London." She read it without expression until she smiled and cried, "A poem of mine has been accepted for publication."

She stood and went over to hug a smiling Sir Thomas and Lady Georgiana, still seated at the table. "Thank you both for helping me finish the poem."

Georgiana replied, "The creativity is yours, we made only minor suggestions."

Sir Thomas asked, "Did they pay anything for it?"

"Publishing it is reward enough. . . do you think they might have paid me something as well?" she asked, looking bewildered. She examined the letter further. "It asks, "Since you no longer reside at Staley Hall, please inform us where we may forward a check for two guineas.' Can you believe it?" Sarah exclaimed. "They are going to pay me for doing something I delight in doing."

"We have always known we had an authoress in our society," Thomas smiled. "Even Anna recognizes your special talent with words. Now it has been made official."

Georgiana added, "Indeed, I am sure this will be the first of

Virtue and Vanity

many publication notices for you. Are you working on something now?"

"I have not been very diligent with my writing during our two months in Paris, but I have written a few poems and," with a look of embarrassment she added, "I have made some notes of ideas I have for a novel." She looked at Sir Thomas, "I am sure you think novels are a waste of time. . . ."

"Indeed, not," he replied. "Stories that are thought-provoking, exemplify triumph of right over wrong, and show us proper moral and social behavior are sorely needed in our society."

"I am not sure my simple story would do all that, but it will give me an admirable goal."

Georgiana added, "With your sweet spirit and positive outlook on life, I do not think your novel could be anything less than what Sir Thomas has described."

Sarah blushed and answered softly, "Thank you for the compliment. I will certainly let you read my writing before I send it off for a publisher to look at. I do not want to include anything that would reflect on you in an unfavorable light; but, I find so many things about high society, such as those at the ball, amusing and contradictory that I would like to include a few of those things. So many people think life would be perfect if they were able to move in a higher social circle. . . I would like to point out some of the good and bad things about it."

Thomas laughed, "Indeed. I am glad you see beyond the polished facade these people present. Just be careful not to make your characters too close to any real person. . . of course, few arrogant, pompous fools would recognize a description of themselves."

An envelope dropped to the floor. Georgiana picked it up and said, "I was so excited to hear your good news, Sarah, that I forgot about my letter." The family chatted amiably while Georgiana perused her correspondence. When she completed reading, she looked up and said, "This is from my dear sister-in-law at Pemberley, Elizabeth Darcy. It appears her children will be here in a few days for a visit. Andrew and John will be participating in a fencing tournament and Maria insisted on coming along to visit us."

Sarah was delighted to hear that her cousin Maria, who was her own age, was coming to visit. Maria had grown into a graceful, lovely young woman who was an easy conversationalist; though, she seemed to talk incessantly about the opposite sex. Maria would help divert Sarah's attention from that of the fraternal twin Darcy brothers, who were two years older than herself. John's dark blond hair, muscular build and outgoing manner made a favorable impression on everyone. John seemed to have inherited all the liveliness of his mother, while the dark-haired Andrew reflected the quiet moodiness of his father.

That night in her own bedroom, Sarah once again explored her mixed feelings towards Andrew and John.

John tended not to pay much attention to her since she was quiet and studious. She enjoyed the animated atmosphere he brought, but felt as an onlooker when he entered the room. John was the type of man she wished a brother, if one had been born, would have been like.

Andrew, on the other hand, always evoked mixed feelings in her. At one time, she had very strong affection for him. Her mind returned to that fateful event eight years earlier.

Chapter Three

"What are you looking for?" the twelve year old Sarah Bingley asked as she ran up to sit by the fourteen year old Andrew Darcy. He was sitting on the bank of the Derwent river, not too far from the bridge to Pemberley. The spring day was bright, with birds singing nearby.

Andrew turned the botanical atlas towards her and pointed to a purple-flowered plant. "I am still looking for a foxglove for my collection. Some doctors use it as medicine."

"May I help you look for it?" Sarah asked.

"Why. . . yes." He studied her for a moment before adding, "If you sincerely wish to help, I would enjoy the company. The other children think it silly to be collecting plants," Andrew looked at her seriously, "but to me they are botanical specimens."

She had heard the other children belittling Andrew on several occasions, but to her it was fascinating that he was so interested in, and knew so much about, beautiful plants. She smiled. "I think I may have seen that flower on the other side of the bridge," Sarah said as she stood and raced away to see if her memory was correct. Moments later, Sarah returned triumphantly with the a delicately colored purple blossom.

Andrew stood and said, "A foxglove! I really appreciate your help. You are not like the other girls."

Sarah beamed. At that moment, Andrew began to be special in her eyes.

After studying the atlas together to verify the new discovery, Andrew said, "Would you like to see the rest of my collection of flora and fauna?"

"Yes," she replied.

They turned and walked across the stone arched bridge back to Pemberley. Her fourteen year old sister, Laura, was standing on the bridge. She turned to watch them--Andrew carrying his atlas and Sarah holding the flower like a prized possession.

Laura said, "Do not tell me you are helping Andrew with his beastly collections. That is not very ladylike, Sarah."

Sarah tried not to cringe from her older sister's comment. She considered Laura much more beautiful than herself and difficult to disagree with.

Andrew said to Sarah, as they passed Laura on the bridge, "Don't pay attention to your sister. She does not understand our secret." Sarah was not sure what their secret was, but it made for a great diversion to act as though she and Andrew shared a mysterious confidence.

As they climbed the grand semicircular staircase inside Pemberley, they could hear the complaining voice of a maid, "Mrs. Reynolds, must I clean Master Andrew's museum? He has bugs and plants and only God knows what. I never know what to throw out or to clean."

"Just do your best. . . I understand his room will never be perfect," replied Mrs. Reynolds, the housekeeper.

Andrew smiled widely as he and Sarah trooped by the two women and entered Andrew's "museum." The ten foot by twelve foot room was lined on one side with shelves filled with all sorts of bottles containing biological specimens. Across from the shelves, several glass-encased collections of butterflies and flowers hung on the wall.

Sarah stood looking at the flowers on the wall as Andrew put the foxglove away. "Andrew, the flowers are quite pretty."

"The two large collections on top were done by my grandfather, Mr. Darcy. Unfortunately, he died many years before I was born. The smaller collection closest to us is my first display."

Sarah spent a pleasant afternoon while Andrew showed her his treasures. She helped identify some of the flowers on the wall as they went through the pages of the atlas. As they were called to supper, she realized this room was a special place for Andrew. She felt she understood something about him that no one else did.

The next day, Laura, Sarah and the Darcy twins were near the bridge when Laura proposed, "We need to have a make believe wedding."

John was on the verge of dashing away when Laura caught his arm and said, "John, you will play the minister." Laura marched

Virtue and Vanity

him to the front pillar of the bridge. She then pulled a puzzled Andrew next to her and said, "Now, John, say the words to. . . ."

Laura was interrupted as the two boys bolted away, leaving Laura and Sarah standing alone, looking after them. Laura spoke her thoughts out loud. "Those boys seem skittish about getting married. I wonder why they are so reluctant."

Sarah, sensing a unique feeling she would later come to understand as jealousy, said, "Why do you want to scare Andrew by practicing a marriage ceremony with him?"

"Look, little sister, whether Andrew wants me or not, the older sister must marry the older brother. Having a pretend wedding might help get his thoughts flowing in the right direction."

Stammering, Sarah asked, "What if Andrew does not love you?"

"Boys are so foolish, they do not know what is destined for them," Laura sighed and continued, "but, it is only a matter of time before he succumbs to my beauty and charm."

Sarah found it difficult to controvert her older sister and turned away from Laura in disgust. Laura ran to her side and said, "Between us, Andrew is mine. I want the grand status of the Darcys."

Sarah burst into tears and ran away.

The following day, the Darcy and Bingley children walked stealthily into the parlor of Pemberley, where their parents were sitting engaged in lively conversation. Andrew, the elected spokesman, approached Mr. Darcy and asked, "Father, may we go to the fair at Buxton?"

"Who is going to take you?"

"Good old Reynolds has offered to take us in the carriage."

Mr. Darcy looked at the well-dressed, grandfatherly servant who, with his wife Mrs. Reynolds, had served at Pemberley since before his own birth. He recalled some of the pleasant diversions the faithful servant had provided for him as a child and the watchful, protective eye he always felt when in Mr. Reynold's presence. He knew his children would be well-cared for and kept from harm during the excursion. So, he answered, "If I refuse permission, I shall never hear the end of it from your lively mother. However, I cannot speak for the Bingleys."

The entire room turned to look at Charles and Jane Bingley.

Charles gave a look of deference to his wife. Jane said, "I see no problem in Laura going, but Sarah must not go."

The extreme delicacy of Sarah's constitution had hitherto deferred Mrs. Bingley from having her inoculated against smallpox. Sarah had been scrupulously kept from all miscellaneous exposure in the neighborhood. Now, as her child's weakness was promising to change into health and strength, Mrs. Bingley planned for the inoculation in a few weeks.

Sarah began to cry very quietly and ran forward to place her head in her mother's lap.

Andrew approached and said, with gentle pleading, "Aunt Jane, it will be a sore disappointment for Sarah if she cannot come with us. Could she join us if she stays in the carriage?"

Looking up hopefully, Sarah softly added, "Oh, please mother. Even from the carriage I may see the sights and hear the delightful sounds. It will be a wonderful diversion for me."

For a few moments, the beautiful face of Jane Bingley showed a struggle, then her amiable spirit quickly decided in favor of her younger child, a girl who possessed a spirit so like her own. "How can I say no to you, my love," Mrs. Bingley said as Sarah jumped up and hugged her tightly.

Elizabeth looked at Mr. Reynolds, as he kept his respectful silence behind the children. "Mr. Reynolds, you may take all the children, but Sarah is to stay in the carriage at all times."

"I understand, ma'am."

The carriage was called for and took off with its passengers, who were delighting in the bright spring morning. As the fair was approached, they passed an occasional colorful booth.

During the ride, John exclaimed, "I shall want to see the jugglers most of all. How about you, Andrew?"

"I have heard they might have a lion or tiger. I have never seen a real lion before."

"Boys, boys, boys," cried Laura in a condescending tone, "I shall want to see the beautiful dresses of the actresses on stage."

Sarah remained quiet, with a resigned but hopeful look on her face. When the booths became more numerous, Laura cried, "Oh, please, let us stop here!"

Mr. Reynolds told the driver to stop. The Darcy children

Virtue and Vanity

and Laura clambered out the door and raced off, leaving Sarah and Mr. Reynolds watching them from the door of the coach.

Sarah said meekly, "I cannot see where the others went." She then sat back with a despondent look.

Mr. Reynolds observed her with compassion and then moved over to the carriage door and said, "Very little activity is occurring here." He poked his head out the door and ordered, "Driver, move ahead to any booth selling toys. Keep a sharp look out for anyone with smallpox."

In short order, the carriage stopped in front of a booth filled with trinkets and toys.

Mr. Reynolds alighted and went over to the booth. He asked Sarah to point out any toys she wanted. She was now ecstatic, although she had difficulty getting Mr. Reynolds to understand the descriptions of the toys she was interested in.

Andrew watched where the carriage had stopped and then walked to the booth before proceeding to the carriage. "Why don't you get out and walk over to the booth?" Andrew asked.

"Mama told me to stay inside the carriage."

"I do not see anyone with smallpox around here and surely your mother would not object to a few steps over to a booth." Andrew turned to Mr. Reynolds and raised his voice, "Mr. Reynolds, may Sarah come visit the booth?"

After mumbling something about Mrs. Bingley, Mr. Reynolds said, "I cannot say no to such a sweet creature. . . Sarah, come over her and choose as many toys as you can carry."

Andrew opened the carriage door with aplomb and bowed as Sarah stepped out of the vehicle. He then followed her over to the booth.

Mr. Reynolds encouraged her to fill the skirt of her white frock. Andrew held the toys up for her to see before handing them back or placing them in her skirt.

Laura, Maria and John soon appeared and enjoyed watching Sarah collect her trinkets. Mr. Reynolds promised the children, "You shall all have your chance to buy some toys, but Miss Sarah will select hers first so she will have something to entertain herself with while you are all venturing around the fair."

Unnoticed by the group, a little boy approached. Maria

turned and said innocently, "Little boy, what's the matter with your face?"

Andrew turned and shouted, "Smallpox!"

Sarah dropped her apron-skirt with all its toys and fell to her knees.

"Oh, my God!" exclaimed Mr. Reynolds, while Laura and John started shooing the little boy, "Go away! Go away!"

Andrew grasped Sarah's upper arms and helped her up. He then escorted the trembling girl back to the carriage.

Laura and Maria climbed in to sit by the crying Sarah. Through her tears, Sarah said, "Oh, Laura, I have disobeyed Mama! I did not mean it in the least. I forgot all of her commands. I do not care if I get smallpox, but I do not wish Mother to grieve."

Overcome by emotion, Mr. Reynolds sat down next to the booth and said, "Lord help us! What poor, sinful creatures we are."

Andrew returned to Mr. Reynolds and pulled the reluctant servant back to the carriage. The somber group returned to Pemberley. As the carriage arrived, the Darcys and Bingleys stood near the tall front entrance doors in front of the grand manor house.

At first, no one spoke or stirred in the carriage. After a delay of a few moments, Andrew emerged with Mr. Reynolds following behind. The young man and elderly servant drew to silent attention before the expectant and now alarmed parents. "What is the matter, Andrew?" asked Mr. Darcy. "Why have you returned home so soon?"

"It is all my fault, sir," replied Andrew, looking down at his feet.

"What is your fault?"

"I encouraged Sarah to step down from the carriage. . . ."

Here, Mr. Reynolds interrupted. "It is my mistaken judgement, since I gave permission."

"What the devil are you both talking about?" As Mr. Darcy said this, Mrs. Jane Bingley began running to the carriage.

She opened the door and Sarah began sobbing, "Oh, Mama, there was a boy with smallpox there."

Mrs. Bingley gathered Sarah up in her arms and supported her as they moved into the hall.

Mrs. Darcy said to the group, "This is no time to worry

Virtue and Vanity 17

about blame. We need to see about warding off the infection." Elizabeth's last statement was uttered as she turned to follow her sister, Mrs. Bingley into the hall.

The contrition of the trembling Andrew and the sorrow of Mr. Reynolds could not but help obtain the pardon they requested from the Darcys and Bingleys. However, it was months before Mr. Reynolds could walk at ease around Mrs. Reynolds. Her umbrage of "How could you be so careless?" was heard many times.

Every precaution possible for warding off infection was taken in regards to Sarah. Her clothes were burned. She was given a thorough bath and put to bed.

After four days, just as the household was beginning to believe she must have escaped the disease, Sarah began running a high fever. The surgeon was called for and, after examining his patient, he came to the assembled group and said to Mrs. Bingley, "Your child clearly has symptoms of smallpox."

"Will she live?" Mrs. Bingley asked with bated breath.

"I am sorry to relate this, but she has several signs indicating a severe prognosis. You must prepare yourselves." After closing his black bag, the surgeon gave a few more instructions and left the shocked and silent group.

Mrs. Bingley ran up the semicircular stairs of Pemberley as Mr. Bingley said to the group, "We want to spend as much time as possible with our angel." Then Mr. Bingley followed the footsteps of his wife.

Andrew ran down the hall to the chapel of Pemberley, where he entered the quiet, empty chamber and threw himself onto the kneeling pad and began to earnestly pray. "Oh, God. I have not always been the boy I should be. Forgive me my sins. It will be my fault if my dear cousin dies. Please be merciful and spare her life. You see, she is special to me. Indeed, sometimes I feel she is the only person who understands me."

After many minutes of desperate prayer, Andrew heard the chapel door open and looked up to see his father enter and approach, sitting close to where his elder son knelt. While Andrew expected his father to upbraid him, Mr. Darcy remained silent. Finally, after several minutes, Andrew said, "I am praying for Sarah to get well. . . you see, if she dies, it is all my fault. . .Do you think

God will grant my prayer?"

Mr. Darcy bid his son to rise off his knees and come sit next to him. As the boy lowered himself to the pew, Mr. Darcy placed his arm over Andrew's shoulders and said, "The Almighty has surely heard your prayer. God has not always answered my prayers the way I have wanted. I remember at eighteen. . . I prayed desperately for my own mother, who was not to be prevented from moving on to eternal glory."

"However, at a later time, my prayers for your own mother's health were granted. She survived and delivered you and your brother."

"What was the difference?"

"I do not know, my son. God always answers prayers, but sometimes it is in the negative."

"But, if Sarah dies, I will be a murderer."

"No, Andrew, you will not be. Yes, you were disobedient and share part of the responsibility; however, the final outcome is in the Lord's hands. That is a far cry from desiring her death and trying to bring it about."

Andrew buried his face against his father's strong chest. He knew that his father had done all he could to prevent Sarah from contracting the disease and had called in the surgeon at the first sign of fever. There in his fathers arms, he began to feel that, perhaps, his prayers had been heard. If God was truly even more loving than an earthly father, then He could be trusted to care for Sarah.

A somber mood reigned over the inhabitants of Pemberley for the next four days as Sarah's fever raged. On the fifth day, her fever broke and the exhausted Mrs. Bingley was uncertain if her barely responsive child was on the verge of death or recovery. The surgeon came to see how his patient was faring.

The medical man entered with a pessimistic look and examined the now pox-covered child. After a minute, he began to smile. Turning to the anxious parents, sitting on the other side of the bed, he said, "I believe she is going to make it."

A jubilant Charles Bingley hugged his wife and then ran out the door to spread the good news.

Jane Bingley bowed her head and began to cry. The sur-

Virtue and Vanity

geon waited until Mrs. Bingley had regained her composure and then continued, "I do not know how many scars will be left on her face and body as a result of this infection."

"I do not care about scars," Mrs. Bingley interrupted, "God has spared my child."

"You will want to bathe her face three or four times a day with warm milk and water to help reduce the scarring."

At dinner the following day, Jane Bingley finally joined the rest of her family at the table.

Elizabeth remarked, "It is very good to see you down here taking your meal."

Her sister replied, "I am glad Sarah has begun to sip broth and speak a little to me. I feel she is well enough that I can leave her for a few moments."

The family ate quietly for awhile and then Jane Bingley looked lovingly at her elder nephew and said, "Sarah is asking to see you, Andrew."

"Do you think I should?" replied Andrew as he looked back and forth from his aunt's face to his mother's.

Mrs. Darcy replied, "It is your decision, son; but, I cannot imagine anyone refusing a request from dear Sarah."

Andrew drew in a breath, "I should very much like to see her, but I do not wish to upset her. . . it is my fault she contracted the pox."

Mrs. Bingley smiled reassuringly, "Neither Sarah, nor anyone else, blames you Andrew. She did what she wanted to do."

"Than I shall visit her."

After the evening meal, Mrs. Darcy and Mrs. Bingley escorted Andrew to the upstairs sickroom. Upon reaching the door, Andrew walked behind his mother and aunt until they reached the bedside. The women turned sideways and revealed an expectant Sarah, who was sitting up and sipping a cup of tea.

Andrew had not expected Sarah's face to be entirely covered with pox blisters. What he had previously considered as a pretty face, was now horrific.

Sarah sensed his discomfort and tried to cheerfully say, "I am feeling much better than I look."

20 Ted and Marilyn Bader

Before she even finished her statement, Andrew turned and ran from the room screaming, "It's all my fault."

Mrs. Darcy went to the door and commanded, "Andrew, come back."

Whether he heard or not, he did not return.

Sarah began crying as her mother placed loving arms around her. As her sobbing subsided, she asked, "Mother, may I have a mirror?"

"It is not much different than when you looked yesterday."

"Will these pox marks ever go away?"

"The doctor said that most, if not all, will likely disappear."

"What if they do not?"

"We will still love you as much or more--any remaining marks will only remind us how precious you are to us and how close we came to losing you. Love is more important than beauty."

"But, mother, Andrew hates me. . . ."

Elizabeth interrupted, "I am sure Andrew does not hate you." She sat down on Sarah's bed and took the girl's hand. "He feels so guilty over his disobedience and his part in causing your sickness, that it hurts him to see you still suffering the effects of the pox."

Sarah brightened a bit, "I hope I recover completely so we can be friends again."

Over the ensuing weeks, Sarah regained her health. The pox disfigurement slowly healed, with the exception of one large scar over her left temple. With gentle help from her mother, she soon learned to comb her hair over the lesion; and, while this hairstyle was not always fashionable, it served to preserve her reputation as being handsome in a pleasing way.

The following year changed her life even more. Her home, Bingley Hall in Yorkshire, had possessed a somber atmosphere for several months during her mother's illness. Servants whispered and her father, Charles Bingley, was quiet and moody. Sarah grew alarmed at the change, as she considered her mother and father to be the happiest, jolliest people in the world. Watching her mother's beautiful face become emaciated, even a young Sarah could grasp the inevitable outcome.

Virtue and Vanity

The night before the death of her mother, Sarah was called to her bedside. She would never forget the hollow face of her mother. She always wanted to remember the lovely woman in the magnificient green dress, wearing the elegant white pearl necklace, portrayed in the picture displayed in the family gallery.

Her mother said in a weak voice, as she drew her youngest daughter to her, "I will not live much longer. There, there, do not cry, Sarah. The Redeemer has a place prepared for me and all those who follow him." She paused and drew a deep, ragged breath before continuing, "Please promise your mother you will always think the best of people and choose goodness."

"I will, Mama," was all the reply Sarah could make before she buried her face in her mother's gown.

"Remember," her mother continued, "that cultivation of the mind and virtues of the heart will lead to personal loveliness." Continuing her hold on Sarah, she drew Laura near.

"Laura, you are richly endowed with the dangerous gift of beauty; hitherto, you have escaped from the snares of folly and frivolity. My heart's prayer for you is that you may be safe from the dangers that await you, in the passions of others, and in the tenderness of your own heart."

"I will try to be good, mother," Laura sobbed.

Two days later, as Sarah watched the casket borne by pallbearers go down the avenue and turn right, she felt her mother had departed from her forever. Her father never recovered from his broken heart and he seemed to just dwindle away. He died just a few years later.

Sarah reacted to her mother's death in a spiritual way by developing a regular prayerlife and joy in attending the parish church. Laura, on the other hand, immersed herself in complete attention to the gaiety of society. Her beauty won her ready acceptance to any circle she desired.

Chapter Four

The next morning, a bright day in Paris, Sarah joined Sir Thomas and Lady Staley outside the embassy as the Darcy offspring arrived in a carriage.

Maria descended first and moved to hug her aunt and uncle. "I have missed you both so much." Looking between the twosome, she said, "I see you still glow with love for each other."

Georgiana pulled back, "Are you not a little old to be so impertinent?"

"Without my 'impertinence', you two would have never gotten together," Maria laughed. "Besides, now that you are not close by to tutor me, mother says there is little hope of my becoming a refined lady."

Then, another melodious feminine voice was heard, as Laura Bingley stepped down to a surprised receiving group. "So, I decided to come along and see that she behaved herself properly."

Reaching out to hug Laura, Georgiana said, "We did not expect that you were coming; but, it is a delightful surprise."

Laura replied, "I found out about the trip and decided to tag along at the last minute. I have so wanted to see the elegance of Paris for myself." She turned to Sarah and said, "Are you taking advantage of everything this romantic city has to offer? You must tell me all the details of the wonderful things you have done here."

"Actually, I have done very little other than helping in the embassy."

"Just what I suspected," Laura replied in a superior tone. "It looks like I shall have to lead the way to fashion and favor."

By this time, Andrew and John were out of the carriage. Andrew said, "Uncle Thomas, it is most pleasing to visit you. I hope we will not burden you too much."

"Not at all," Sir Thomas replied. Then he added with a smile, "Of course, I am assuming that John has outgrown his propensity for pulling pranks."

John put on a very serious face, "Why Uncle Thomas, why

Virtue and Vanity 23

would you worry about such a thing. I have certainly matured beyond childish behavior." As he reached out to briefly hug Thomas, he added, "Besides, if you recall, I learned at an early age that it was not wise to play tricks on you. You are better at it than I am."

John moved on to acknowledge Sarah. "It is good to meet you again, cousin."

"Thank you," Sarah replied as she curtsied.

Andrew seemed a little stiffer as he repeated his brother's greeting.

The group moved into the embassy entrance. Sir Thomas said, "We have an authoress among us. One of Sarah's poems will soon be published."

Maria went to congratulate her cousin, when Laura said abruptly, "It is not good for a woman to appear to have a mind and a heart. If you show yourself too clever, no man will ever want you." Then, turning to Georgiana, she asked, "Do you not agree, Auntie?"

"I beg to differ, my dear Laura. A woman may be accomplished in whatever she wishes."

As the group followed their hosts upstairs, Sarah was vexed with her older sister. Laura was vain and almost cruel at times. It was displeasing to see Maria and Laura on such intimate acquaintance. Maria evidenced her mother, Elizabeth's liveliness; yet, she did not seem to have inherited either parent's good sense. Sarah hoped that being in close quarters with Laura for a prolonged period would not adversely affect Maria.

Maria then asked her aunt, "Is there to be an embassy ball tomorrow night?"

"Yes, just a small one to welcome you to Paris."

Maria and Laura then said in unison, "I cannot wait for it."

Larua added, "To think, my first ball in the city of romance. How exciting. I brought the most enchanting dress I could find; but, I shall certainly want to meet with a Parisian seamstress later in the week to order more sophisticated gowns." She paused before the small mirror as they climbed the remaining stairs, "Indeed," she murmured, "with the right gowns to accent my fine attributes, the gentlemen of Paris will not be able to resist."

24 Ted and Marilyn Bader

The next evening, the embassy ballroom was once again brightly lit. Madame Duval stood with Laura, Maria and Sarah as the arriving guests were greet by the Staleys.

Madame Duval said, in nearly accent-free English, "I am afraid, girls, there there will be few beaux for you to entice tonight."

Maria had readily warmed to Madame Duval because of her friendliness and constant talk about the opposite sex. She wished to hear more and asked, "Is anyone coming we would be interested in?"

"I am aware of a handsome young French officer, Lieutenant Fabry, who will come as an aide to my cousin. Then to Maria she added, "You msut not look so eager, my young friend."

Maria blushed, "Oh, but I would like to dance with him."

"Be assured, I will introduce you."

"Now, for you Miss Laura and Miss Sarah, I have not hear of any other. However, there are two handsome Englishmen approaching us now."

Andrew and John neared the group. Laura said, in a voice loud enough to be heard by the brothers, "Oh, they are just country bumpkins. I wish to meet the quality men of Paris."

"If that is so, you may have to wait for another night," was the elder woman's reply.

Andrew bowed and asked Laura, "Would you favor me with the first dance?"

Laura haughtily replied, "I am sorry, but I believe I will not dance this evening."

Without any change in his expression, he turned to Sarah. She looked down, but her hand automatically reached up to make sure her hair was pulled forward correctly.

"Would you, Miss Sarah, favor me?"

Sarah smiled and nodded affirmatively.

At that moment, the group turned to see two officers, dressed in French blue, stiriding towards them from the reception line. The lieutenant approached Madame Duval. He, and the officer with him, stopped to bow. "Madame Duval and company, allow me to introduce my comrade, Captain Wiley."

As Madame Duval introduced the young women, she

Virtue and Vanity 25

brought Maria forward. Lieutenant Fabry, with a flair, asked Maria, "Would the lovely young English woman favor me with the first dance?"

Maria tried to act as though she had done this many times before and replied, "I have nothing else to do."

Captain Wiley bowed before Laura, "May I have the honor of dancing with the brightest jewel in the room tonight?"

Laura willingly extended her arm as the Captain escorted her away. The dance was announced. As Andrew came to take Sarah's hand, she quietly said, "I must apologize for my sister's rudeness."

Andrew replied, "It is not your affair. Your sister is her usual self. She has stayed much too long with the insufferable Countess Westbrook."

The dance began and during one of the face to face moves, Andrew looked at Sarah and said, "But you are not your sister. You have always been much different."

Sarah blushed and looked away.

Upon their next encounter, Andrew said, "Rose petals falling from my heart. . . ."

"Where have you heard that?" was Sarah's immediate inquiry.

"I believe it is from your poem," he answered as he moved close once again.

"How did you find that out?"

"You forget, you lent it to Uncle Thomas and I saw it on his desk. . . are you angry?"

"No, it will soon be published."

"Congratulations."

At the end of the dance Sarah felt the friendly grasp of Andrew's hand. He said with an earnest look, "May I escort you to the veranda?"

Sarah held out her arm in assent. Arriving on the small porch which could only hold two comfortably, Andrew looked down and said, "It is a beautiful garden below us, is it not?"

"I see you are still very interested in plants and gardens."

"Yes. I am. . . you must tell me all about Paris."

"You forget, my cousin, that I have scarcely been here two months myself." His presence put her at ease, so she continued,

"We have been settling in. As you know, I am governess for the children and that takes up most of my time. I am also trying to improve my conversational skills in French. Sir Thomas has been a most patient instructor."

Andrew turned and looked at her with a face that asked for mercy. "May we discuss a treaty of friendship?"

"Whatever do you mean?"

"I apologize for my blunder in causing your smallpox. . . Can you ever forgive me?"

"You forget it was my own choice to be disobedient. . . I have longed to tell you so. I have missed our amiable times together."

"Yes, yes, it is so for me also. . . whenever I see a foxglove I am reminded of your help long ago. May we put our hands together in friendship?"

As they did so, Andrew and Sarah continued their movement towards each other, which became a prolonged mutual embrace. Sarah cried softly and Andrew sighed deeply as he whispered his pledge of friendship to her.

After the next dance ceased, Andrew escorted Sarah back to a large table where the other young couples had returned. Andrew sat by John and Lieutenant Fabry. Andrew said to Lieutenant Fabry in halting French, *"Mon frére et moi, nous sommes ici. . . ."*

The lieutenant held up his hand and said, "The captain and I speak English."

Andrew continued, "Ah. . . , as I was saying, my brother and I are here for the fencing tournament tomorrow. Though I have little chance of winning the prize, since my brother is the best swordsman in England."

Captain Wiley stood, came to attention and clicked his heels. "It is an honor to meet my chief opponent, for many consider my swordplay to be of championship quality."

John stood and extended his hand, "My brother exaggerates my abilities."

"Not from what I have heard," Captain Wiley said. "Your reputation has preceded you."

At the end of the evening, Laura and Madame Duval were in conversation together as Andrew and John approached. John said to Laura, "Is Captain Wiley as much as you expected?"

"He provided a pleasant diversion this evening and is all right as far as junior officers go; however, I am looking for someone of higher quality."

"Would you like to meet a Marquis?" John asked.

Laura's countenance glowed with excitement, but she soon sneered, "How would you know an aristocrat of that rank?"

Unflappable, John continued, "On our last visit here, the Marquis de Mascarille introduced himself. His father is acquainted with our father."

"I do not believe it."

John turned to Madame Duval, who added, "I have heard of the Marquis de Mascarille, but I have never met him."

After Madame Duval's statement, Laura visibly softened and inquired, "When may I meet such an aristocrat?"

Andrew and John exchanged delighted looks and Andrew said, as he looked at Madame Duval for permission, "Perhaps we can arrange for him to call at Madame Duval's, the day after tomorrow."

"He is most certainly welcome," the matronly matchmaker answered. She then turned to Laura, Sarah, and Maria. "I will send my carriage early in the day, so we can prepare for the visit." She then turned her attention back to the Darcy brothers and said, "I am not sure to what I owe the honor, but you, sirs, are always welcome."

John bowed, "My brother is a much better speech maker and philosopher than I am. However, we need to excuse ourselves in order to prepare for tomorrow's tournament."

Chapter Five

"The match goes to Lieutenant Fabry," shouted the announcer. A dejected Andrew Darcy sheathed his foil and came to stand in front of Sir Thomas and the English entourage. John and Maria rushed to hug their brother. Maria gushed, "You were marvelous!"

"You always say I'm marvelous."

With a pat on Andrew's back, John said, "Good show, old boy."

Before taking his seat, Andrew said "I wish I had parried his right thrust better. If our coach had been able to travel, I am sure he could have improved my play."

Sir Thomas replied, "Your moves were excellent. Your skill allowed you to make it to the third round--that is quite an accomplishment at this level of competition."

"We will always be proud of you," Lady Staley said with a smile.

Sarah hoped to give Andrew a look of encouragement, but as he sat down, his attention turned to Laura, who refused to give make eye contact.

John continued to win in the third and fourth rounds and the group from Derbyshire eagerly awaited his championship match. John stood before them and said, "At last it has come. I am matched with Captain Wiley." He paused for a moment and looked at Laura, "Shall I beat him?"

She replied, "By all means. His arrogance is irksome; it will serve him well to be bested."

Both John and the group were silent for a few moments, reflecting on Laura's last statement, when the announcer interrupted, "And now, the final match, between Mr. John Darcy and Captain Wiley."

The contrast in colors was striking as John Darcy, with the British-red jacket, stood next to the light blue French uniform of

Virtue and Vanity 29

Captain Wiley.

They separated, bowed, and the match was on. It soon became apparent that the struggle was one of quickness and nimbleness, on the young Mr. Darcy's part, and that of strength and masterful moves on Captain Wiley's part. Sarah detected a look of surprise on the French officer's part when John eluded his well-set traps.

As the match progressed, Sarah could see that both combatants were tiring and she worried for her cousin. She prayed silently that neither man would be injured. She noticed that Andrew sat on the edge of his seat, with his eyes glued on his brother. His hands occasionally made slight movements as though he were holding a foil and participating in the match.

At the final break, John motioned Sir Thomas and Andrew over and asked, "What should I do?"

Andrew replied, "Mr. Coning repeatedly said to fight with your head and not your heart. The French captain is overconfident and that is making you angry."

"I know that," snapped a breathless John. Softening his voice, he asked, "What should I do?"

"You must remember to hold the handle of the foil like a bird. If you hold it too tight, you will kill it; if too loose, it will fly away."

Andrew and John turned to look at their uncle who mused, "Perhaps you should take advantage of his overconfidence."

"And?"

"The French love their *coup de grace*. Retreat, cower, anticipate, dodge, and the rest is up to you."

In the final moments, John was backed up as though he were beaten. Captain Wiley made the final victory lunge, only to miss John, who twirled and pinked a surprised Captain Wiley. The obvious winning move silenced the home crowd, but the English side went wild with cheers. These accolades continued as the referee held John Darcy's hand high at the end of the match.

"Well done, nephew," Sir Thomas shook his hand and congratulated John as he came off the stage. "I only wish your father and mother could have been here to see your dashing performance."

"I knew you would win," Lady Staley said with a big smile.

Inhibitions aside, Laura and Sarah rushed to John's side and he lifted both in the air, one in each arm, as he twirled around and in the process kissed each one on the cheek. He put them down and Sarah saw him spot his twin brother. John walked over and shook his brother's hand with all the warmth and meaning of an English handshake. Such brotherly love soon evolved to a hug. As they did so, John said, "Were you not such an excellent sparring partner, I should have never grasped the championship ring."

"I am proud to have the best swordsman in England and France as my brother," Andrew replied.

Sarah was moved as she saw Andrew genuinely congratulate his brother. She wished Laura would someday likewise exhibit such sisterly warmth.

Chapter Six

Sarah had mixed feelings as her hair was being fixed for the day. She was quite pleased at her cousins doing so well in the tournament. The pleasure that came with John winning the championship felt like that which any sister might feel towards a brother.

On the other hand, the invitation to Madame Duval's house filled her with trepidation. She must spend the entire day with her sister, Laura, with whom she had never spent an agreeable day. Early in life her sister had been domineering and disrespectful. After their mother's death and the subsequent preoccupation of their father, the sisters mutually decied to separate. Laura went to live with Aunt Caroline, the Countess of Westbook, and Sarah moved into joyous peace at Staley Hall.

Over the past four years, Sarah had observed that her sister's sojourn with her snobbish Aunt Caroline did nothing to improve Laura's disposition. Sarah hoped to see an improvement in her sister and planned to place the best interpretation on any behavior; none the less, she would at least try to guard her own feelings.

With dressing completed, Sarah descended the stairs to meet her sister. Laura looked quite beautiful in her white day gown and wide-brimmed hat.

Sarah said, "You are quite handsome in your dress."

"Thank you, sister. I think you look well. . . but your dress seems rather nondescript. Do you not realize that we are to meet the Marquis today? Perhaps, I should help you select something more suitable."

"I am afraid there is not time, we must be prompt on such an auspicious occasion." Continuing with a sad smile, Sarah said, "Besides, sister dear, I fear you would find my entire wardrobe consists of nondescript gowns."

Laura leaned closer to Sarah and said, "Smell my perfume! It is the latest fragrance in Paris." After the obligatory sniff, Laura grabbed Sarah's arm and led her out the door. As they stepped outside, Laura released her grip and clapped her hands with joy.

"What a perfectly lovely day. The sun seems to shine as never before--I am sure it will bring out the fine sheen of my golden hair. I will have to make sure the Marquis sees me outside in this glorious light."

Sarah's mood began to brighten with the outside air and the thought that her sister might be agreeable. At least if Laura was busy thinking of her own beauty, she would be too self-absorbed to pick at Sarah's shortcomings.

Stepping into the carriage, Laura exclaimed, "I wonder what this young Marquis looks like. It would be difficult to marry an ugly face--but then, if he is charming and rich enough, I suppose I could endure a plain face and form."

"Marriage? Is this what you are thinking of?" Sarah queried.

Laura looked surprised and answered in a condescending tone, as though explaining something to a child. "Of course. I am at that age when a woman needs to consider marriage. And, as Aunt Caroline has taught me, I hope to marry well."

"Do you not think a Marquis a bit out of our class?"

"All noblemen wish for a pretty young wife."

"I think I would be cautious when dealing with such an aristocrat."

"That is all right for you, I daresay. With your lack of coquetry you have little hope of marrying well, if at all."

Laura looked at Sarah, "I am sorry for being so beastly to you. I am afraid it is an old habit. You are such a good woman. Everyone here speaks so well of you. Perhaps, I am ashamed of myself."

Sarah remained quiet and tried to smile in a friendly manner. After a moment, Sarah said quietly, "Sister, we have very little dowry."

"Yes, that is true, but as Madame Duval says, 'A handsome woman needs proportionately less dowry than others.'"

"Still, this Lord may take little notice of us."

"If that is the case, then I shall just marry Andrew Darcy."

"Andrew?" Sarah said with more emphasis than she cared to show.

"Yes, Andrew. . . Oh, I know he is not the most gallant

man, with his stuffy scientific endeavors; but, with the Darcy fortune, Pemberley would be splendid."

"Has he said anything to you?"

"Not in words. But I am sure if I set my sights on him, I can fix his intentions."

Sarah wished to quickly divert the conversation before her sister could discern the displeasure she was struggling with and asked, "Do you think Maria will be at Madame Duval's?"

"She hopes to be. If her brothers finish their business, they will bring her by."

The carriage arrived in front of Madame Duval's residence. Madame Duval came out to greet them.

"Have you had any visitors yet?" Laura asked eagerly.

"If you mean the Marquis, no," replied the elderly chaperone as she escorted them into her parlor. The threesome sat down as Madame Duval said, "My cousin, the general, is always complaining of my matchmaking; but, it provides so much diversion to introduce women to an appropriate beau."

"Now then, girls, have you sent out any invitation cards?"

Laura replied, "We have not received any cards. I suppose we are not yet known."

"You must forget your provincial English custom of waiting for cards and invitations. In France, it is the newcomer who is supposed to send his cards around to the people they are desirous of visiting and then wait for a response."

Sarah asked, "Isn't that presumptuous?"

"Not at all. In France, we assume the newcomer wishes to be alone unless he indicates otherwise. A much better social introduction scheme than what you English or the Americans have."

"You will also be amazed at another custom of France in that we matchmakers often place advertisements in the paper stating that a certain person is in quest of a wife or husband."

Astonishment filled the faces of Madame Duval's two guests.

"Shall I tell you of my latest success?"

The sisters nodded.

"I recently helped a charming girl with a good fortune of four hundred thousand francs. She was of the mercantile class. Four and twenty proposals were made to this young lady. In every case she was permitted to decide for herself. When matters went so far as to render an interview desirable, it was arranged for the parties to meet at the house of a mutual friend, where they might see each other, or dance together."

"Over the twelvemonth, the suitors of my young protegeé formed a curious list. Nobles, wealthy *roturiers*, soldiers and *savans*. One was too tall, another too short; this one too ugly, and that one too handsome. One was too noble, an odd objection I must say, and another objected to because he was a dandy. I heartily approved of her latter objection since dandyism is almost conclusive evidence of a frivolous mind. She finally choose a warm hearted son of a judge and they have been happily married since."

"Your story is most remarkable," Sarah said thoughtfully.

Laura eagerly asked, "What do you know about the Marquis de Mascarille?"

The elder woman replied, "Very little. I have only heard the name. He shall have us at a disadvantage until we learn more of him."

With a smile, Laura said, "At the end of the day, we shall know the answers to all our questions. Aunt Caroline has schooled me well in the art of alluring a gentleman and enticing him to tell the essential information. . . besides, men love to talk about themselves."

Sarah sat on a smaller chair beside her sister and said thoughtfully, "Unfortunately, we will only learn about him from his own lips. It may be difficult to determine the truth in his answers."

"Sister, be not so skeptical. A man of true quality would not intentionally deceive us."

"Perhaps not, but I am sure we shall only see his best face today."

Madame Duval then asked Sarah, "Good miss, please stir the fire, that the teakettle may boil."

Sarah did as requested.

"You have done it well, now it burns purely. Well, Sarah, you shall have a cheerful husband if you can keep a fire hot for tea."

"I am not interested in marriage now," Sarah said as she took the teakettle and poured servings for her two companions.

Virtue and Vanity

"Sugar?" Madame Duval asked.

"Yes," replied Laura as Sarah said, "No."

"Cream?"

Again, Laura said, "Yes," while Sarah said, "No."

Madame Duval exclaimed with tongue-in-cheek, "Well, Sarah, if you always say no, you will never be married."

Sarah thought about taking umbrage at her chaperone; but, seeing the woman's jolly face, she realized the remarks were meant only to be teasing.

A servant stepped in to announce the arrival of Miss Maria Darcy. Madame Duval stood to welcome her guest, "Miss Darcy, it is so good to have you come. You must tell me something about yourself."

Laura interjected while Maria sat down, "Her brothers call her the Princess of Pemberley."

Bewildered, Madame Duval asked "I did not realize our guest was royal," as she began to curtsey.

"Please, no," Maria laughed. "I am not a princess; only my brothers say so, since they think I am pampered and spoiled."

"You know they are right," Laura continued.

"Why should I care?" Maria replied, "since my wants are taken care of, all I need is to marry well."

"I hope the Marquis is interested in marriage," Laura said.

"Is he coming to propose today?" Maria asked breathlessly.

"My dear girls," Madame Duval interrupted, "you must not be so hasty. As Moliére says, 'Marriage comes after a series of adventures. A suitor must first express the finest sentiments. After meeting her he keeps the loved one in ignorance of his passion, but visits her frequently. With each visit, he poses some question about the passion of love to intrigue the wits of the company. The day of declaration finally arrives and you should banish the suitor from your presence by your refusal. Then, little by little, he returns to repeat the outpouring of his passion, and at last draws from us that confession which is such an agony to make. After that, come rivals who try to interfere with the settlement, the persecution of parents, jealousy caused by mutual misunderstanding, despair, abduction and so on.' That is how these things are managed in best style."

36   Ted and Marilyn Bader

Laura and Maria began to laugh towards the end of the hostess' speech and even Sarah could not smother her own mirth.

Regaining her composure, Laura replied, "I like your suggestion, except for the first refusal part. I am afraid I should never be asked again."

"Ah, you understand not the passion of the strong sex. If it is done in a manner suggesting you are under constraint, it will only lead to a greater display of affection."

At that moment, a servant announced the Marquis de Mascarille. "Show him in," replied Madame Duval.

The Marquis entered with two men, dressed in black and red livery, trailing him. The Marquis was a young, middle-sized gentleman who was slightly overweight, had hair down to his white collar and was dressed in the finest fashion of the day. He immediately turned and accosted the two servants with him, "Hold, fellows, hold! That was the most jarring carriage ride I have ever had. I think you scoundrels must wish to break my bones."

The first driver said, "Is this the thanks we get for carrying you from the carriage to the steps?"

"I should say so indeed. Would you have me leave the imprint of my shoes in mud? Go away."

"Pay us then, Sir."

"Eh? What?"

"I ask you, Sir, to give us our money, if you please?"

The Marquis then struck the driver lightly with his rod, "How dare you, rascal? Demand money from a man of my rank?"

"Are poor men paid with that? Can we dine off your rank?"

"I will teach you to know your place. As scum, you would dare to bandy words with me?"

The Marquis lifted his rod again, but the second driver stepped forward and pulled out his whip, replying, "Come, pay us at once."

"What?"

"We mean to have our money at once."

The Marquis looked at the whip and replied, "Well, that is quite reasonable."

"Be quick about it, then."

"Now that is the way to talk. But your mate is a rascal who

doesn't know how to negotiate properly. There! Are you satisfied now?"

The second driver replied, "No. I am not. You struck my mate and. . . ." He lifted the whip again.

"Gently! Gently!" The Marquis then gave money to the first driver.

"Here is to pay for the blow. A man can get anything from me if he goes about it the right way. Go now, and be sure to come back later to carry me to the Louvre."

With the drivers dismissed, the Marquis turned to meet the foursome who stood to curtsey. The Marquis bowed and said, "Fair ladies, you will no doubt be surprised at the boldness of my visit; but your reputation has such magic that I could not resist a visit."

Madame Duval replied, "If you are in pursuit of merit, sir, our presence should not be your hunting ground."

Laura finally recovered and added, "If you see any merit, it must be that which you have brought yourself."

"Ah, it is awkward to deny the first statements of so lovely a lady. Rumor did not lie when she whispered of your brilliance."

Sarah then caught his attention and braved, "Your courtesy is too lavish in the generosity of its praise. My sister and I must not take your sweet flattery too seriously."

The Marquis began looking around and Madame Duval replied, "Will our Lord be seated?"

The group moved to sit down, while the Marquis continued, "Tell me now, can I feel safe in this house?"

His hostess replied, "Why should you fear?"

With a smile, he sighed, "Ah, the theft of my heart, the assassination of my liberty." He then looked at Laura, "I can see eyes, or very wicked eyes, capable of the cruelest assault upon my freedom."

Sarah saw her sister amazed at such forward language so early in the meeting. Even Madame Duval was at an unusual loss of words for a few moments. She finally recovered and playfully replied, "My Lord possesses a lively temper and wit!"

Laura said sweetly, "You need not be afraid. Our eyes are guiltless of any evil purpose."

Madame Duval then intervened, "My Lord, would you care

for some tea?"

"Indeed."

Sarah went to fill his tea cup. Upon reflection, she felt uncomfortable. She realized a feeling that had been growing since the aristocrat's arrival: this gentleman was either without honor or not the man he purported to be. She could not decide why she felt this way. Perhaps it was his appearance or the inconsistencies of his demeanor. But what did she know? How many high lords had she met?

The Marquis continued, "Well now, ladies, what do you think of Paris?"

"It is as exquisite as we expected," Laura replied. Then, with a slight pout, she continued, "But we have no one to show us around."

Madame Duval raised her eyebrows while the Marquis said, "If you ladies would allow me the honor, I should be delighted to introduce you to the finest of circles. All of the wits of Paris call on me. . . ." Focusing on Laura, he continued, "What would you like to see first?"

"I delight in portraits."

"Portraits are difficult, and demand a depth of mind," pausing for a moment, the gentleman continued, "you shall see some of mine which will not displease you, I think." He then turned to Sarah and asked, "What should you like to see or hear?"

Sarah stammered briefly and then said, "I am fond of riddles."

"Ah, that taxes one's ingenuity. I made as many as four of them this morning, which I will give you to guess."

Laura then said, "My sister is modest. She has published her first poem."

"Ah, poetry is it? I must recite to you an extempore I composed yesterday when on a visit to the Duchess."

"You must give it to us," Madame Duval requested.

"Listen carefully," the Marquis invited.

> "Oh, oh! My mind was at ease,
> And its own thoughts pursued:
> When, with no thought of harm,
> your fair visage I viewed,

Virtue and Vanity 39

Oh, eye, that by stealth
hath encompassed my grief,
My heart thou didst ravish!
Oh, fie on thee, thief!
After her, after her, after her, thief!"

"How gallant," Laura exclaimed.

"Everything I write, you see, strikes a dashing note. I take care to avoid the pedantic."

"How exquisite," the adoring Laura continued.

"Did you notice the beginning? 'Oh, Oh!?' Uncommon is it not? Surprise. 'Oh, Oh!'"

"Yes. I find 'Oh, Oh!' Admirable."

"A mere trifle!"

Laura turned to Sarah, "What think you of our poet?"

She hesitated and then replied, "It rhymes well."

"Indeed, it does," her older sister rejoined and turning back to the Marquis continued, "You have such good taste."

"I flatter myself that it is not entirely undiscriminating."

A servant entered and said, "Madame, the coachmen for the Marquis have arrived.

The Marquis stood and bowed, "With painful purpose, I must sever myself from this delightful company. I shall return tomorrow and escort you all to the Louvre."

The women rose and curtsied. After the gentleman left, Madame Duval broke the silence by asking aloud, "What think you of our Lord?"

Laura enthusiastically replied, "How gallant. I eagerly await his return. He missed the chance to view me outside in the sunlight." She gently played with a tendril of hair that framed her face and continued, "but perhaps we shall have a sunny day tomorrow." Turning to Sarah she asked, "Sister, what have you to say?"

After a moment, Sarah slowly answered, "He seems vain and conceited."

Maria piped, "A Lord of such rank has a right to be vain and conceited."

"Pooh. Pooh, sister. You are bound to dislike anything I care for." The young ladies then turned to look at their hostess.

The normally ebullient woman thoughtfully said, "The

gentleman certainly warrants further inspection. I hope my inquiry about him is answered soon."

The servant re-entered and announced, "A French officer, Ma'am."

"Well, show him in," replied the hostess.

In uniform, Captain Wiley stepped smartly into the room and bowed.

Looking directly at Laura, he said, "I have come to pay my visit from yesterday's ball. Never have I enjoyed such beauty and grace in such a picturesque setting."

"Thank you," was Laura's limp reply.

"Please sit down," encouraged Madame Duval.

"I am unacquainted with the gentleman who preceded me. Who is he?"

Laura, in a superior tone, replied, "The Marquis de Mascarille was kind enough to call on us."

"You don't say. I am not acquainted with the man."

"I suppose he is far superior to your circle of friends."

Madame Duval interrupted Laura and said, "We are honored by your visit. It is not often such gallant men are in my parlor."

The Captain smiled, "*Au contraire*, Madame, it is my pleasure to be allowed to visit such lovely ladies."

Sarah then volunteered, "I suppose we are prejudiced in favor of our cousin, but we congratulate you on your championship match with him."

"Thank you, Mademoiselle," he replied. "I am hopeful it will, how do you say, turn out differently next time."

"If my cousing, John Darcy, is your opponent, I shall have to cheer for him," Laura said without enthusiasm.

"Of course," the Captain replied.

The room was uncomfortably quiet for a minute as Sarah observed a puzzled expression on the officer's face. Captain Wiley stood, bowed towards Madame Duval and said, "Thank you, Madam, for allowing me to pay my respects. *Bon jour*."

As he left, the room fell silent. Sarah was at a loss for words. Her sister had appeared alternately hot and cold to two very different gentlemen.

Virtue and Vanity   41

Laura rose and walked to the window. Madame Duval then inquired, "Far be it from me to pry into your thoughts, Laura, but I am wondering at your reception of Captain Wiley?"

"I have lost interest in him. . . He was a pleasant diversion at the ball, but with a Marquis as even a remote possibility. . . I do not wish to scare the aristocrat away. Besides, Captain Wiley is just a junior officer."

"Where do you think senior officers spring from?" Madame Duval rejoined.

"Yes, of course, you are right," Laura glared at Sarah and continued, "Do not look at me like that, Sarah. Indeed, if I wish to fix the attention of an aristocrat, I shall do so."

Sarah replied, "I dare say as a man of the world, he will not be oblivious to your attempt. His character seems so, well, superficial."

"I cannot wait until the Marquis returns tomorrow," Laura said, looking at Madame Duval.

Leaning over to Maria, Madame Duval whispered, "This will be fun to observe," and then she said aloud as she stood, "Yes, yes, of course you must return to my home and stay the whole day."

"Excellent. You are so kind to us." Laura replied.

Chapter Seven

Sarah sensed an unusual atmosphere in the embassy residence during the evening meal. Edgar and Anna were enjoying the opportunity of dining with the adults. While Anna's eyes flitted from person to person, Edgar's eyes rarely left John.

Sir Thomas spoke, "John, the congratulations are still pouring in for your fencing victory."

"Thank you, Sir Thomas. I hear, however, that I am not the only one to be congratulated."

"Oh?" his uncle queried as John chuckled and Andrew exhibited difficulty keeping his face straight.

The young men turned to pointedly look at Laura as John said, "We hear you have an aristocratic admirer."

Laura, at first, gaped with a slight blush and then stiffened to look superior. "Yes, it is true. The Marquis de Mascarille visited Madame Duval today."

"I was told you would 'steal his heart and assassinate his liberty'. . . " John began chuckling again.

Glaring at Sarah, Laura said, "I wish my sister would not expose everything we do."

"It was not my doing," replied Sarah in a determined manner.

"Indeed. We heard it from other sources," a smiling Andrew replied.

"Don't look at me," Maria volunteered.

"So, you think me an adventuress, one who has no business with a Marquis?" Laura said indignantly.

"Beware of your virtue," John replied, "this fellow has a reputation of, what shall I say. . . breaking many feminine hearts."

"You need not worry about my virtue."

"Well, do not believe this fellow too much," John said.

"I implicitly trust someone of his rank, especially when he was recommended to me by you, my dear cousin."

John looked directly at her. "We did not recommend him.

Virtue and Vanity

We simply said that if you wanted someone of high rank to call upon you, we could arrange the first visit. As I said, do not place too much confidence in him."

Conversation around the table ceased and all went back to quietly finishing their meal. A tired looking Anna leaned her head against the side of her mother, Georgiana.

Sarah asked, "Did Anna have another spell today? I should feel remiss if she did and I was not here."

Georgiana put her arm around Anna and said, "No, but I am afraid she has a headache and does not feel much like eating."

Andrew said, "I am sorry if we have been too boisterous for her."

"No. She enjoys the presence of her cousins."

Sarah came around the table to take Anna's hand and signaled to Edgar that he too should excuse himself. Edgar eagerly turned to his father and asked, "Father, may I have permission to join the men after dinner? I want to hear more about the fencing contest."

Sir Thomas nodded permission. "I believe your cousins will enjoy having such an attentive audience."

As Sarah led Anna upstairs, the young girl asked, "Will you read to me before bedtime?"

"Which fairy tale will it be tonight?"

"How about *The Lion and the Princess*?"

Smiling, she said, "That is just the story I was hoping you would ask for."

Meanwhile, Laura and Maria joined Lady Staley in the adjoining room as Maria excitedly described the Marquis' visit. Georgiana raised her eyebrows and then furrowed them during Maria's story. "I think I should be very careful, if I were you, Laura."

Laura's face was quizzical. "Aunt Caroline taught me that people of high rank are inherently better than others. . . even if they have a few flaws, we should overlook those because their other ingrained qualities will compensate for them."

Georgiana continued with even more concern, "A gentleman's rank tells you nothing of his character." Softening her voice she said, "As you probably know, I was once mildly attracted to a duke who proposed to me. I decided against him. . . ."

"A duke," Laura gasped. "I never heard about this. How could you refuse a duke?"

"Didn't the Duke give you the Gainsborough painting?" Maria asked.

"Yes, he did."

"That explains why you didn't keep it to hang in your own home," Maria mused. "I always liked the painting but not the man who gave it to you."

"Even my little dog didn't like him," Georgiana said. "That should have told me much about his character."

"But a duke," Laura exclaimed, "and someone who was obviously quite generous with his wealth. . . how could you?"

Lady Staley held up her hand to silence the ambitious young woman, "I had an uneasiness about him. . . there were many little things about his character that warned me he would not be a good choice for marriage."

"Surely you could have overlooked a few little imperfections."

"No. A woman should not have to spend her married life trying to pretend she doesn't recognize her husband's flaws. Indeed, it is important to marry a man you can both respect and love." Georgiana looked at Laura and said sincerely, "Thank goodness my negative feelings continued. . . later the Duke's libertine behavior proved my decision was the correct one."

Laura straightened a bit in her seat and asked a bit haughtily, "So, you have let this one bad experience color your view of the aristocracy?"

"Of course not," Lady Staley said. "I have met some men who have both rank and integrity. I am just saying you need to be careful with your feelings and do not judge the man solely on his position in society. Try to find out what he is like as a person."

"That is the whole point of our meeting at Madame Duval's home. . . it gives me an opportunity to get acquainted with him."

"Use the time well. And, remember, most anyone can appear to be something other than what he is for an hour or two." Relaxing her pose, Georgiana said, "Enough of lecturing. Why don't you two girls tell me what you like about the Marquis?"

"He is the highest ranking. . .," Laura began and then

stopped.

Maria said helpfully, "He talked of art."

Laura beamed, "And he likes poetry. He even quoted a poem he wrote."

Both girls fell silent. Georgiana said gently, "I was not aware that you were particularly fond of poetry."

"I am not overly fond of reading prose or poetry, but I do not mind hearing an occasional poem quoted or read," Laura replied. "Aunt Caroline says that only refined gentlemen can truly appreciate the arts."

"What did Sarah think of the poem the gentleman composed?" Georgiana asked.

"Sarah said it rhymed well," Maria said.

"What other traits does the Marquis possess which appeal to you?"

Laura thought for a moment and then said, "We really did not have much time to converse; but, he is such a fine gentleman. Any one who meets him would hold him in high esteem. He has offered to introduce us to his social circle."

"We are meeting him again tomorrow," Maria added.

"Perhaps that will give you opportunity to learn more of his character," Georgiana said. "I have found one can tell a lot about a man by the way he treats his servants and those beneath his station."

"We are beneath his station and he treated us with great charm."

"Would any gentleman do otherwise with three lovely young ladies?" Georgiana rose and said, "Now if you'll excuse me, I would like to check on Anna before she goes to sleep." On her way out of the room, she patted Laura's shoulder, "Just be careful, my dear. I should not like you to be hurt."

Chapter Eight

"I cannot wait for the visit of the Marquis," Laura said as Sarah, Maria and Madame Duval were again seated in the latter's parlor, preparing their tea.

Madame Duval said, "I still have not heard any response to my inquiries about him. However, it seems Laura that you are interested in his attentions, whatever his character may be."

"Of course, why should I not? It is only a dream to marry a Marquis; however, a girl can always make a wish."

"Well, if you wish to fix his attention, I suggest you engage in coquetry. You must not seem interested in his advances. After your initial interest yesterday, this will serve to inflame his passion."

"Coquetry is an art form known best to the ladies of France. I certainly would like to try my hand at it." Laura stood and went to stand in front of the mantel. "You have some lovely hand fans mounted here. Tell us about them."

Madame Duval rose and pointed to the first one, which was black. "I do not know how much of what we French call the *eventail* you are acquainted with, but continental ladies have fans for every status. The one you are pointing to is one for mourning. If you look closely, there is a funeral scene in the picture."

"Oh," Laura said and pointed quickly to the next one, "What is this one?"

"This means the fan carrier is expecting a child, as you can tell by the babies pictured on it."

By this time, Maria and Sarah were standing behind Madame Duval and Laura. Maria said excitedly, "Madame. Tell us about the language of the fan. Do the movements mean the same as in England?"

"I have not been to England, so I do not know if there are differences." She picked up four hand fans and gave one to each young woman as they backed up to form a circle.

"If you let the fan rest on the right cheek it means 'yes'."

Virtue and Vanity

Maria ventured, "So, resting on the left cheek means 'no'?"

"Yes, of course," their hostess replied.

Laura asked, "Please show me the position that says, 'I want to know you better.'"

The young women laughed as Madame Duval used her left hand to hold the fan coquetishly in front of her face. She then continued, "Whatever you do girls, don't place the half-open fan to your lips."

"Why?" asked Maria innocently as Laura and Sarah tried to smother their mirth.

"Maria, my dear, that position means 'kiss me'."

Maria's face colored.

At that moment, a servant entered. "The Marquis de Mascarille has arrived."

"Wait a moment," their hostess said, "we need to put these fans away. . . there, now you may show him in."

Laura whispered to the others, "I am glad we do not need fans today. I am not ready. My fan might say the wrong thing."

As the Marquis bowed and entered the room he said, "Ah, the most enchanting women in France."

"Please, sit down, my Lord," Madame Duval said, gesturing toward a chair.

Looking at Laura, the visitor complied and continued, "How would Lady Bingley like to visit the Louvre?"

Laura's face blushed slightly at the first time use of "lady" appended to her name. She looked at Madame Duval and then spoke, "I do not think I would be interested."

"You surprise me. Why only yesterday, you said you loved portraits." Leaning forward in his chair, he continued, "I should like to show you some of my own work, which is on exhibition."

"I know so little about you, my Lord."

Leaning back into his chair, he smiled slightly, "Ah. I see your reluctance. Of course, you wish to be introduced into society before making the circle of sights."

Laura did not reply but tilted her head in a coquettish manner.

The Marquis continued, "Would you allow me to escort you to the ball tomorrow evening?"

The ladies were silent and the aristocrat continued, "Of course, I mean your happy quadrille."

Madame Duval replied, "We shall be honored to be escorted by our lord."

"Excellent. My carriage will call at eight o'clock."

The visitor stood in a stance reminiscent of a peacock and asked, "What do you think of my accessories? Do they match well?"

He looked at Sarah, who replied, "Very well, my Lord."

"What do you think of my stockings?"

Laura eagerly replied, "They are the best of taste. I, myself, wear only the finest of stockings."

Maria blurted out sarcastically, "I must confess that I have never seen a more perfect and elegant ensemble."

The Marquis cried out sharply, "Gently! By jove, ladies, you use me very ill! I must complain of your treatment, indeed, I must. This is not fair."

Laura replied, "What is the matter, my lord?"

"You both besiege my heart at once. Attack me on both flanks. The sides are not equal. I vow I will cry murder."

Sarah whispered to Madame Duval, "He certainly has an original way of putting things."

"An admirable wit," Laura said.

"My heart hangs by a single thread. . . ." here the Marquis paused and the servant announced, "Two English gentlemen, Mr. Andrew Darcy and Mr. John Darcy."

The brothers walked into the room with John holding a riding stick under his arm. Those already in the room stood as Laura raised a superior tone. "What are you two doing here? Can you not see we are entertaining a Lord?"

Madame Duval quickly reassured, "Of course, you are welcome. I believe you know the ladies. This is the Marquis de Mascarille."

As the Marquis bowed, John slapped him on the back several times with his riding stick and said, "There you are, you rascal. We have been looking for you for the past three hours."

The aristocrat replied, "Oh, oh, oh! You never told me there was to be a thrashing in the bargain."

Maria stepped forward and tried to restrain her brother,

Virtue and Vanity   49

"John, do you realize what you are about?"

Laura stood aghast as she watched the happenings.

Andrew said, "You are a fine one to play the man of rank."

His brother then ordered, "Take off that funny coat and return to your duties."

Laura raised her voice indignantly, "What is the meaning of this?"

As the questioned Marquis began to take off his coat he said, "It was a wager, my lady."

"What? To let yourself be insulted like that?"

John and Andrew began laughing. The Marquis looked at the two brothers, "You have won the wages, Jacob," John said between laughs. "Why do you not explain it?"

With his coat in his arms, the Marquis, or shall we say Jacob, turned and said, "My masters bet me that I could not fool you as did the Marquis de Mascarille from Moliere's play, *The Precious Provincials*, did."

"I should have smelled a rat," Madame Duval said. "I thought the title familiar, although it is difficult to remember a play from the 17th century."

"You have done quite well," John said as he approached, "but, now you must return to your duties."

"Thank you, sir," was Jacob's reply.

As the pseudo-aristocrat left, Laura angrily said, "I hate you, John Darcy. You are low and despicable. I know you are the one behind this, since you are always playing tricks."

At this, the brothers renewed their mirth, while Madame Duval merely smiled and sat back to enjoy the entertainment. Maria, who had always enjoyed John's pranks, could not suppress her giggles.

Sarah felt guilty about her secret pleasure at seeing Laura so infuriated. She restrained her smile and said, "I was fooled also. This will just teach us to be more careful next time."

"Oh, be quiet! The only thing worse than being tricked is to have a moralizing sister," the vexed Laura replied as she collapsed onto a sofa.

Sarah asked Maria, "Would you be so kind as to ask your brothers to leave since they are so obviously enjoying Laura's distress."

Maria firmly pushed the mirthful John towards the door as Andrew controlled his laughter long enough to say, "Prolonging of our visit is clearly not desired. We beg leave of you."

Madame Duval replied, "I must say you have given us a most colorful diversion. I shall keep a careful eye on you and your brother in the future." She then moved to pat Laura's hand and said, "All is not lost, my dear. You have a natural gift for coquetry. Surely, you will interest many other suitors in Paris. Perhaps we can regain the interest of the Captain."

Virtue and Vanity   51

Chapter Nine

Following the private morning church service a few days later, the ladies gathered in a small reception room on the lower floor of the embassy. "I simply cannot stand being upstairs on such a warm day," Laura grumbled as she continued to fan herself. "I had no idea Paris could be so unbearably hot!"

"If it is of any consolation to you, Laura, I believe this warm weather to be quite unusual," Sarah said.

"Does it being unusual make it more comfortable?" Laura snapped.

"No, of course not sister."

"I'm sorry, Sarah," Laura responded. "I am a weak person if weather makes me reply ungracefully."

Trying to add some cheer, Maria said, "I am glad we can use the downstairs rooms this afternoon. . . the heat is surely unendurable on the upper floors."

"Most of the well-to-do Parisians have deserted the city for the cooler comfort of their country homes."

Lady Staley suggested, "Perhaps this would be a fine afternoon to stroll through the Tuilleries–with the trees, fountains, and its pleasant situation near the river. The gardens might offer a respite from the heat." Looking at Laura's doubting face, she added, "And, it is the place for young ladies and gentlemen to be seen on a Sunday afternoon. Since everyone dresses in their finest, it is an excellent time to see the latest in Paris fashions."

Laura's attendance was not to be doubted after Lady Staley's statement.

Soon, it was arranged that Andrew and John would escort the young ladies to the gardens. Sarah quickly offered to take Edgar and Anna also, allowing Georgiana to rest during their absence and offering the children a time to enjoy the amusements of the park.

They gathered in the entry hall, even Edgar and Anna were dressed as though to receive guests. John looked down at Edgar

52   Ted and Marilyn Bader

and said, "Are you going to the park without a boat to play with? What kind of young man are you?"

At the mention of the toys, Edgar's eyes lit up, but he quickly asked, "Do you not think I'm a bit old for such playthings, cousin John?"

John leaned down and said, "I hope not, because I think sailing a boat would be great fun on such a day as this. Perhaps you'd allow me the pleasure of setting it sail a time or two—I have always been fascinated with boats."

"Yes, sir. I will go get the best one straightaway!" With that, he bounded up the stairs.

Sarah laughed softly, "I wish I had some of his energy. He seems to not even notice the temperature."

Soon they were strolling down the Rue du St. Honoré. The young ladies' parasols, of course, matched their outfits. Laura and Maria kept their perfumed handkerchiefs close to their faces in an attempt to ward off the horrible smells intensified by the warmth.

"How can they call this place civilized, when they still have so much garbage and sewage around? This is simply disgusting!" Laura said.

"Thankfully, we are ahead of the French in those areas," John said.

"Yes, London is much more pleasant to visit now than it was several years ago," Sarah said. "Most houses in London have indoor water supplies, whereas here even the Palais Royale still hand carries its water. However, Paris has an advanced gaslight system that they say will soon be offered for use in individual homes. When we reach the park area, you will notice the finely crafted gas lamps. At night, they are quite beautiful."

"Spoken as a true member of the ambassador's household," Andrew teased.

Sarah was careful to keep Anna shaded with her parasol as the young girl walked between her and Andrew. As they turned onto Rue Royale, heading to Place Louis XVI, Edgar was enthusiastically telling John about the last time he had sailed his boat at the park. John was carrying a hoop, another popular diversion at the park.

As they entered the Place Louis XVI near the entrance to

Virtue and Vanity

the gardens, Sarah's pace slowed dramatically. Andrew asked, "Is the heat too much for you, Sarah? Shall I find a spot where you can sit for a moment to collect yourself?"

Sarah smiled wanly, "Thank you for your concern, but I'm quite all right. . . it's just thoughts of all that has happened in this place, especially during the reign of terror in 1792." Looking at Andrew's quizzical expression, she reminded him, "This was formerly called the Place de Concorde. I can hardly walk past this area without shuddering at the thought of the hundreds of people who were sent to the *guillotine*."

"What's a guillotine, some cold place that makes people shiver?" Anna asked.

Forcing a reassuring smile, Sarah said, "Someday, we will learn about the French revolution in our studies; it is certainly not something we need to worry about on such a sunny day as this."

Andrew hurried their pace toward the Tuilleries and asked, "Does not the word *tuille* refer to a type of tile?"

"Yes. It seems a strange name for such a lovely place, but the name was chosen because tuille kilns existed here for many years prior to it becoming a garden in the 16th century." Sarah answered, thankful that Andrew had quickly changed the subject from that of the gruesome guillotine.

Edgar rushed up to Sarah, "May I show John the best spot for sailing my boat?"

"When we near there. For now, please stay near us."

"May I roll a hoop? I will stay out of the way of the grownups," he continued.

"Yes, but make sure you don't wander off."

"It sure would be nice to take my shoes off and walk on the grass," Edgar said as he started to wander away.

Sarah stopped him abruptly, "Do not even mention such a thing aloud. You know how the French feel about their grass areas. They are to be seen and not walked upon."

"Yes, Miss Sarah," Edgar said contritely, for his parents had made this point to him clearly when they first came to Paris. "I still don't understand it, but I will not mention it again in public."

"You may go roll your hoop then," Sarah said.

The path was broad, of fine gravel, with trees along each

54   Ted and Marilyn Bader

side. In fact the trees almost became small forests in some areas of the park. The group slowly strolled in the shade. While Laura and Maria seemed enchanted to watch the elegantly dressed procession coming from the opposite end of the park, John seemed to simply wander along after them. Andrew stopped quite frequently and commented on the elms, chestnuts and sycamores lining the walkways, while Sarah listened intently. Anna was quite happy to be walking along with Sarah and Andrew.

Andrew gently pulled Anna and Sarah over to the side of the path for a moment. "Look down this row of trees," he indicated the row with his arm. "It is simply amazing that the French plant the trees in such straight rows. British tradition has been to plant groupings of trees, or simply start with the trees that are there and cut away the ones we don't want. This is most unusual. . . actually, it's quite attractive. I shall have to try an area like this at home."

Sarah smiled at him, "This reminds me of when we were children and you would teach me about the plants on the estates."

He smiled in return, "Those were delightful times, indeed." Then with a slight frown, he added, "Am I boorish, talking too much about the flora of the park?"

"Not at all," Sarah replied, "I enjoy it very much."

Andrew then knelt down by Anna and pointed out to her, "See the black magpies on the ground ahead. The french call them *pies bavardes* or what we call *chattering magpies*. If you listen, you can understand why they named them so." Then he stood as he saw his brother approaching.

John explained, "Laura and Maria have decided to rest awhile on that shady bench. I think Laura is still quite angry with me and only let me escort her to the park so she would not be seen walking unescorted through the streets."

Sarah added, "That, plus she is probably finding it hard in this unusual heat to muster enough energy to act properly indignant. It was a rather unkind trick," she finished with a slight smile.

"Perhaps Edgar would like to join me for a time of boat sailing?"

Smiling, Sarah said, "I am sure nothing would please him more." She turned to where she had last seen Edgar and gasped,

Virtue and Vanity   55

"Wherever did he go? He was told to stay near us."

Laying a comforting hand gently on her arm, Andrew said, "His enthusiasm probably got the better of him and he wandered a bit. Perhaps he is already at the pond, happily sailing his vessel."

"Indeed, that is most likely exactly what happened," John said. "Why don't you show us this pond he likes to sail on and along the way, we'll keep a sharp lookout for him." John extended a hand to Anna, "Miss Anna, since the other ladies have deserted me, will you do me the honor of showing me the way to the pond?"

Anna smiled and took the proferred hand.

Andrew cupped Sarah's elbow in his hand as they walked. "I am sure he is fine. John used to wander away all the time. Occasionally boyish excitement overrides common sense."

"I am sure you are right. I should have kept better watch."

"Not at all. Edgar is twelve, almost a man. He knew to stay with us."

"Yes. . . I suppose it is just this heat giving me such an oppressive feeling. . . almost a premonition of danger."

"Certainly it is just the weather. It seems to have brought a strange quietness over the city."

"Yes, that is it exactly. I could not pinpoint the strange feeling I had as we were walking down the streets. It seems there is an unearthly quiet. Almost as though it is the calm before the storm." Sarah said.

Andrew said, "I am sure Edgar just wandered off."

Soon they reached the pond and stood beside John and Anna gazing over the water, around the edges, looking for the familiar face. Suddenly Anna pointed and tugged at Sarah's skirt, "Miss Sarah, there's Edgar's boat, but I don't see him anywhere."

Sarah had never felt so near fainting before. She was thankful that Andrew's hand on her elbow offered a firm support. "Do either of you see him? What shall we do?" Her voice was not unduly loud, but was rising with intensity, "Where shall we look? He would not voluntarily leave his boat!"

With his free hand Andrew patted her arm, "We will find him, Sarah. Do not upset yourself and Anna."

At the reminder of Anna, Sarah took some calming breaths and said, "Of course. Where do you suggest we begin?"

56 Ted and Marilyn Bader

"Let us divide up and search different sections of the park."
He quickly laid out a plan for John to go one direction, Sarah and
Anna another and himself another. "As you walk past the forest
areas, look carefully down each row. The way the trees are planted
in such straight lines, it should be easy to spot him if he is among
the trees."

Sarah and Anna walked quietly through their assigned section. They were quite discouraged when they returned to the pond.
They took a seat on one of the nearby benches.

"Here comes cousin Andrew!" Anna said. Then her face
fell, "He is alone."

Andrew joined them on the bench to wait for John. When
Sarah saw John approaching with Edgar, she started to rise to rush
to the lad, but the gentle touch of Andrew's hand on her shoulder
restrained her.

John and Edgar came to a stop before the bench. "I am
sorry, Miss Sarah," Edgar said with his head bowed in contrition.

Sarah took his hands in hers and said gently, "You are forgiven. I am just thankful you are all right."

John mumbled, "At least one of the Bingley sisters is for-
giving."

Edgar leaned forward and whispered to Sarah, "Thank you
for not running forward and scolding me like I was an infant."

"You are quite welcome. Now shall we hear of your adventure?"

"Some boys invited me to sail my boat with them. . . to see
who could get their vessel furthest out onto the pond. It was very
difficult because the air is so still."

"Yes, we also noticed the stillness," Andrew said.

"I forgot that I should come and tell you about going to
the pond. After the race, I could not get my boat back," with a grin
he added, "unless you'd allow me to take my shoes and stockings
off to wade in after it?"

John swatted at him playfully, "Even I know that would
not be appropriate behavior for the Ambassador's son."

"So, the boys and I started rolling hoops to see who could
go the furthest without tipping their hoop over. I was doing very
well, too, until Cousin John found me."

Virtue and Vanity 57

"Indeed he was," John said. "However, a good captain never deserts his ship. Let us see if we can retrieve it."

A gardener loaned them a shovel and with it the men were able to create enough motion in the water to bring the small boat to the other side where Sarah and Anna grabbed it. Then they enjoyed the puppet shows before going back to where Maria and Laura were seated.

"Are you two lovely ladies ready to return to the embassy?"

Laura glared briefly at John before acknowledging that it was probably time to depart. Maria seemed unsure whose side she should take in the unspoken quarrel; but, she understood Laura's embarrassment and so she acted a bit peeved with her brother.

The group decided to walk back by a different route. Andrew carried Anna most of the way, since she had gotten quite tired on the excursion.

While the group walked quietly, the air was heavy and still, yet the atmosphere had changed. Each home or business they passed, where people were gathered, seemed abuzz with nervous energy and chatter. . . like the building of a storm.

John stepped into one of the establishments and asked, "What is happening?"

"Why should it matter to you British?" a man snarled.

An older gentleman said, "Don't take it out on those around you, Jacques." Turning to John he said, "All of Paris is in an uproar over the King's latest proclamation in the government newspaper. It goes against the charter! He surely cannot do it! Take a copy of the *Monitor* with you. It might be best, though, if you read in the safety of your home."

Chapter Ten

"The King of France has done it," Sir Thomas exclaimed to the seated members of the Staley and Darcy entourage.

"What has Charles X done now, dear?" Georgiana asked.

"He has sharply limited freedom of the press, dissolved the deputy chamber and asked for an unprecedented third set of elections in one year."

Lady Staley stood with Sarah behind her and asked, "Shall I retire with the women and children?"

"No, you need to hear about this emergency situation first-hand as we are all likely to be engulfed in it."

The ladies sat down as Anna climbed into Sarah's lap and Edgar edged closer to his mother.

"Why do you think he has made such a confrontational move?" Andrew asked.

"It is clear he feels his power and prerogatives are slipping. . . however, this will likely make matters worse. I daresay, his moves are a gamble. He will either restore his power, or lose the throne, or worse, lose his head like his grandfather."

"What is your forecast?" Andrew rejoined.

"I don't know for sure. The devil in these matters, just like war, is their unpredictable nature."

"What form of government do you think will emerge if the King loses?" asked Andrew. All parties listened intently to the explanation of Sir Thomas.

"A revival of the republic is possible. The Bonapartists have never been happy with the restoration of the Bourbons forced upon them by the allied powers. It makes my leg ache to think about the possibility of such an event."

Sarah observed that the evening was almost a briefing on the tumultuous events of Paris. She was always impressed with Sir Thomas' way of including Georgiana, and often herself, in his world. She felt less frightened knowing his viewpoint was both experi-

Virtue and Vanity 59

enced and logical. She also knew it was not often the case with husbands and hoped someday that her future husband, whomever he might be, would also be so inclusive.

Three days later Sir Thomas ushered Andrew and John into his study and motioned for them to be seated. "Thank you, for answering Edgar's summons." He then returned to the door to close it.

Sitting down on his overstuffed chair, he continued, "I would like to request of you what I hope is a low risk mission for His Majesty's government. I have no extra guards or couriers left as we are down to the minimum for the defense of the embassy."

"Your wish is our command," John exclaimed with Andrew nodding in agreement.

"As you are aware, the revolutionaries have blocked many, if not most, of the roads going in and out of Paris. Therefore, a carriage is out of the question and you will have to walk many miles to deliver a message."

"Yes, of course," John said.

"May we ask what the content of the message is?" Andrew asked.

Sir Thomas paused for a moment, and then answered, "I suppose it will not protect you, as it might a soldier, to keep you ignorant of the contents. The situation for the King of France has deteriorated. It seems clear that Charles X can no longer be the monarch. From our reports, the royal troops have lost control of Paris and alternate forms of government are being discussed at the Hotel de Ville. One of the King's ministers has contacted me to inquire as to the possibility of Charles X seeking exile in England."

"My standing orders as ambassador allow me to grant temporary exile to foreign citizens of any level of importance without consulting London. A permanent stay must, of course, be sought from the foreign office once the exile is on English soil. It is this letter of permission I want you to take to the palace at St. Cloud, across the Seine River."

"How are we to dress and arm ourselves?" Andrew inquired.

"I have thought much about that. I do not wish for you to have a near miss with the guillotine as I did after the last war. So, I

60 Ted and Marilyn Bader

will ask you to travel as British citizens so as to not invoke any charges of spying. I have tried to balance two attitudes of the French. First of all, now they have an intense antipathy to foreigners after emerging from an economic depression which the common man rightly or wrongly ascribes to the large influx of foreign laborers. Also, the proud Frenchman still stings from the Allied defeat at Waterloo. With you as English representatives, he may decide to vent his aggression. You will recall it was not too long ago that one of my predecessors, the Duke of Wellington, was shot at in the streets of Paris."

"Second, the leaders of the revolution are not eager to anger foreign powers since they fear another invasion to prop up the Bourbons and undo the revolution. As such, they will probably show you extreme deference as diplomats of the British crown."

"Should we carry arms?"

"No. You will probably be less threatening unarmed; further, you would probably be disarmed at the first barricade."

"May I go, Father?" Edgar popped up from behind the sofa near the door.

"How did you get in here?"

"Father, you take a long time to close the door." Edgar approached John's chair and stood by it.

"I think it is too risky," his father replied.

"But you said it was a low-risk adventure," his son rejoined quietly.

"Your sweet mother would break diplomatic relations with me if I authorized such an action."

"If I petition mother for permission to go, will you allow it?"

Thomas deliberated for a moment and replied, "I appreciate the mature manner of your request. If you obtain your mother's sanction, I will consider the matter."

Edgar scampered out of the room.

Sir Thomas turned to a map and said, "I would suggest you take the Rue du Fauberg St. Honoré in front of the embassy as far as you can and head to the *Arc de Triomphe*. Our latest reports are that this latter route, along with the *Bois de Boulogne* for the last third of your journey, are still under the control of the Swiss guards

Virtue and Vanity 61

and royal troops, respectively."

"It is the middle third of the route which is chaotic. The revolutionaries are uneven as to their actions at the barricades. As a reuslt, I am giving two passes to you: one, signed by General LaFayette, will hopefully be respected by the revolutionaries; and a second one, an official diplomatic pass should get you past the royal checkpoints. Do you have any questions?"

"When do we leave?" John eagerly asked.

"I think this evening would be best. The night will give you cover. Be ready at 8 o'clock and you will still have some light left. Your contact on the palace grounds will be at the top of the *Grande Cascade*, a series of waterfalls. He will be wearing British red clothing. The King's minister does not wish you to enter the palace as this would arouse suspicion. Officially, the King is being firm about not abdicating."

At eight o'clock, Andrew, John and Edgar assembled in the vestibule of the embassy. Lady Staley had a worried look as Edgar hugged her and stepped back, "Don't worry, Mother, everything will be fine; besides, I need to go to talk my cousins out of any minor difficulties." Lowering his voice he said, "John's French is atrocious and Andrew's is not much better."

Sir Thomas stepped near her and said, "He is at that age when young men go off to sea or join the army. He cannot be our little boy forever."

"I know," she bravely replied.

John said, "Andrew, why don't you lead the way with Edgar between us and I will form the rear guard."

The threesome moved into the summer sunshine of the evening, which poured into the cobblestone street. They soon disappeared from sight of the embassy. The district was very quiet, without any sign of rebel activity. Andrew felt like a commissioned officer on an important mission as they headed in a northwesterly direction. He had always been thrilled at Sir Thomas' stories about his involvement before and during Waterloo. He also appreciated for the first time that an officer must not only think about the mission, but the safety of his men. Andrew had great respect for his brother's physical skills and intelligence; though most observers ceded the advantage to himself concerning intellectual and academic affairs. It was for this reason he carried the two passes and communique in his pocket, and felt responsible for the success of their adventure.

Passing the *Arc de Triomphe*, they encountered their first barricade. Though it appeared to be a royalist stop point, Sir Thomas had warned them that some of the troops were increasingly defecting to the revolution. Thus, the mere sighting of a uniform was not equivalent to monarchal control.

"*Bon jour, monsieur,*" the first sentry said.

Someone shouted behind the sentry, "*Vive la chartier!*"

"*A bas de la roi!*"

Andrew eyed the sentry in royal uniform and observed his uniform to be unkempt. The soldier had either been at his post far too long or had loosened his uniform to express support for the revolution. The cries from behind the soldier, "Long live the charter" and "Curses on the king" took Andrew a few moments to interpret.

The sentry again said, "You are English, no? Why should you be given *laissez-passer*?"

Andrew reached down into his pocket to pull out the note from General Lafayette as planned for this moment and handed the note to the guard.

The guard unfolded only the top third of the paper, then clicked his heels and stood completely erect. The paper was returned with only one arm as he then waved them through the barricade with the other hand.

As they left the barricade behind them, the trio heard: (French: "They are important diplomats from the British embassy").

Farther down the road, John asked, "By the way, Andrew, which pass did you hand the sentry?"

Looking down at the document clasped in his right hand, Andrew became chagrined as he saw the British diplomat pass.

John said, "I thought so. You gave the wrong document. It is diverting to see my smart brother make such a *gaffe*."

"I admit the mistake; however, it produced the desired result."

"True."

Virtue and Vanity

As they approached the *Bois de Boulogne*, Edgar asked, "May I lead the way? I know a route off the main trail which Father showed me."

The light was now diminishing to *gloam*, the term the Scottish use to describe that peculiar reflected light of summer just before shades of darkness begin.

They made their way through the new growth of trees in the area that had been deforested when the Prussian army bivouacked there ten to fifteen years earlier during the occupation of Paris after Waterloo.

The threesome easily crossed the bridge over the Seine. Royal troops treated them as well as at the first barricade in Paris.

At the end of the bridge, Edgar said, "Why did we not ask which way to the *Grand Cascade?*"

John replied, "We did not want to alert them to our secret mission. Sentries talk. Let me lead now."

He started walking off to the left in what was now becoming darkness. If a crescent moon had not shed a modicum of light, it would have been utterly dark.

After a short time, Edgar asked, "Shouldn't we be there by now?"

"Yes, I think so," replied Andrew.

John stopped, "I think we are lost."

His brother said lightly, "Well, well, the adventurer and pathfinder is lost. . . it is most diverting, except I sense that Edgar may become frightened."

Edgar responded by pulling his two cousins near him and sitting down.

"Some couriers we are," John mused, "we cannot find our way."

Andrew said, "I am beginning to suspect that the adventures told by Sir Thomas were probably only his glorious ones and not the misadventures."

His brother said, "We probably need to be quiet and get our bearings."

As they did so for a few minutes, Edgar asked, "Is that water splashing?"

"Yes," John agreed.

64   Ted and Marilyn Bader

"Then that direction is likely our meeting point, the Grande Cascade. Now I know why Uncle Thomas had a good reason for picking it as its sound would help guide us in the dark," Andrew said.

Each stair step of the upper falls was two foot high by six feet wide. The three stair cases formed an impressive monument as the trio found the top of the falls.

While they were waiting for their contact, the trio gazed out upon the garden between their position and the well-lit palace. At one point, a group of ladies escorted by two guards passed within 50 feet of their position. After they passed by, John said, "Oh, oh. . . who was that angel that just passed by?"

"Not likely anyone you are eligible for. . . ." Andrew guessed.

Their contact appeared at the prescribed hour wearing a white wig and the red suit. The communique was given. Before departing, John, sensing the gentleman to be of some importance in the court, ventured to ask, "Earlier, a beautiful woman passed by with an entourage. She was wearing a light blue ball gown and she had raven black hair."

"You must be referring to Mademoiselle Magdelan. She is the keeper of the wardrobe for the Dauphine." After a little more conversation, the Frenchman bid them *au revoir* and disappeared in the darkness.

The threesome retraced their steps down the hill to the Seine and through the *Bois de Bolougne*. They decided to return by the same route since they had gotten through the revolutionary barricade without incident the first time.

However, it was now midnight and instead of a lone sentry, a group of 8 - 10 men sat around a large bonfire passing bottles of wine and engaging in drunken singing. None of them appeared to have uniforms on, but rather smudged and typical working class clothes. As the trio approached, two of them stood up and said, "*Halte–lá! Qui viva?*"

John, Andrew and Edgar stepped forward.

A fellow around the fire yelled what would be politely interpreted as, "Dirty English scum. We should've wiped them out at Waterloo."

Andrew took a further step forward and asked for the leader.

Virtue and Vanity

A lean but surly looking fellow, unshaven and unkempt, came forth. Andrew handed him the pass from General Lafayette and watched him study it. He was not sure the Frenchman could read. The leader soon dropped the note and said, "We don't care about any General Lafayette. He is a *vieux moustache* (old mustache)." Looking up he said, "We will take you boys into custody and see what you have."

John pulled his brother back and stepped forward to challenge, "I bet I can beat the lot of you one by one with the sword."

"What?" bellowed their leader. "In the last war we said one Frenchy was worth ten Englishmen."

"Give me a sword."

"It will be a pleasure."

John turned to Andrew and Edgar and whispered, "Run! Save Edgar."

As John turned back to the fire, a sword was handed him and the first round began. Andrew took Edgar's hand and began slowly backing up until they were in blackness. They then ran in a wide semicircle toward the *Arc de Triomphe* with Edgar falling down several times. They heard the swordplay clanging for more than a hundred yards before the sound faded. They continued to walk and run the last two miles of the Rue de Fauberg St. Honore towards the embassy. At intervals, Andrew carried the exhausted Edgar.

The outside gaslights of the embassy were burning brightly as the guard was obviously watching for them and opened the gate immediately. Andrew held Edgar's hand as they stumbled into the courtyard. Edgar's knees were torn and bloody, but they both stood up and were hugged by Sir Thomas, Lady Staley, and Sarah.

The joyous meeting was soon ended as Sir Thomas asked, "Where is John?"

"We ran into trouble on the other side of the *Arc de Triomphe*. We were going to be taken prisoner when John offered to duel the ten men one by one with a sword. That action allowed us to slip away. We must gather a party and return."

Sir Thomas said, "I haven't anyone to spare." He turned to the guard and said, "Get me my pistols and two for Mr. Darcy. We must leave immediately."

As they exited the embassy gate, a familiar voice asked from out of the darkness, "Are you fellows going to find some action?"

Sir Thomas stopped and said, as John stepped out of the darkness, "You old cavalier, you gave us a start."

"How did you get out of there?" Andrew asked proudly.

"I disarmed the first man. The second swordsman recognized me from the tournament and stopped after a minute and bowed. After telling the group who I was, they all bowed and allowed me to pass."

Chapter Eleven

The next morning, Clara, the housekeeper, came to Sarah's bedroom door and said breathlessly, "Little Anna has had another seizure just a few minutes ago."

Sarah grabbed her housecoat and hurried with Clara to the second floor bedroom. She said, "I'm afraid the heat and worrying over Edgar and her cousins yesterday was too much for her. Has Lady Staley been notified?"

"No, they were called out to the Mayor's office. We have sent a messenger to inform them."

Arriving at Anna's bedside, Sarah observed her beloved charge slumbering in a confused state. She carefully sat on the child's bed and began gently stroking the girl's hair into a semblance of order. Then she took the small hand in her own. With tears in her eyes, she looked up to see Clara still standing by. Smiling weakly, she said, "With her hair straightened, it appears more that she is taking a brief rest, rather than suffering the after effects of a seizure."

Clara nodded to a group of servants gathered in the hall, as if to inform Sarah of the resources at hand, and asked, "What can we do to help the poor dear?"

"Please bring me a cold compress and let us change the bedsheets."

The servants disappeared with alacrity to bring the desired items. The little Staley girl was a favorite in the household and was doted upon by all.

Sarah began sponging Anna's forehead and whispering softly to her "God will take care of you." After several minutes, she motioned to Clara to help her change the sheets. Trying not to disturb the exhausted child more than necessary, the two carefully changed the soiled bedding and gently washed the sleeper. Then Sarah dismissed the housekeeper and the staff, who seemed to be milling about the hallway. "Quiet rest is what she needs now. I will sit here until her mother arrives."

After an hour, Anna opened her eyes, focused on Sarah, and asked, "What happened?"

"You had another seizure."

"Why do I have seizures?"

"I do not know."

Anna looked away and quietly said, "I heard one of the servants say it might be a demon. Is that true?"

Sarah smiled at the weak, bewildered girl. "No, my child it is not. Your spirit is so gentle and full of love. . . no one could ever seriously level that charge at you."

With a sigh, Anna turned back to look directly at Sarah, "Then, why do I have fits?"

"The doctors say they only know some of the causes: such as alcohol, fever, or too much excitement. I am afraid there is not much known about your condition."

"Will I always have it?"

"Again, my child, no one knows. The doctors say some children outgrow it, while others do not." At this, Sarah leaned down and hugged Anna. "I love you. I think the Almighty watches carefully over little ones like yourself. Please rest a while longer. I will be here if you should need me and your mother will join me as soon as she is able."

As she sat watching Anna rest, Sarah began to wonder what kind of person would even suggest that such a delightful child could possibly be demon possessed. Oh, she knew people were superstitious, but no one acquainted with Anna could think there was anything but goodness in the girl. Somehow, she felt it her duty to make sure none of the servants who came in close contact with Anna would ever say such a thing again.

Later in the day, Sarah received a message that Sir Thomas and Lady Staley were to be detained overnight in Lyon and that they would plan to return in the evening on the morrow. "Oh, dear," Sarah said to herself. "They apparently did not receive the message about Anna's seizure and I have no way of contacting them. Hopefully, she will sleep quietly tonight."

Sarah constructed a pallet so she could sleep by Anna. She laid down and listened to the child's quiet breathing for a long time before falling asleep. She awakened to the distressing sound of her

Virtue and Vanity

charge's rhythmic thumps. She instantly moved over onto Anna's bed and began gently caressing her hair and speaking softly to her. After Anna calmed into a post-seizure state, Sarah wanted to get medical help. Who could be trusted? The servants might be afraid to help. She certainly couldn't leave Anna to her servants. She naturally began praying for her charge. After a few minutes of seeking direction, her mind turned to Andrew. She would go to him.

As she stood outside Andrew's door with her candle, she felt a little foolish in her night clothes as she knocked repeatedly. After a delay, a yawning Andrew opened the door. He saw Sarah and his facial countenance rapidly focused. "What is going on?"

"Anna had another seizure. Can you take one of the servants and find her doctor?"

"In the middle of the night?"

"Please."

"I am at your service. I shall dress quickly and meet the servant downstairs."

Sarah returned to wait in Anna's room for what seemed an interminable amount of time until the French physician entered with Andrew behind.

The doctor bowed and spoke in broken English, "Your friend was, how do you say, insistent." He then leaned to examine Anna. "I am afraid she is very ill. She has had several seizures today, no?"

"Yes."

He then lapsed into a rapid flow of his native language, which she could only partly follow. She could make out his cursing the lack of some medicine. After he became quiet again, she asked, "Are you having difficulty finding a medicine?"

"It is true, mademoiselle. I wish we had *Assafoetida* drops to treat her fits."

"Where can we get them?" Sarah asked.

"None are to be had in Paris."

After a moment, Andrew asked, "*Assafoetida* is a plant species from Central Asia, is it not?"

"Yes," the doctor nodded.

"Then perhaps one of my fellow botanists in Paris will have some." Without explanation, Andrew nudged the servant out the door and left.

At the doctor's instruction, Sarah placed cool compresses over Anna's forehead and they sat down to wait.

Sarah awakened at a noise in the embassy and noticed the darkness outside was becoming a pre-dawn grey. Andrew burst into the room and brought a few dry leaves to the doctor. "Can you use these leaves? My Parisian colleague just brought some back from his eastern expedition."

The doctor put his glasses on and exclaimed, *"Oui, oui mais bien sûr!"*

Sarah and Andrew anxiously watched the doctor grind the leaves with his mortar and pestle and then liquefy the powder. Using a sipping dish, Sarah assisted the doctor in gently rousing Anna and helping her take the solution.

After an hour, Anna fell into a restful sleep.

Early in the morning, Sir Thomas and Lady Staley unexpectedly returned to the embassy. Sarah and Andrew met them at the foot of the stairs.

Sir Thomas said, "A messenger overtook us on the way to Lyon. We turned around immediately."

Sarah hurriedly told of the events and of Andrew's assistance. Sir Thomas and Lady Staley were not comforted until they beheld their peaceful Anna.

The adults quietly stepped outside Anna's room to continue talking.

"Thank you, Andrew for helping with Anna last night," Sir Thomas said as he shook hands.

Lady Staley said, "She is resting so peacefully now. I am glad you came to our aid."

Andrew rose in Sarah's esteem and gratitude as the Staley's continued to talk about Anna's condition and as they heard the servant tell about Andrew's persistence in enlisting the aid of a fellow botanist in Paris.

Virtue and Vanity 71

Chapter Twelve

A week later, Sarah gazed absentmindedly out of the second floor window of the embassy, watching the activities of the people on the street below. The quiet sounds of conversation drifting up to her were interrupted by the harsh sounds of a carriage rapidly approaching the embassy. As the driver pulled the lathered horses to a quick stop, Sarah was surprised to see Andrew Darcy step down and rush towards the embassy entrance. The glimpse Sarah had of his face filled her with alarm, for his countenance was troubled.

She went to the landing at the top of the stairs and watched his rapid ascent. He seemed surprised to see her, perhaps a bit disoriented.

Sarah signaled a servant to take the gentleman's coat and as soon as they were alone on the landing, Andrew whispered, "Something terrible has happened. . . ."

"Pray tell, what is the matter?"

"John is in jail for murder," he blurted.

"No. It cannot be."

"I need to speak to Uncle Thomas, immediately."

"Yes, of course," Sarah said as she grasped his arm and began to walk. "Come this way, he is in the parlor."

As they entered the room where Sir Thomas and Lady Staley were seated in conversation, Sarah quickly released Andrew's arm and rushed to sit by her aunt. Andrew paced back and forth for a moment before mumbling, "It is entirely my fault."

"Andrew, calm down and tell us what the problem is. . . it cannot be as bad as. . . ."

"It could not be worse! John is in jail for murder!" the young man barked.

"What!?" Sir Thomas jumped to his feet. "Tell me what happened."

"John appears to have fatally wounded Captain Wiley in a duel."

72   **Ted and Marilyn Bader**

Thomas took the young man by the shoulders, "Sit down, Andrew. John certainly knows that dueling has been outlawed. How did this come about?"

Andrew sank into the chair and ran his hand, nervously, through his hair as he continued. "Captain Wiley challenged him to the *code de honeur*. John might have been able to ignore it, except the French captain began speaking horribly about Laura."

Lady Staley interrupted, "What did he say?"

"Well, he called Laura a 'slut' and other words I do not wish to repeat. He egged John on by continuing to insult her. As a result, John accepted the challenge to fight the Captain." He looked chagrined, "I am sorry to be the bearer of such tidings."

"Nonsense. At least we know you will tell us the truth, no matter how uncomfortable it might be," Thomas said. "Pray, tell us all."

"Lieutenant Fabry was Captain Wiley's second and I, obviously, became John's. Instead of waiting until the morning, we proceeded to a nearby field, where John chose pistols as the weapon. I had little apprehension for the skill of John, but I little thought of how a *code de honor* is settled. . . . I should have talked my brother out of it." He stood and paced again, "Now, I may lose my only brother." He turned to Sir Thomas, "How will I ever explain this to my parents?"

"We will pray that the situation is not as glum as it appears," Sir Thomas said. "You stated that Captain Wiley appeared to be fatally wounded. Is he dead?"

"I do not think so; however, the attending surgeon is quite pessimistic."

"Where there is life, there is hope," Lady Staley said without much conviction.

"Where is John now?" Sir Thomas asked. "Was he injured at all?"

"He lies in the city jail. He has some cuts, but of what concern is that when his life is threatened?"

"Let us go there immediately," Sir Thomas said. "This will require all the diplomatic skills I have learned. Though the revolution is over, we have little ability to predict the new government's response. Georgiana, I trust you will pray for us while we are on

Virtue and Vanity 73

our errand."

She surprised him by standing and saying, "I will be in constant prayer, but. . . ."

Sarah interrupted and completed Georgiana's statement, "We wish to accompany you."

Thomas furrowed his eyebrows for a moment and then replied, "A jail is not a place for women to visit; but, I can see you are both intent on your purpose, so you may come along."

Sarah asked, "May I have just a moment to run to my room. I should like to take a few items that may be of use."

As she left the room, she heard Georgiana ask, "Shall we inform Laura and Maria? They are at Madam Duval's."

Sir Thomas replied, "There is not time. They will find out soon enough."

The group was quiet as the carriage raced to the jail. As they arrived at the stone entrance, Sarah was sick to her stomach with apprehension about John. Sir Thomas showed his credentials and talked with the guard for several moments before they were led into the jail.

Sarah noticed a distinctly unpleasant odor emanating from the entrance of the gloomy building. The smells became overpowering as the guard led them down a flight of steps, to a dimly lit landing.

Catcalls rang out and whistles were directed at the women. Sarah decided to keep a stony face and not react to the cacophony. She was thankful that her limited French prevented her from understanding many of the words they used.

The guard yelled at one point to the surrounding cacophony of sounds, "Tai toi"! (Keep it down). He then opened the door and let the ambassador's group in.

John stood in his blood stained clothes and mustered a rakish smile as he bowed, "Welcome to my resplendent quarters. The servants will see to your every desire."

Sir Thomas said, "John. This is serious. Even as Ambassador, I may not be able to disentangle you from this affair."

Lady Staley softly asked, "John, what happened to your leg?"

"Only a nick from my opponent. It is not my leg I am worried about, but my neck."

Sarah rushed over and knelt down on the filthy floor to examine his leg. She removed a clean cloth and flask from her package and began wiping off the dirt and blood from around the wound, thankful for the small bottle of water she had brought along.

As she ministered to his injury, John looked at his uncle and asked, "What are we to do?"

"I really do not know. Napoleonic law is quite different from English Common Law. I don't know how we can prove your innocence. We will find the best lawyer in Paris for you."

John asked, "Is Captain Wiley dead?"

Sir Thomas replied, "We do not know. I will ascertain his status as soon as possible."

Lady Staley asked, "Is there anything you need?"

"I do not think even you can get rid of the vermin--both two-legged and four-legged. However, I think you are permitted to send food, since I see other prisoners receiving food from the outside."

His aunt replied, "Of course, we will arrange food to be sent."

John then asked quietly, "Must you tell my parents?" There was no answer immediately forthcoming, so John raked his hand through his hair and answered it himself, "Yes, yes. Of course you must."

"Time to go," the guard interrupted. By this time, Sarah had bandaged his leg wound reasonably well. She handed John the remaining water in the bottle.

As the foursome left the prison, Andrew was the first to speak.

"I am not sure John fully understands his predicament. Uncle Thomas, what are his chances of. . . of. . . ."

"Execution," his uncle filled in the sentence. . . . "I do not know. In England his situation would more hopeful, since family connections mean a lot there. Here, at this moment, I can not think how we shall begin to procure his release if the captain dies. Fortunately, General D'arbley has not yet been purged by the new govenment. "

The group remained solemnly silent for the remainder of

Virtue and Vanity 75

the trip to the embassy.

Word had been sent to Madame Duval's and Laura and Maria were impatiently waiting for their arrival. "What has happened to John?" Laura asked as tears continued to run down her face. "Is it true he shot Captain Wiley defending my honor?" Sarah thought it had been a long time since she had seen her sister lose her composure.

Lady Staley took Maria on one side and Laura on the other and explained the situation as they entered the embassy and ascended the stairs. At the top of the landing, Laura cried out, "He should not have done it! I deserve whatever names the Captain called me. Why did John risk his life for my honor?"

Sarah saw her sister begin to cry in earnest and run to her room. Sarah's attitude softened toward her sister as she saw real concern exhibited. Had Laura not been touched by their cousin's plight, Sarah would have concluded her sibling had a heart of stone. Maria looked shocked, bewildered, and very frightened; she clung to her aunt as though trying to absorb some of her strength.

Sir Thomas quickly departed to determine the status of Captain Wiley.

Sarah ascertained the Staley children were accounted for and Georgiana was settled in the parlor, trying to console Maria. Andrew spent most of the time pacing, seemingly unaware of the others waiting with him.

The few hours Sir Thomas was gone seemed an eternity for Sarah and her companions. Occasionally they would attempt to talk. The group could not decide if John's main fault was his desire for pranks or his intense pride in family.

Maria said, "His pranks have always provided a great diversion. Perhaps if I had not laughed so at his antics, he would have outgrown his delight in trickery."

Andrew put his arms around her, "Little sister, I am sure John would have found fun in teasing others regardless of your response. It is not your fault, you could have done nothing to stop him."

Sarah experienced anxiety at a depth she had not sensed since the loss of her own mother. Her cousin, John, felt like a brother to her. Losing him would create one more void in her life. Aunt

Elizabeth was very close to each of her three children. What would this horrible loss mean to her and Uncle Fitzwilliam?

Eagerly, Sarah searched her uncle's face upon his return. His inscrutable look left her unable to decide if he had discovered favorable information during his excursion.

Finally Georgiana asked him, "Please, tell us what you found?"

"I think the French surgeons are very much like our English surgeons," he said as he sat down. He was quiet for a moment, gathering his thoughts before continuing. "I went to the house where Captain Wiley lies in a first floor room. I met the surgeon, who clearly speaks very little English, so I was thankful to be fluent in French. He emphasized to me the gravity of the officer's condition and pronounced that he is likely to die. Then, he looked at me and asked if I were going to pay him since my relative had caused the wound. He said the magistrate would take it into account if we paid for the damages."

"I sincerely doubt it will make any difference, except to place a double fee in his pocket." Thomas looked uneasy as he continued, "Perhaps it was not the place for wit, but I looked at him and said I would pay as the ancient Greeks paid. His eyebrows were raised in surprise as he replied, 'But, monsieur, that means I will only be paid if the patient lives.'"

"So be it," I said as I pushed past the downstairs group and made my way up to the bedroom where Captain Wiley was lying. The captain was conscious and as I entered he said, 'Ah, the English Ambassador.'" Thomas looked at the concerned faces gathered around him in the embassy and said, "I think we can have enormous relief as to our French captain. He does not appear to be mortally wounded. Having seen many men live and die from different wounds in the past war, I would say he does not look like a man about to die."

The tension in his loved ones faces seemed to abate as he continued, "When I asked the captain about the surgeon's gloomy prognosis, he replied that surgeons 'always give the worst prognosis possible, so as to extract the highest fee; and then, when the patient recovers, they take credit for extreme skill in effecting the restoration.'"

Virtue and Vanity 77

"I am afraid I laughed, which caused Captain Wiley to laugh and then groan from the pain it caused in his chest wound," Thomas said. "I assured him that surgeons were no different in England."

"He was quite amiable, but then his eyes became inflamed as he said, 'I will recover. . . if only to challenge the diabolical Englander again.' Since he seemed to be getting quite agitated, his friends asked me to leave." Sir Thomas stopped here and pulled out his pipe and tobacco.

"Well, Uncle," Andrew impatiently asked. "What do you propose? Are we to leave John rotting in jail until the captain is healed enough to challenge him again?"

Sir Thomas sighed, "I do not know. I have called the General. When he arrives, please have him shown in at once. Otherwise, I would prefer to be undisturbed." As he left the room, he muttered, "There must be some way to help the lad."

Andrew paced in the parlor for the next hour as Lady Staley, Sarah, and Maria tried to keep a conversation going. Laura remained in her room. Anguished sobs could be heard through the closed doors.

Finally, the General arrived and was promptly escorted to Sir Thomas' study. The group waiting in the parlor grew more agitated as they anticipated the General solving John's dilemma. Their hopes for an immediate solution were dashed as an hour passed. Georgiana tried to settle the group back into a semblance of peaceful waiting, "Sometimes, dear Thomas can be verbose."

"I just hope the General does not still hold a grudge against our family for the way they treated Uncle Thomas before your marriage," Andrew said.

Georgiana smiled at Andrew, "You may rest your mind from that worry. The General, while not overly fond of the English as a whole, has come to respect and care a great deal for the Darcy family." She patted Sarah's hand as she added, "The D'arbleys treat Thomas and myself as though we were their children. The General would assist Thomas in any way he could, even if John were his personal enemy."

Andrew sank into a chair. "Then John must be in a grave situation, indeed, if two such diplomatic men cannot think of a way to extricate him."

Booted steps were heard approaching. Lady Staley, Andrew and Sarah all stood, huddled together, to await the news. Thomas entered and gave Georgiana a brief hug. "Let us sit down and I will tell you the hope General D'arbley has offered."

Sir Thomas continued, "The prefect of police is the General's friend. If Captain Wiley's wound does not appear fatal to an independent opinion of a second surgeon, then John can be released into our custody."

Georgiana gasped, "Surely, we can find such a second opinion if the Captain is in condition to be threatening a second duel."

"I assume there would be additional conditions of his release." Andrew said.

"Yes, but he would be out of that filthy place." Thomas took Georgiana's hand and continued. "If. . . no, when he is released, he will have to remain with us a week and then, if all continues to go well, I can claim diplomatic immunity for John and he may leave the country if he promises never to return."

Virtue and Vanity 79

Chapter Thirteen

John enjoyed traveling, but rarely did he look so happy as when the Staley's took him, Andrew, Laura, and Maria to board the ship for their return to England. "I never thought I would feel this thrilled at the prospect of returning home to Pemberley," John said as he gave Sarah a brotherly hug goodbye.

"And at the start of your visit, we never thought we would be so delighted to see you leave our home!" Thomas laughed as he patted the young man on the back. "You were always a quick study John--I hope you learned this lesson well."

"Yes, Sir," said John, then glancing at Laura, he added, "but, I am still not sure what I would have done differently."

"Talk to your father, John," Georgiana said. "He is a very wise man."

"I will," he said as he returned her hug. Looking at both Sarah and Georgiana, he said, "I still cannot believe two such elegant ladies visited me in prison. Thank you." He quickly moved on to tease the Staley children one last time. He picked Anna up and swung her around while she squealed with delight. Gently setting her down, he turned to Edgar.

The boy extended his hand for a manly goodbye. "Thank you for giving me pointers on fencing."

John shook the proffered hand. "Just remember what trouble I got into by being too willing to fight. Save the fencing for tournaments."

"Yes, sir."

"You were an excellent companion on our courier adventure. Without your sharp ears we might never have found the Cascades."

"Thank you, sir." Edgar's eyes glowed with pleasure.

Laura embraced Sarah in a tender hug and quietly said, "I have certainly learned a lot during my visit to Paris." She pulled back and looked into Sarah's eyes. "It was such a help to have you with me during this trying time. . . I have never truly appreciated you, little sister; but, well, thank you."

Sarah could hardly believe this was the same Laura who had arrived in Paris a few weeks ago. Perhaps, someday, she and Laura might become friends.

Maria moved in to say goodbye to Sarah. "This is such a joyful homegoing compared to what it might have been."

After saying goodbye to the children, Andrew shyly approached Sarah. He did not hug her, but reached out and clasped her hands. "Thank you for all your help. You have a gift for nursing. . . I shall never forget the sight of you kneeling in that filthy cell to care for John. I am glad we are friends again."

"So am I."

"May I write to you?"

"I would enjoy receiving correspondence from you," Sarah replied shyly. She stood with the Staley family as the ship pulled away, taking the Darcy offspring and Laura back to England.

As Sarah held out a hand to assist Anna into the carriage, the little girl looked up at her and said, "Why are you crying, Sarah? Mama said we were happy Cousin John was able to go home."

Surprised to find a tear streaking down her face, Sarah gave a shaky smile, and said, "I must be so happy that I am crying. That happens sometimes." Satisfied with the answer, Anna settled into the coach next to her brother, Edgar.

Chapter Fourteen

The city settled into a peaceful routine following the short-lived revolution. While the embassy dealt with many problems, none were as exciting as assisting with getting permission for the King to go to England for his exile.

Encouraged by the sale of her first poem, Sarah began her first novel. She used quiet moments in the evening to work on her story. The children enjoyed playing in the Tuilleries, so she often had an opportunity to sit in the shade and write while watching the children.

Each letter from her Cousin Andrew made the day special for Sarah, and for the children as well, since she often shared the missives with Edgar and Anna. Andrew frequently mentioned some scientific fact or curiosity that Sarah could use in teaching the children about the world they lived in.

John was not much of a correspondent. He was often at sea as he began to rise stepwise in the command of the merchant ships he sailed on. When he was at home in Derbyshire, between voyages, he would add a note, with his typical bold flourish, onto Andrew's letters. Edgar particularly enjoyed John's notes.

Laura never wrote, nor even replied to Sarah's infrequent letters to her. Maria wrote to Sarah, though not as regularly as Andrew.

Sarah had made few personal acquaintances while in Paris her first two years, so she was rather surprised when a servant announced that she had a visitor waiting in the family parlor. Usually callers wanted to see Sir Thomas and Lady Staley.

She told her maid to watch over the children while she attended to her guest. Then she quickly checked her toilette before going to the parlor and asked a servant to bring a light tea for her guest.

Entering the room, she felt more like the guest than the hostess as Madame Duval greeted her. "Sarah, my dear, I do hope I am not imposing by visiting when you did not send me your card or request a visit; however, I have such a splendid opportunity to share with you that I simply had to come straightaway. Please join me here on the couch."

"You are most welcome here any time," Sarah said as she took her seat. "Would you like me to send a servant to call Lady Staley to join us?"

"No, indeed, her presence is not necessary and I am sure she is busy with other duties. I came with the intent of talking to you." Noticing Sarah's uplifted brow she patted the young woman's hand and continued, "There is nothing to worry about, my dear. In fact, I bring wonderful news!"

Relaxing a bit, Sarah said, "I shall be pleased to have you share your good news with me." Seeing the servant waiting to enter the room, she nodded to indicate permission and then said, "Shall we take tea while we chat?"

Sarah poured the tea while Madame Duval began, "Please do not make a rash decision about my request since, as I once told you, our French customs are quite different than what you are used to."

"I have been called many things, but rash is not one of them."

"Excellent! Then you will keep an open mind. This is such a wonderful opportunity that I wanted to share it with you before I place the advertisement."

"The advertisement?"

"Yes. As you know, I enjoy my role as a matchmaker." Clasping her hands together she continued, "Blossoming love is such a joy to watch; and, what a thrill to know that my actions help to bring it about."

"Who are the fortunate people you have brought together?"

"Oh, I was talking in general terms. I am afraid I get so caught up with the excitement that I have gotten sidetracked from the point of my visit. Now, I came to tell you about a fine gentleman who is widowed. He has at least one child and is seeking a new wife. Wisely, he has asked my assistance in making the acquaintance of an appropriate young lady." With a huge smile she continued, "I had just written up an advertisement to place in the newspaper on his behalf when I realized that you would be perfect!

Virtue and Vanity 83

So I came directly to tell you about him."

"I am sensible of the honor of your consideration in this regard, but I am not sure I wish to marry, at least not in the near future. I am quite content with my writing and caring for the Staley children and. . . ."

Madame Duval said, "Of course you do not wish to show interest in marrying; but, I have learned to pay little heed to such statements. I warrant that introduction to the right man will change your opinion. Now, let me tell you about this gentleman. Your future with him would be secure. He is a count, with a beautiful country estate." Spreading her hands for emphasis she continued, "I have been told that his chateau is so large as to almost be called a castle."

"A count. I would not be appropriate for a man of such rank." Sarah mused aloud, "If he is interested in meeting me, perhaps he is like Laura's supposed Marquis."

With a laugh, she said, "Do not concern yourself about that. In contrast to the prior escapade, I have thoroughly researched this gentleman. You are exactly what he is looking for, and his family is well-known here in France. General D'arbley's villa is not far from his."

"Oh," said Sarah simply.

Undeterred by Sarah's unenthusiastic response, Madame Duval continued, "He is in his late thirties and quite a handsome man."

Caught up in the story, Sarah mumbled, "Looks are not that important to me."

"Of course not," the matron replied with a smile, "but they certainly should not be held against the man. *Oui?*"

"*Oui.*"

"He is known to treat his servants well. . . ." She went on to detail his many attributes and then said, "He is looking for a quiet woman who could be happy living in the country. He is not concerned about her station in life, but he does need someone who has been in society enough to know how to play the role of hostess." With a pat on Sarah's hand she said, "After living here at the embassy, you have learned much about being a hostess and I know your first choice would not be to live in a large city all your life."

84 Ted and Marilyn Bader

"That is true," Sarah quietly said.

"But of course. I have an eye for matchmaking. You fit his desires perfectly," Madame Duval continued. "He desires someone of fine moral fortitude, who likes children. . . someone well educated. . . . You see, I have thought of everything. I know you have been concerned that men do not want a woman of intellect, but the count must feel differently if he asked for a woman with education! Will you consider meeting him?" she pleaded.

All was quiet for several moments. Sarah took a sip of her now cool tea and quickly set it down. She looked intently at her guest, "I cannot believe I am not refusing outright. . . ."

"It is your sense of adventure, I daresay."

Smiling ruefully, Sarah said, "Perhaps you are right." In a somewhat uncertain voice she asked, "Where would such a meeting take place?"

"The count will be in Paris for the ball next week. Your initial meeting could be there, so you would be well chaperoned, and if either of you are not interested you could easily spend your time with other people or retire early."

"That sounds like a good idea." Thinking for a moment Sarah asked, "If, perchance, we did have some interest, when would we meet again? I would not want to be rushed in such an important decision."

"Apparently Count Frontenac is not eager for immediate marriage since he said that after the ball, the remainder of his time in Paris will be taken up with business. If further meetings are to be scheduled, he would like me to bring the young lady to his chateau in a fortnight."

"I am glad he has business in Paris other than to find a wife. That way he will not have wasted a trip if I decide. . . I mean if the young lady decides not to pursue a relationship," Sarah said. "If I meet him at the ball and decide I do not wish to become further acquainted, what happens to your role as matchmaker?"

"I would then put the advertisement in the paper and begin to sift through the deluge of respondents."

"So I would be under no pressure? My attending the ball would not imply any commitment on my part?"

"Of course not, my dear," Madame Duval answered with

Virtue and Vanity

excitement as she perceived that Sarah was actually considering the meeting. "Sometimes even expert matchmakers like myself make mistakes. My role is to provide an introduction for appropriate people and then they decide if they want to pursue a relationship." With a wink, "If you don't like the count, it may still be of use to you by providing an interesting story to add to your novel."

Sarah thought, *Madame Duval certainly knows how to persuade me. . .* and then she smiled, "Perhaps you are right." Refreshing their teacups, she said, "If Aunt Georgiana finds it acceptable for me to do so, I will agree to go to the ball."

"Wonderful!" Madame Dual exclaimed. "I am sure you will find the count intriguing."

"Please, do not get your hopes up too much. I am quite content with my life as it is."

"Yes. Yes, but when you meet the right man you will soon change your notion of contentment."

"Perhaps so," Sarah said wistfully.

Throughout the week preceding the ball, Madame Duval visited almost daily–giving Sarah suggestions about her upcoming visit to the ball. In an early visit, she encouraged Sarah by saying, "I am acquainted with a lady whose beauty, taken in the common acceptation of the word, would not obtain her a second look, but in the elegance of her manners, in the dignity of her carriage, in the taste and disposition of her attire, and in the thousand inexpressible charms which distinguish the gentlewoman, she is so powerful that none can behold her without captivation."

Sarah responded, "To whom are you referring?"

Her visitor replied, "To you, of course. Sarah your unstudied manner brings a wonderful feminine attraction that the French coquette cannot even approach; however, I would suggest attention to your walking. The gracefulness of a French lady's step is always a subject of commendation." Madame Duval then had Sarah walk back and forth several times and with a little coaching was quite pleased at her charge's response.

On another visit she gave Sarah a recipe for skin cream, with instructions to use it regularly.

Finally, sensing that she was making Sarah nervous, she said,

86   Ted and Marilyn Bader

"Just be your delightful self, my dear. I am sorry for giving you so many commands these last few days. I am a silly old woman and sometimes forget that a beautiful young girl does not need to overly decorate herself. Decide for yourself what to wear and simply plan to enjoy the ball whether you find the count attractive or not."

Sarah relaxed then and found herself looking forward to the meeting as an adventure. Lady Staley and Sir Thomas had encouraged her to at least meet the count, saying, "You are part of our family and we love having you with us, but we would delight in seeing you happily settled. If you do not go to the initial meeting, you would wonder for the rest of your life if the count might have been the perfect match for you."

"You look lovely, my dear," Sir Thomas said as he personally handed Sarah up into Madame Duval's finest coach. "The poor man will likely be groveling at your feet before the evening is through."

Sarah smiled at her uncle as she settled into the luxurious carriage. "You are too kind, Sir Thomas."

"When you arrive home, please join us in the upstairs parlor and tell us about your adventure." Nodding to Madame Duval, he said, "Take good care of our girl."

"If I let anything but good happen to one of your family members, Sir Thomas, the General would have my head." With that she laughed and signaled the driver that they were ready.

"I am glad you will be with me this evening. I find myself more nervous than I anticipated and will appreciate leaning on you as we make our entrance. My French still has many shortcomings."

"Oh, my dear," said Madame Duval. "I will stay as close to you as possible, but we must make our entrances separately so you receive the proper attention as you are announced." Patting Sarah's hand, she continued, "Do not worry. I will go first and await you at the start of the reception line. Simply pretend you are one of the characters in this novel you are writing–filled with poise and a spirit of adventure."

Sarah laughed shakily, "I shall try my best. Indeed, the night does seem to be filled with an air of excitement."

They continued to chat through the remainder of the brief

Virtue and Vanity 87

journey. Soon they arrived at their host's home and Sarah stood aside as she watched Madame Duval glide into the room. Sarah took a deep breath and prayed for poise and grace as she heard her own name announced and tried to follow the example set. She was truly thankful for Madame Duval's presence as she successfully reached the end of the stairs and reached for the portly woman's arm. The two smiled at each other as they proceeded to the reception line.

Madame Duval presented Sarah to those who had not met her at the English embassy. When they were through the line, she led her young charge to a comfortable sitting area and whispered, "I believe this is the count coming now. He looks very similar to his father."

Sarah glanced up to watch the handsome, dark-haired man approach her. He walked with the air of confidence that seemed ingrained in people of rank. "Surely, such a man does not need a matchmaker to find a wife," she whispered.

When he neared, Sarah stood with Madame Duval who said, "Count Frontenac, it is so good to see you. May I present Miss Sarah Bingley?"

The count bowed low and gently kissed Sarah's hand, "*Enchante.*" He then stood and looked directly into Sarah's eyes. In a wonderfully deep, base voice he asked, "Would you honor me by being my partner for the first two dances?"

Smiling, Sarah curtsied and said, "Certainly. It would be my pleasure."

Sarah felt she had never danced more smoothly as the count expertly led her through the first two cotillions. He quietly managed to give her small signals to remind her of the upcoming step. While he seemed to walk through each pattern as though concentrating intently on the dance, his eyes rarely left Sarah.

As the second dance ended, he returned Sarah to her chair saying quietly, "I wish I could claim you for every dance, but etiquette demands that I fulfill my other commitments."

"Thank you for the compliment, sir."

"It is not a compliment, but a statement of fact." He then turned his attention to Madame Duval, "May I get you some refreshment?"

"That is not necessary, but we thank you. Perhaps you will join us later for some refreshment?"

"I would be honored," he said as he bowed briefly and walked away.

"What do you think of the count?" Madame Duval asked.

Shyly Sarah said, "He seems to be all that you purported him to be. He is certainly an elegant dancer, but it is a bit difficult to judge a man's character after two dances."

Laughing softly, the matronly lady said, "You are not a bit like your sister. She would have happily committed to the man after seeing his good looks and knowing his position in society."

"Perhaps not. I believe she did learn something from John and Andrew's cruel trick. I pray she will be more cautious in the future."

"Yes, I hope so, too; but one can carry caution too far. Take your time and ask the questions you need to, but do not be afraid to trust." As the next dance began, Madame Duval smiled at Sarah. "Well, he may be going off to dance with others, but his mind is set on you. Can you feel his eyes upon you?"

Sarah hoped the blush was not showing on her face. "Yes. He has such intense eyes, it is hard not to notice when he is watching."

As the evening progressed, Sarah danced with several handsome young men; but, she found her attention kept returning to the eyes that watched her. She enjoyed three additional dances with the count and they used the opportunity of one unscheduled dance to share refreshments with Madame Duval and partake in conversation. The count was delighted to learn that Sarah enjoyed children, that she was well educated and to note the grace she had acquired while living in the embassy. He granted Sarah permission to ask any questions she would like.

She carefully phrased her questions, so as not to offend, and was quite pleased with the count's answers. He appeared to be nothing in type like the Duke, whom Lady Staley had warned her about.

When the two ladies deemed it time to leave, all eyes were on them as the Count himself escorted them to their waiting coach. Once again, he bowed over each ladies' hand before he assisted

Virtue and Vanity 89

them into the carriage. He lingered over Sarah's just a bit longer than necessary and then lifted her into the conveyance.

He handed a card to Madame Duval and quietly said, "Will you do me the honor of calling on me before I leave Paris?"

"Indeed. I am your humble servant,"

On the ride back to the embassy, the two women reviewed the events of the evening. Madame Duval said, "The count was quite taken with you. He gave me his card and requested I call on him before he leaves town. I am sure he wants to discuss my bringing you to his estate. Do you want to meet him again?"

"I am not sure," Sarah said slowly. "At first meeting, he certainly appears all that you promised, but we did not have much time to get acquainted."

Madame Duval said, "Exactly why you should meet him again. Seeing his home will tell you much about the man and the slower pace of life on a country estate will allow you time to ask all the questions you desire. . . I am sorry, my dear, I did promise not to push. I so want to see you happily situated in life."

Sarah smiled, "And you think marriage is required for me to be happy?"

"Perhaps not, but being married to a man such as the count and to have your future provided for cannot hurt the chance of happiness."

Both women were silent for a moment, then Sarah said, "I will discuss it with Sir Thomas and Lady Staley."

Madame Duval laughed heartily. "I hope your decision will be in the affirmative. Your curious writer's mind is longing for such an adventure."

Chapter Fifteen

Noting the lovely arrangement on the entry table late the next morning, Sarah said, "Aunt Georgiana, what lovely flowers. Are they from the embassy's garden?"

"No. They are for you. Here is the note that came with them. Why don't you read it while you enjoy breakfast."

Sarah took the note and read it silently.

"My Dear Miss Bingley,
While enjoying a morning walk in my host's garden, I saw these flowers at the point of perfection; their beauty reminded me of you, so I gained permission to have the gardener pick them and deliver them to you.
Thank you for attending the ball last night and for honoring me with so many dances. I should like to have you visit my family at our chateau so we may get better acquainted.
    Respectfully yours,
    Count Frontenac

"This was very kind of him." She handed the note to Georgiana and asked, "What do you think I should do?"

"First, you should select your breakfast. Cook left several items warming for when you awakened."

Sarah smiled and began to gather her breakfast from the sideboard. "What should I do concerning the count?"

"What is your desire?"

"I knew that's how you would respond," Sarah said as she settled into a chair at the breakfast table. "He is an intriguing man. . . he may be my only opportunity for marriage."

"Trust me, my dear, with your many fine attributes, he will not be your only chance."

"But, I do not have the beauty of my sister Laura and I

Virtue and Vanity 91

have this smallpox scar. I certainly do not know, or care about, coquetry."

"You have a very comely appearance; but, more importantly you have inner beauty. As for the art of coquetry, I have never cared for it either. I believe it is better to be honest and communicative and see if a friendship develops." Georgiana added, "You alone must decide what to do about the count; but please, do not marry a man simply because you think you cannot have another, nor because you feel pressured."

Sarah was silent for a moment and then asked, "Would it be unseemly for me to want to get further acquainted with him? I do not know enough about him to decide about marriage; but I must confess, what little I have seen of him, I like."

"The count has made his wishes known and after meeting you he forwarded the invitation. You would be well chaperoned by Madame Duval, so a visit to his home seems the most appropriate way to become better acquainted."

"Perhaps I shall agree to the second meeting," Sarah said softly.

Lady Staley took a sip of tea and said, "You can tell a lot about a man by the condition of his home and his reaction to it. I remember when Sir Thomas took me to his home prior to our becoming engaged. His grounds and the buildings had fallen into disrepair due to lack of funds. He was so embarrassed by their condition that I knew it would not be long before he had restored his home to its original condition. It told me that he had pride and determination to succeed. Also, I saw how he loved his father and the kind way he treated his servants." Looking at Sarah, she asked, "How many children does the Count have?"

"I believe he has only one; but, now that you ask. . . I am uncertain."

"Well, watch how he treats his children or how they respond to him. And keep in mind that he and his family will be at their best, hoping to impress you. If you see any negative behavior, you can depend on seeing it ten times more often if you marry him."

"I never thought about anyone going to an effort to impress me," Sarah said softly. "I shall look beyond surface appearance."

"I am happy you are planning a visit."

When the appointed time came, Sarah shakily climbed into the carriage. "I do hope I will not prove an embarrassment to you, Madame Duval. I am so nervous."

"There is nothing to be uneasy about, my dear. The count has already found out what he wanted to know about you. This is your opportunity to get further acquainted with him and his family. If you like what you learn, that will be wonderful. If you do not wish to continue the relationship, perhaps it will provide fodder for a pleasant diversion in one of your stories."

Sarah relaxed a bit and smiled, "If I do not desire a deeper acquaintance with him, I hope you will not be angry with me for taking so much of your time."

"Nonsense. My delight in life is to watch young people interact with one another. I shall enjoy this little adventure of seeing Count Frontenac's chateau. I am sure we will be treated like royalty."

The journey seemed to last forever, yet once the chateau came into view, it seemed to Sarah that they were arriving much too soon. *Oh, why did I ever agree to this*, she thought. She tightly gripped the seat as she viewed the huge, gothic-looking edifice and saw people gathering at the entrance.

Madame Duval reassured, "Relax, my dear. Just be yourself."

Sarah forced herself to take a few deep breaths before she alighted from the carriage and was greeted by Count Frontenac, his twelve year old daughter, Felicia, and the housekeeper. Apparently, Sarah greeted people appropriately, because soon she and Madame Duval were led through long, dark corridors to the room they would share. "Dinner will be served promptly at six in the main dining room," the housekeeper said. "The maid will bring warm water for you to freshen up and then, perhaps, you would like to rest a bit before the evening meal. Would you like some tea sent up?"

"*S'il vous plaît* (please)," Madame Duval said.

The maid brought their water and then returned to set the

Virtue and Vanity

tea service on a little table in a lovely alcove with a window that overlooked a small garden. She then excused herself, with a promise to return shortly.

"Well, I must say, this sitting area is a pleasant spot. I was afraid the whole house would be as gloomy as the hallways," Madame Duval said as she poured the tea.

"I was thinking the same thing," said Sarah sheepishly. "They seem to have the usual number of candles lining the hallways, yet they seem to give little light."

"Perhaps the dark stone does not reflect the light or it could be that no light from windows can manage to find it's way to the interior of this building. If you should decide to make this your home, I am sure the addition of some mirrors would greatly brighten the place."

The maid quickly returned and unpacked their cases while they finished their tea. "I believe we shall rest a bit before dinner," Madame Duval said.

"Of course, Ma'am. Shall I return at five o'clock to help you ladies dress?"

Madame Duval glanced at Sarah and then said, "Yes, please."

"Enjoy your rest," the maid said as she backed out of the room.

"I am surprised I actually slept for awhile," Sarah said as the two ladies rose to begin preparations for their first meal with the count.

"The rest has done wonders to help you look more at ease."

"Indeed. I am determined to enjoy our adventure from this point forward, without worrying about the future."

"Wonderful. I am sure this visit is one we will never forget," said Madame Duval. "I believe I hear the maid returning, and right on time. The count must have his staff well-trained."

With dressing complete, the maid began to arrange their coiffures. "Oh, your hair is most becoming," Sarah said as the servant finished her work on Madame Duval.

Sarah then took the spot the matron had vacated and allowed the maid to work her magic. As she felt her hair being pulled back and fastened away from her face, she placed a hand over the scar on her forehead. "You must not pull my hair back on this side," she said to the maid.

"I am sorry Ma'am. Count Frontenac gave me specific instructions as to how your hair should be arranged."

A sense of panic welled up in Sarah and she said rather sharply, "It is my hair and I will not have a man, who is not even my husband, telling me how to present myself." Softening at the look on the maid's face, she said with a sigh, "Do not worry, you may fix it as directed."

Madame Duval watched the exchange. "The scar is barely noticeable, my dear."

As soon as the maid left, Sarah pulled some of her hair forward to cover the unsightly spot.

"Whatever are you doing? You told the maid she could follow the Count's instructions."

"So I did; but, I will not go to dinner with my temple showing. If our host makes inquiries, I shall explain that I rearranged my hair to cover a scar. We are certainly not of such an intimate acquaintance that I am required to let him see it."

Madame Duval said, "You look lovely, my dear, and eager to embark on our fact-finding adventure." She slowly turned, "Do I pass inspection?"

"Indeed," Sarah said. "Shall we sally forth and find the dining room?"

Linking arms, they retraced their steps through the dark hallways and down the broad staircase to where their host awaited them. Sarah felt his dark eyes fixed upon her before she saw him. Glancing at him demurely, she accepted the hand he extended when she reached the base of the stairs.

"You look as lovely as my memory of you," the Count said, "even if the maid did not follow my instructions. I shall talk with her later."

"Please do not lay the blame on your servant. I rearranged the hair around my face to cover a small scar."

The Count looked taken aback and the two stood silently staring at one another for a moment.

Finally, Sarah forced a smile and said, "Surely I am allowed the feminine frivolity of wanting to look my best?"

Virtue and Vanity

A shorter, nervous silence followed before the count curtly nodded. Then, regaining his courtly voice, he said, "Of course, Miss Bingley." He then offered an arm to each lady and led them into the cavernous room where they would dine. Felicia was already waiting to the left of the table's head, looking very small in the huge space. The Count seated Madame Duval to the left of his daughter and assisted Sarah to a chair on his right, while he took the seat at the head of the table.

As the servants delivered the *appertif*, Sarah took the opportunity to gaze around the room. The table looked large enough to accommodate twenty or more–*The Count must have been quite serious about needing a hostess*, Sarah thought. Two of the dark stone walls were covered with beautiful tapestries. The outside wall had three good-sized windows, but they seemed small in contrast to the room's vastness. The focus of the fourth wall was a fireplace, larger than any Sarah had previously seen. Above it hung a set of portraits.

The Count noticed her focus and said, with no emotion in his voice, "When we marry, I will of course have your painting done to replace that of Marcella, my first wife. We'll dispose of her painting then."

Felicia started at this and bit her lip.

Poor child, Sarah thought, *surely she would like her mother's portrait to remain and her memory to be cherished.*

"I have never enjoyed people looking at me," Sarah said softly but firmly. "Marcella was a beautiful woman, I would rather have her picture gracing the room. I am sure Felicia would prefer to. . . ."

"That would not be proper," the count said. "We will remove her picture as soon as we wed." Then softening his voice to the courtly one Sarah was familiar with, he said, "We will leave my portrait hanging there until you feel ready to have yours added. Now, let us talk of more pleasant things. Please try the appertif. Our cook is one of the finest anywhere."

Madame Duval gave Sarah a look that said, *He is trying to be pleasant now. Follow along.*

"Do you not wish to say grace?" Sarah asked.

"If you wish, I will do so." He quickly recited a standard

table prayer.

Well, at least he knows a grace, Sarah thought. "Thank you," she said and then tasted the food before her. "Your cook is excellent. This combination is very pleasing to the palate as well as to the eye."

"I am glad you find it so," Count Frontenac said. "The housekeeper has been overseeing menu plans since my wife died; but, of course, you will take over when we marry."

"If we marry," Sarah said kindly, but with emphasis.

Madame Duval turned to Felicia and said, "You are a very mature young lady. I am happy you are in our company this evening."

"Thank you Madame. It is nice to be old enough to eat with the adults."

Sarah hardly noticed what she ate that evening. She could feel the gaze of both the count and his daughter with each of her movements. When a dish of cheese was served, the Count pointed out that the cheese was produced locally. Its creamy, sharp quality was exceptional. Felicia seemed friendly when responding to Madame Duval's questions, but she answered Sarah's queries with a sullen formality. As dinner ended, Felicia courteously wished the three adults *bon nuit* and made her way upstairs.

The count directed the two women to a small parlor. The walls were covered with a cream-colored fabric, which provided a bright backdrop for the many cheerful paintings. A mirror graced each wall, causing the light from the fireplace and candles to dance around the room in a delightful way. "What a lovely, cheerful room," Sarah said as she entered. Glancing at Madame Duval she realized that the matron understood her relief that the building had at least one bright spot.

"This is, of course, the ladies sitting parlor. While it is not a room I particularly enjoy, I thought it would be more comfortable than the men's parlor," the count said. "After breakfast I will give you ladies a tour of the house and the grounds."

"Thank you," Madame Duval said. "We shall look forward to seeing the remainder of your spacious home."

Sarah silently applauded her companion for the tactful statement. The house might be dark, damp and drafty, but it was cer-

Virtue and Vanity 97

tainly large.

The Count told a bit of his family history and answered many questions. After an hour's pleasant chat, Sarah asked, "How long ago did your wife pass away?"

"It has been a year," came the dour answer.

"May I ask how she died? Did she suffer long?"

"I will not discuss it," the count answered and then rose and escorted the ladies to their room. Bowing over each of their hands, he gently touched Sarah's with his lips and bid them goodnight.

Sarah quickly brushed out her hair, washed up and prepared for bed. Then she glanced at her roommate and asked, "Do you know anything about the death of the count's wife?"

"No. I'm afraid not. Why?"

"You do not suppose he had anything to do with her death, do you?" Sarah asked.

"Of course not," Madame Duval responded. Then she said more thoughtfully, "At least, I hope not."

The two stared at each other, with horrible thoughts reflected in their eyes. Finally, the elder lady laughed, "My dear, your writer's mind is looking for mystery where there is none. I must admit I was also giving my imagination free rein."

"You are probably right," Sarah said. "In any case, it is certainly not a thought to dwell on prior to retiring. Let us talk of more pleasant things."

Madame Duval seemed to take forever to prepare for bed. She sat before the mirror and carefully wrapped several locks of hair in rags before putting on her nightcap. With the nightcap and the rags, her head looked like a cushion with its stuffing popping out.

"So that's how you keep those curls framing your face." With an effort, Sarah managed not to laugh and said, "I'm afraid I wouldn't have the patience."

"Usually my maid takes care of it for me," Madame Duval said, "but I learned to do it myself for occasions such as this. After all, a matchmaker must take pains with her own appearance."

"Perhaps you would like a match for yourself?" Sarah teased. "I will keep my eyes open."

"No. No. For me I think there was only one true love," she answered reflectively. With a spark of mischief, "My matchmaking is all my husband's fault. He made me so happy that I want to help everyone else find the same."

Sarah smiled, "You will have to tell me about your husband. He must have been very special."

"Indeed," said the older lady as she began to arrange several containers in front of her. She harshly rubbed one of the strange-smelling mixtures into her skin and tried to talk at the same time.

Laughing, Sarah said, "Why don't we wait til you're done with your toilette, so I can understand you."

Madame Duval smiled and nodded agreement as she fanned herself.

Watching in fascination, Sarah listened as her roommate explained the use of the various items she spread on her skin. Some she rubbed on with a vengeance; others she gently patted on.

Madame Duval spread the fourth and final concoction over her face and neck and turned to Sarah and said, "This is the one I told you to try on your scar. Have you used it yet?"

"No. I forgot and have not even opened the container you gave me," Sarah said with chagrin. Then she looked at the matron, "I noticed when you opened that first mixture, it had a rather unpleasant odor. Does not the smell bother you at night?"

"Oh, no, not this mixture," the elderly lady laughed as she walked over and put a spot of the ointment on Sarah's nose. "You see, it smells delightful. I believe it has some lavender in it. I rinse that first mixture off before I apply the others."

Sarah reached for a handkerchief to wipe it off with, but Madame Duval stopped her. "No, no. If you must remove it, put it to good use on your little scar."

Content that her wishes were complied with, Madame Duval closed her containers and climbed heavily onto the bed. "As I get older, it takes more and more work to look acceptable." Catching Sarah's humor-filled glance she added with a grin, "You find my ointment covered face amusing? Well, as long as there is no emergency in the night, it hardly matters what I look like to sleep. By morning I expect these magic potions to have turned me into a beautiful young princess. . . perhaps I'll give a try for the count."

Virtue and Vanity   99

Then she tucked a linen scarf under her chin and tied it above her nightcap.

Sarah couldn't help giggling at the older woman, who now looked like she had grown rabbit ears. "Well, if I don't recognize you in the morning, please introduce yourself."

They snuffed their candles and laid in the darkness, whispering like school girls. It wasn't until her companion grew silent that Sarah noticed the wind blowing rain against the window. *Well, at least this castle is sturdy and will stand secure against any storm*, she thought as she settled into bed. Just as she began to drift toward sleep Madame Duval began emitting a soft snore, which soon grew into a bed-shaking, sleep-chasing roar.

Sarah tried to block out the sounds of the storm raging outside and of her bedmate's snoring. After a long period of tossing and turning, she finally drifted off to sleep.

A loud noise awakened Sarah and she laid listening for a repeat of the sound. Over the storm's wails, she heard a creaking sound from the hall that sent a shudder up her spine. Then she saw a faint light under the door. Perhaps someone was in the hall with a candle. Why were they pausing at her door? The worst possible thought popped into her head. . . perhaps the count had hastened his wife's demise and now she haunted this castle-like home. Was she anxious to have any potential replacement leave? Did she want to protect Sarah by telling her about the count's nefarious tendencies?

Sarah lit the candle on her bedside table and then wakened her companion. "Madame Duval," she urgently whispered, "wake up."

The matron sat up, looking startled. "Whatever is it, my dear. Are you feeling ill?"

"No, but look. Do you see the light moving back and forth in front of our door?"

"Yes. It appears someone is pacing in the hallway. What time is it?"

"One o'clock. No one should be up and about at this time of night. And, why would they be hovering about outside our room?"

"Oh, my. What shall we do? Do we have anything for our

defense?"

"Surely, no one would harm us," Sarah gasped. "There is but one thing to do," she continued resolutely. "We must find what we can for our protection and see who is there."

The light began to slowly move away from their door. "Quickly," Sarah urged. "You carry the candle and I will take the fireplace poker for our defense."

Slowly, Sarah opened the door. Madame Duval huddled behind her, half pushing her into the hallway. They glanced in the direction the light had moved. A ghostly apparition, dressed in a long white gown, with a white nightcap seemed to float down the hallway, carrying a candle. Then she suddenly disappeared from view.

The two women stared at each other for a moment, both thinking, *Was that a ghost?*

Sarah whispered, "I think I've read too many stories. I feel a bit like Catherine Morland in *Northanger Abbey*." She clasped the older woman's hand. "I am so glad you are with me," she whispered. "Shall we investigate?"

The portly woman nodded her ointment-covered head in the affirmative, pushing the flopping rabbit-ear ends of the linen cloth back away from her face. Together they tiptoed down the hallway, Sarah a bit ahead of the older woman. They were almost to the point where the apparition had disappeared, when a door opened. Madame Duval turned to the doorway and stood face-to-face with a girl they had never seen before.

The girl took one look at Madame Duval's white-smeared, linen-wrapped face and quickly screamed, "*C'est un fantôme!*" and then fainted.

Sarah rushed back to the scene and together they assisted the girl back into her bedroom. "Perhaps it is best if you are not her first vision when she awakens, Madame, since the potions have not yet had time to finish their work."

"Oh, my dear. No wonder the poor thing was frightened," Madame Duval said as she put her head in her hands. "To see an unknown figure looking like a ghost with its head tied on. . . the poor girl."

As the girl began to open her eyes, Sarah said, "*Soyez*

Virtue and Vanity   101

tranquille! Tout va bien, ma petite (Don't worry. It is all right, my little one.)." Smiling to reassure the girl she continued, "My name is Sarah Bingley. What is your name?"

"I am Cassandra Frontenac." She glanced at Madame Duval and then whispered to Sarah, "What is wrong with her? Was she injured?"

Sarah chuckled and whispered back, "No. She thinks the ointment will help make her look more beautiful and the cloth is to prevent the ointment from soiling the bedclothes."

Cassandra looked doubtful at these two strange-looking apparitions, but managed a tentative smile as Sarah introduced her to Madame Duval.

"Did you see someone in the hallway with a candle? Is that why you were coming out?" Sarah asked.

"Yes. I thought it might be my little sister. . . she walks in her sleep. I was going to check on her and," glancing at Madame Duval, "I was startled to find a stranger."

"Very tactfully said," Madame Duval replied with a smile. "That must have been who we saw. Perhaps we should check on her. The last place we saw her was just a little further down the hall."

"She is most likely back in her room then," Cassandra said. "It is at the end of the hall."

The threesome relaxed a bit and Sarah said, "Shall we tuck you back into bed after giving you such a fright?"

"Yes, please," Cassandra said. "Felicia was wrong. You are nice," she continued as she settled into her bed.

Sarah smiled as she pulled the blankets around the girl. "How many sisters and brothers do you have?"

"I have four sisters. You met Felicia. Susannah is the sleep-walker, she's the youngest. In the morning you'll meet Nanette and Josephine. Father said we were all to look our best to be introduced after breakfast."

"We had all better get some rest then if we are to look our best," Sarah said. "I shall look forward to seeing you again in the morning." She extinguished the girl's candle and whispered, "Good night. Sleep well."

Chapter Sixteen

Sarah awakened in the morning to find Madame Duval sitting at the little table in the alcove. She looked up at Sarah's approach and said, "Good morning, my dear."

"Good morning. I am sorry for the sleep you lost because of my foolish imagination."

"Not to worry, my dear. I think the castle-like atmosphere of this place and unknown details of Countess Frontenac's death made us both quite susceptible to jump to conclusions last night. Now that I look back on it, it was the most diverting experience I've had in some time."

Sarah laughed, "I was so afraid. . .then I felt foolish when we found out it was just a little girl sleepwalking. I was almost disappointed it wasn't a ghost."

Soon the two ladies were dressed for the day and joined Count Frontenac in the dining room. He was having a cup of tea and reading a newspaper. Felicia sat quietly beside her father, who rose when the twosome entered. "Good morning," he greeted, "please join us. Felicia, let the cook know that we are all assembled."

"*Oui*, Papa," she said as she scooted off to comply with her father's directive.

As they enjoyed the delicious pastries, Sarah said, "We met Cassandra last night. She seems a delightful girl."

The count snapped, "I had planned for you to meet the children when they looked their best this morning." Then regaining control of his voice he said, "I hope she did not disturb you. If she did, I will take care of the. . . ."

"Not at all," Sarah said. "It is our fault. We nearly scared the poor child to death."

Felicia giggled as Madame Duval briefly retold the story. The Count did not seem to find the adventure amusing.

The count said, "As you can see, your duties as my wife will

Virtue and Vanity

keep you quite busy."

"If we should decide to wed, I would be happy to assume the responsibilities of the household. However, I do hope to continue my writing career."

"My wife found little time to keep her diary updated, but perhaps you are more organized. In any case, I am sure such a trivial pursuit will not distract you from your responsibilities to your family."

"Madame Duval must not have told you that I write poetry for publication and am currently working on a novel."

He clenched his jaw, glanced at the matronly woman for a moment and then back to Sarah, "I believe she did mention that you had a poem or two published, but you will find it unnecessary to allow your thoughts to be displayed in such a public way when we are married. You will have no need for finances beyond what I provide and there will be little time for such foolishness."

He does not even seem open to discussing the idea of my writing, Sarah thought. *In fact, he acts as though writing for publication would be an embarrassment to him. My stories are like my children, I cannot give them up.*

After breakfast, the other children were ushered in. Sarah's heart went out to the motherless group. Little Susannah smiled shyly and said, "I am sorry if I scared you last night."

Sarah knelt down before her. "My imagination is what caused me to be frightened. You cannot help your sleep walking." She smiled and the little girl took her hand as she met the other girls.

Cassandra grinned at Madame Duval, "It worked! You look much nicer this morning."

The count snarled, "How dare you talk so to an adult. You are to be on your best behavior. If you cannot do that, you may excuse yourself."

"Yes, Papa. I'm sorry," the little girl said as tears welled in her eyes.

Sarah whispered in her ear, "You are right. She does look much better this morning." Then as the count's attention was drawn away by a servant, Sarah pulled out her handkerchief and dried the tears that threatened to overflow the girl's wide eyes.

Count Frontenac turned and announced, "Now, children. The nanny will take you for a stroll while Miss Bingley and I discuss our forthcoming wedding."

Turning to him, Sarah said, "You assume too much, Sir. I have not been formally invited to be your wife."

"The invitation to come here was the same as a proposal. The evening we met at the ball, I found you to be acceptable."

"I was told the purpose of this trip was for me to get better acquainted with you and meet your family and. . . ."

"You have done so. Have you not?"

Madame Duval stood by, silently watching this exchange. She smiled a bit as she saw Sarah was not allowing herself to be bullied by the man.

"Indeed. I have met your children and learned more of your character since we came here."

"Fine. Then let us plan the wedding." The count turned to Madame Duval. "I have looked at my schedule and believe the 14th would be an acceptable day for the wedding."

Sarah stood aghast. "Just a fortnight away!"

"Yes. As you can see. The children need a mother and I need someone to manage the household and act as hostess."

"I have heard nothing about the other duties of a wife," Sarah said.

"That is all that can be expected. I have all the children I care to. The room you slept in last night would become yours. I do not want a lover, just a wife."

"What of the scriptural injunctions for a man to love his wife as his own body?"

"Do not bring scripture into this matter. As my wife, you may teach the children whatever nonsense you wish regarding religion. I will hear none of it."

Sarah pressed her lips together, afraid even to begin to respond to such a statement. *Does he not care anything for his children? Surely he has some sort of religious beliefs he would like to see instilled in his offspring.*

"May I ask what your beliefs are?"

"I do not believe in organized religion of any sort," he snapped. "Now, let us discuss more pleasant matters."

Virtue and Vanity 105

Not to be so easily diverted from a topic that was so important to her, Sarah asked, "Do you believe in God?"

"Children and weak-minded people need to believe in an all-knowing deity, I do not. I have no objections, however, to a church wedding ceremony since that is what people expect." Returning to his courtly manner, he smiled and said, "But, let us talk now of our wedding. The dressmaker will call later today to take your measurements and let you select the style of your dress. Please do not consider the cost. It is important that my bride wear the finest materials available so people know. . . ."

Sarah turned to Madame Duval, "Would you leave us alone for a moment please." As her chaperone left the room, Sarah turned back to the now broadly smiling count. *Does he not have an inkling of my feelings?* she thought. Taking a deep breath, she began, "I am honored that a man of your stature would seek me to be his wife."

He nodded, pleased that she recognized he was stooping beneath his level to offer marriage to her.

Looking directly into his eyes, she said, "I have had opportunity to closely observe Sir Thomas and Lady Staley's marriage. By being part of their household, I have come to the realization that when I wed I want the kind of relationship they have."

"Of course, your experience in a diplomatic household is one of the reasons I selected you," he said, taking her hand.

She pulled her hand back. "You mistake my meaning, Sir. I have learned much more from the Staleys than proper etiquette. They have taught me, by example, that when I wed I want a relationship based on shared beliefs and a deep love. I am sorry; but, I cannot marry you. Madame Duval and I will be leaving as soon as we can complete our packing. Thank you for your hospitality."

The Count was stunned. He did not even ask for further explanation.

In the coach, on their way back home, Madame Duval said, "As much as I enjoy making a match, I am glad you refused him."

Sarah glanced at the matron, "I thought you believed we would be a perfect match."

"I knew a lot of facts about the count before our visit and those details made me think he would be good for you;" she shuddered a bit, "but, being in his home, seeing his temperament, I knew you were not destined to be together."

"Then you are not terribly disappointed?"

"No, indeed. I shall find some young woman who wants no love or emotion expressed, cares little about her religion, but desires security and social position."

Sarah relaxed and laughed then. "You were right, though. I think parts of our little visit will one day be found in one of my novels."

The remaining two years in France were very quiet for Sarah, affording her time to write a novel incorporating many of the events which took place at the embassy residence. Her story included a duel over a lady's honor. . . an event her critics said "so seldom occurred as to not be a legitimate activity for a novel. However, the details were so well-written, that one could almost envision such an absurd scene taking place between two hot-headed young men." One of her stories included a gruff English baron in a haunted castle. At first Sarah was afraid the count might recognize himself, but then with a laugh she recalled his disdain for women writers and realized Count Frontenac would never read such a story.

Many events were hosted at the English Embassy. Sir Thomas was valued for his wit and honesty and Lady Georgiana was often requested to play her harp at state dinners. The peaceful atmosphere which suffused the embassy following Georgiana's performance provided the perfect setting for the diplomacy which followed.

One evening, several months before the Staley's departure, Madame Duval and General D'arbley were present at the English Embassy for the early evening meal. Conversation flowed around the table pleasantly. Madame Duval quietly turned to Sarah and asked, "My dear, where have you been keeping yourself? I have not seen you at the balls over the past year and you have not visited me for six months or more."

"I have been watching Anna and Edgar," and with her color heightening with embarrassment, she added, "and writing my book."

Virtue and Vanity 107

In a friendly tone, her inquisitor continued, "Must writing a book make you live in a nunnery?"

"Not at all," Sarah said, relieved that Madame Duval was not condemning her for striving in the unladylike field of literature, but was merely chastising her for not participating in social activities. "I have little desire to be in society at the current time."

"For someone like yourself, to be seen is to be courted," the hopeful matchmaker said.

"I have no matrimonial desires that could be fulfilled by my attendance at local balls."

"Tush, tush, my lovely young friend. You do not want to become an old maid?"

"I try not to think too much about my marital state." Looking at the elder woman she asked, "Why should celibacy be so contemptible? For now, Anna, Edgar and the characters in my stories comprise my children." Stiffening her chin she added, "They seem sufficient for me."

Madame Duval smiled conspiratorially and said, "I dare say, if the right man appears you will be willing."

"Indeed, you are probably right. I wonder, though, how many men would appreciate a woman with a heart and mind. As you know, the count abhorred the thought of an authoress. I fear most men have the same prejudice. I surely could not marry such a man."

"The man was a fool! There are many that would esteem a woman for such talents, and have high approbation for her."

"I hope there is one at least," Sarah quietly said.

Thomas left the room soon after Madame Duval and General D'arbley departed. Sarah asked Lady Staley, "Why did Sir Thomas seem so ill at ease this evening?"

Quietly Georgiana explained, "The foreign office has asked Sir Thomas to misrepresent His Majesty's intentions regarding a plan of great import in the Mediterranean."

Sarah nodded knowingly, "And Sir Thomas is unwilling to initiate and maintain such deceit."

"You are right. Despite his four years as ambassador, the foreign office said they will ask for his resignation if he does not follow their plan."

"And?"

"He spent this evening purposefully avoiding the subject with General D'arbley. He refuses to lie to his friend, even in the name of national duty. He realizes deceit is sometimes necessary in wartime, but France is not our enemy now and we are not at war. He is upstairs, drafting his resignation. We will soon be going home to Staley Hall."

Virtue and Vanity   109

Chapter Seventeen

Arriving in the front parlor of his ancestral estate, Thomas exclaimed, "It is good to be home at Staley Hall. Four years away has been too long."

Georgiana declared, "I have missed our garden and roses." Slipping her arm through her husband's, she added, "I have grown to love Staley Hall even more than Pemberley."

Edgar turned to Lady Staley, "Mother, may I go up to the playroom?" He barely waited for her nod of ascent before dashing up the stairs.

Anna grabbed Sarah's hand and exclaimed, "Let us go see if my room is still the same."

"I do not think anyone has redecorated since we left," Sarah said as she attempted to keep up with her young charge.

The little girl skipped to a small table, with two chairs, placed in front of a tall window. She sat in one of the chairs and her perpetual smile drooped a bit.

"What is the matter?" asked Sarah. "Are you not feeling well, Anna?"

"I feel fine," she said. Looking content, she asked, "Do you remember the private tea parties we had?"

Sarah returned the child's smile, "Yes." Carefully lowering herself into one of the tiny chairs she added, "I think this table set has shrunk while we were gone."

Anna smiled fully now. "Indeed! That is just what I thought."

"On our return trip home, your mother suggested that we might need to purchase a few new furnishings for your room."

"Did she? That would be grand."

Sarah thought, "This dear child always seemed surprised that anyone, even her loving parents, would want to buy things for her."

Lovingly, Anna stroked the small table top. "If we buy a

larger table set, may we keep this one in the playroom?"

"Of course, but is there a special reason you wish to keep it close by? We could always store it in the attic."

"The attic would be all right. I think it would be nice to have if a very young girl should visit."

Sarah smiled at the girl's thoughtfulness. "Indeed, that would make a young girl feel at home." Turning to leave, Sarah said, "I will be across the hall, in my room, if you need me for anything."

After dinner that evening, Sir Thomas sat back in his oversized chair and lit his pipe as he spoke to Georgiana. "Oh, to be a gentleman farmer again. We will need to repair the estate road and begin worrying about crops and weather more than affairs of state."

"Yes. Now, no more worry about a stream of Parisian socialites."

At that moment, Mr. Hand entered the room. "Good evening, sir."

"Hello, Mr. Hand. We have received the news of your marriage to the good woman, Miss Reston. I am sorry Lady Staley and I were unable to get home soon enough to see the marriage of our foreman."

"Thank you, sir."

"From what I see, you have done an excellent job of maintaining our estate during our absence. May we visit your cottage tomorrow and bring our wedding gift then?"

"Yes, sir. Would you be kind enough to bring Miss Sarah Bingley along, also? The Mrs. and I wish to ask her something."

Sir Thomas replied, "We will extend your invitation."

As Mr. Hand was leaving, a servant entered and announced, "Miss Darcy to visit."

"Let her come in," Georgiana replied. "What were we saying about not having a stream of visitors?"

"Ma'am and Sir," she curtseyed as she entered. "I am delighted to have you in residence once again. I have sorely missed my forays to your house. I would like to talk, but I came to speak with Miss Sarah. Is she in?"

"She is upstairs in her sitting room."

Virtue and Vanity

111

Quickly, Maria made her way to the small suite of rooms. Sarah was pleasantly surprised to see her guest.

Maria came in and sat down and talked of meaningless things for a few moments. Then, twisting her handkerchief in her hand, she said shyly, "I suppose you wonder at the true reason for my visit."

"I always enjoy chatting with you about any subject."

Looking down at her shoes, Maria softly said, "I wish to ask you about a young gentleman who is pursuing me."

"Oh?"

"Mr. James Johnson, a respectable and rich young farmer has begun to pay attention to me."

"How would you have me advise you?"

"Oh, Sarah," she blurted. "I am beginning to believe myself simpleminded. I have none of your good sense."

They were quiet for a moment and Sarah asked, "As you probably realize, I do not know Mr. Johnson."

"Do you not see? While he is a gentleman, he is so far below my status that I wish he would stop paying attention to me. I have always wanted men to be attentive, but not to become serious." She continued on, "Oh, he is a good sort of man; however, I have become aware of my ignorance lately and would not only like to marry a gentleman, but an intelligent and clever one to help make up for my own deficiency. Mr. Johnson is neither wise nor clever."

"Then why ask me what to do? I am not married, nor have I had a good deal of experience in warding off ardent admirers."

"You are the most intelligent woman I know." Maria said. "Indeed, you write novels."

"Characters in a novel can be manipulated at will. Living creatures are not so pliable. Perhaps you should talk with your mother."

"She might think me silly."

"If you do not wish to talk to your mother, Aunt Georgiana is a good listener."

"How could I ask her?" Maria said. "If it were not for my playing matchmaker, she and Sir Thomas might never have gotten together."

Here they paused for a few moments and Sarah finally said, "What is it you wish from me?"

"How can I tell Mr. Johnson to leave me alone?"

"Why not say it in a forthright manner?

"I do not wish to hurt his feelings."

"That is kind of you. However, sometimes untarnished truth, told in a sympathetic tone, is the gentlest approach of all."

"Why?"

"I believe we must discover truth and then adjust ourselves to it. I find the sooner I try to do this, the happier I am."

They were then quiet again momentarily. This time Maria broke the silence. In an awed voice she said, "You deserve a very wise husband." Her face glowed as she added, "You would be the perfect match for my brother, Andrew. He is the wisest man I know, apart from my father."

Sarah was taken aback for a moment and then replied in a strained manner, "While I greatly esteem your brother, I am afraid such a notion is impossible." With a forced smile, she added, "Maria, you are beginning to remind me of Madame Duval."

Maria waited a moment, studying Sarah. "Mother says I should not pry into other people's affairs, so I will not ask you further about Andrew. For myself, I need an intelligent and wise gentleman. Do you have any suggestions?"

"I am afraid not. In my absence, I have forgotten all the gentlemen in the neighborhood. But I promise to keep my eyes open, and I will let you know if someone seems appropriate."

"That is exactly what I wished for," Maria said delightedly. "In two weeks, there is to be a ball at Pemberley. Come and peruse the gentlemen then."

"On your behalf, I shall do my best."

The next morning, the Staleys and Sarah set out for the foreman's cottage a quarter of a mile from Staley Hall. Sarah enjoyed the crisp early October day with the brightly colored leaves.

As they approached the cottage, she noticed six small trees with their root-balls wrapped with cloth, ready for planting. When the newlyweds opened their door, the visitors were ushered in amidst dozens of roses festooning the sitting room. The Hand cottage,

Virtue and Vanity   113

while only three rooms, had a very large living and kitchen area.

Lady Staley exclaimed, "I love roses. Where have you found all of these?"

Mr. Hand replied, "I guess you wouldn't know. While you were gone, Mr. Andrew Darcy resumed his grandfather's tradition of sending fruit trees and roses to every newly married couple in the parish. Indeed, my father told me that Grandfather Darcy was responsible for most of the fruit trees in the area."

"How lovely," Sarah exclaimed to Mrs. Hand as Mr. Hand continued, "Mr. Andrew Darcy is becoming quite a favorite around these parts. What a fine young man—just as dependable as his father. While you were gone, he often came to see if he could help in any way. Some of the new species you see in the flower beds were given to us from the Darcy nursery. Looking at Lady Staley, he said, "You must be proud to have him as your nephew."

"Indeed," was Lady Staley's reply.

Sarah found herself listening quite intently to the discussion. *Why did Andrew Darcy spark an interest in her that no other man did? Oh well,* she thought, *he is unobtainable to me.*

As they sat down to tea, Mrs. Hand, a handsome young woman about Sarah's age spoke up, "Miss Sarah, my husband and I were wondering if you would help us start a Sunday School. Most of the worker's families on our estate have become interested in Methodism. As you know, the purpose of such a school is to teach the children to read and write. The circuit Methodist minister encourages literacy so the children can read the Bible and other helpful books."

"Oh, I don't know if I should," was Sarah's first reply.

She then looked at Sir Thomas, who said, "Sarah, Mr. Hand has already spoken to me about this. While Mrs. Staley and myself continue to attend the parish church, I have also had an interest in Methodism. They are doing a fine job uplifting the poorer folk – many of whom do not feel comfortable with the higher classes who attend the Anglican communion. It is your choice, of course, but we would support your effort and time in doing so."

Eight-year-old Anna piped up, "Can I help you, Miss Sarah?"

"Of course, you are an excellent reader. Well, it appears I

have already made a decision. Let us give it a try."

The following Sunday morning, Sarah and Anna returned to the foreman's cottage. When the door was opened, more than a dozen eager children's faces were focused on her entrance. Sarah stepped inside with Anna. Mrs. Hand stepped forward to welcome Sarah and said, "Welcome. Class, this is Miss Sarah Bingley, who is going to teach us how to read and write."

"Thank you. I brought along my charge, Miss Anna Staley, to help. She is an excellent reader."

Mrs. Hand said, "No doubt you notice several mothers and fathers present. They, along with myself, would also like to read and write. May we also join the class?"

Sarah was unprepared for this. She had anticipated a handful of children. Not only was the class larger than she'd planned for, now it included adults. She wanted to turn and leave. However, as she surveyed the faces of the adults present, she saw the same eagerness as in the children and her heart melted. "Why, of course," was her reply. "We will start off by learning the letters of the alphabet."

Virtue and Vanity 115

Chapter Eighteen

A few days later, a late evening knock at the door of Staley Hall preceded Mr. Darcy's entrance into the parlor, where the adult Staleys and Sarah Bingley were sitting.

Mr. Darcy's face showed grave concern as he spoke, "There has been a riot at Westbrook estate. At least one building has been set afire. For all we know, the remaining estate may be burning as we speak." Continuing to pace nervously, he added, "Our information estimates as many as fifty men may be involved."

Sir Thomas motioned him to sit down, "We will help in any way we can. What can we do?"

"I would have you go to speak with the group of men. Perhaps you can reason with them and get them to desist."

Georgiana then spoke with alarm, "Brother. You are the most respected man in the county. Would they not listen to you?"

"Unfortunately, I think not. As magistrate, I have had to sentence several of the ring leaders for past misdeeds. I fear my presence may inflame them."

Sir Thomas turned to his wife, "A magistrate is helpless without a militia, and we have none in Derbyshire now. If your brother shows his face, he may be lynched." He gently grasped Georgiana's hand, squeezing it reassuringly as he turned back to Mr. Darcy, "Are any of the men of Pemberley involved?"

"No, but they are afraid of what the mob may do. The workers of Pemberley are loyal to us, but we can only muster, at the most, twelve men." He leaned forward in his chair. "I doubt any of the rioters are angry with Pemberley Hall. This difficulty has been brewing while you have been absent in France. There have been land disputes involving the Westbrooks. With a shortage of arable land, and the sometimes arrogant attitude of the Westbrooks, it has boiled over. I have tried to reason with the present Earl of Westbrook, but he is both dogmatic and senseless."

"What plan do you have?"

116　　　　　Ted and Marilyn Bader

"We will maintain a defensive position at the bridge of Pemberley. If we fail, Staley Hall may be next in line." He glanced quickly at Georgiana as if to ascertain if this talk were too straightforward for her. Seeing her resigned, but trusting expression, he continued, "If the fighting begins, Elizabeth plans to take the women servants to Becker's Point, halfway between our estates. I suggest Georgiana do the same with the Staley Hall servants." Looking at Georgiana now, he asked, "Do you know the way to Becker's Point?"

She smiled briefly at Thomas, "Indeed. If I were blind, my heart could still lead me to it."

"Good," Fitzwilliam continued as he headed out the door, "Elizabeth will send a runner if it becomes necessary."

Thomas and Georgiana looked at each other as she asked, "Are you sure you should go?"

Thomas stood and paced slowly, "My unsought after calling appears to be diplomacy. To avoid such service would be cowardly." Sitting beside Georgiana, he took her hand once again. "If the warning comes, take Edgar and Anna to Becker's Point and enough money to make it to the Darcy home in London." Looking at Sarah, he added, "Perhaps you could help by preparing a small satchel of clothing and such for the children and yourself, should evacuation become necessary."

Quietly, but firmly, Sarah said, "I would be of more use if I came with you to assist any of the injured. I am sure Lady Staley can manage the children."

Sir Thomas looked at Georgiana for her response and then back to Sarah. "I value your skill as a nurse. A riot is certainly no place for a lady; but, neither was a jail a proper place. You were invaluable then, I am sure you will also be helpful tonight. You must agree to stay back in the carriage and, if things get out of control, go directly to Becker's Point."

"Yes, Sir Thomas." Sarah smiled calmly. "I have a small bag of supplies readied for emergencies. I shall retrieve them and my cloak and meet you out front in a moment."

As she stood to leave the room, Sarah heard Thomas say, "That girl has a real gift for healing. Did you see how calm she was?"

Sir Thomas was waiting out front by the carriage as Sarah

Virtue and Vanity

exited the house. "Reverend Henry Westbrook and his son, Paul, are waiting for us at the rectory."

Reverend Henry Westbrook was a longtime close friend of Sir Thomas and a brother to the current Earl. While not in the immediate line of succession, since the Earl had a son, he had an abiding interest in his family home. As a popular parson, he probably had little to risk in going with Sir Thomas. His adopted son, Paul, was seven and twenty, college-educated at Cambridge and now recently out of the army to prepare for the ministry.

As the carriage with Sir Thomas and Sarah Bingley stopped at the rectory, Sarah observed Paul to be a tall and handsome man as he entered the carriage. His father calmly climbed into the carriage and shook Sir Thomas' hand with all the meaning an English handshake gives. While little emotion appeared evident, Sarah knew the two older men to be loyal, long-time friends.

"In the thick of it again, eh, Thomas?"

"I cannot seem to avoid it. Why are you going? You certainly could remain at the parsonage."

"It is my family home, you remember; besides, many of the men know that I have long been on their side in the dispute."

Sir Thomas turned to Paul, "And what is your interest?"

"I came to see to the safety of my father. As a former regimental officer, I may know some of the men."

"Good," was Thomas' reply.

Both of the Westbrooks looked at Sarah, as though just now noticing she were in the carriage. "Miss Sarah," the Reverend began, "I must confess, I am quite surprised to count you amongst our number. Are we taking you to Pemberley to help Elizabeth?"

Sarah could not help but note the hint of hopefulness in his voice. "No, Sir," she replied with a slight smile. "I shall be going with you to the riot."

Sir Thomas quickly interrupted, "Sarah is a gifted nurse. She insisted on coming in case she could be of help. However, since it is no place for a lady, she has agreed to remain in the carriage unless she is needed." Turning to Paul, he asked, "Since you have had military experience, would you remain with Sarah and see to her safety?"

"It would be my honor," the young man replied.

"Keep a close watch on the rioters as I talk with them. If you sense things are getting out of hand, take off immediately. Sarah knows where the family is to meet."

"But, Sir, how would you and my father retreat if need be?"

"We will watch out for each other. Your duty is to Miss Sarah."

"Yes, Sir; but, if flight is necessary, I will return as soon as I have deposited my charge in a safe place."

Sarah wished she could demand to stay no matter what. After all, if things turned ugly, they would truly need her assistance. However, she knew that Sir Thomas would never agree to allow her to place herself in jeopardy. So she sank back into a corner of the carriage, as though hoping they would forget she was there, while the men discussed the best way to approach the mob.

As the group approached the Westbrook estate, a thick odor of smoke began enveloping the carriage. A cacophony of sounds assailed them in growing strength as they drew close: men shouting, a hammer banging, the harsh crackle and pop noises of a building on fire.

Sarah found herself praying earnestly, as she was sure her three increasingly somber companions were doing. The carriage stopped about 100 feet from the burning stable. The glow of the fire cast an eerie pall on the faces of Thomas and Mr. Westbrook as they exited the carriage. Thomas quickly instructed the driver to turn the carriage around and beat a hasty retreat if Mr. Paul Westbrook were to give the signal.

As the former ambassador and the rector approached the mass of men milling about the stable yard, Paul stepped down and stood outside the carriage. Sarah moved to the other seat, facing the stable, so she could see the events. Perhaps it was not ladylike, but she wanted to know what was happening.

There appeared to be about four dozen men, gathering into a tighter group as the two negotiators approached. Sarah could see a man standing on top of an overturned farm wagon, about twenty yards away. She could hear him shouting, "We need to control ourselves and the way we make our demands or the militia will intervene."

"Burn 'em," someone in the crowd shouted.

Virtue and Vanity   119

The apparent leader saw Sir Thomas and Reverend Westbrook approach. He shouted, "Sir Thomas Staley is here!"

Sarah heard many things shouted in response. Fortunately, she did not understand all their words, but she heard voices call out, "We don't need no blueblood." "Let him speak." "Lynch him." "Let him have his say."

The voices began to settle down as Sarah realized the extreme tension of the mob.

Sir Thomas stepped on top of the wagon, while the elder Mr. Westbrook stood behind. Thomas surveyed the crowd calmly for several moments and the group quieted. Then he began in a loud voice, "Ye men of Derbyshire and veterans of Waterloo. . . ."

A voice piped up, "What does a gentleman like you know about 'loo?"

Another shouted, "He's a veteran, with a wound to prove it, stupid."

Laughing at this, the atmosphere became much less tense and more attentive to Sir Thomas as he continued, "You men have legitimate grievances. I am here to listen and represent your concerns to the King, if need be. Violence and arson will not get you what you want. If you persist, the militia will come and trade your freedom for jail or worse."

"The Westbrooks are heavy on the land and village," someone cried out.

"A Westbrook family member is here, ready to listen to you." The group whooped it up, until they realized it was "only" Mr. Henry Westbrook.

"Why'd you bring the good parson by? We have a dispute with his worthless older brother, not him."

"He promises to urge his family to settle the dispute in the proper way. He will listen to the grievances you have and try to arrange an agreement."

Here a favorable shout went up. "The parson is right good at speakin'."

Sir Thomas continued, "I, too, pledge to represent your interests, but only on the condition that you disband and promise not to form an unruly mob again."

With this last statement, Thomas jumped off the wagon to

shake hands and to speak to the men one by one. He almost appeared to be running for parliament, though most of the men could not vote. The tenseness disappeared and the crowd began to melt away. After the last man left, Sir Thomas and Mr. Westbrook came over to the carriage and told the waiting twosome that they were going to inspect the damage.

Mr. Paul Westbrook climbed back into the carriage and said, "I am glad this mob has been dispersed. I hope the district can regain its calm."

"I always thought of Derbyshire as a peaceful retreat. This episode took me quite by surprise."

"I am sure it did," he said. "May I say, it took me quite by surprise to see you looking so calm and pleased to be attending a riot."

"Indeed, I am not 'pleased' to be attending. . . ."

"Of course not. I am sure you could not have changed that much in eight years."

Sarah smiled slightly, "You always have had a unique way of. . . ."

"Upsetting you?" he asked innocently.

"Not exactly the word I would have selected," she chided, "but close. You have changed for the better. I sensed a strength in you tonight and a knowledge of how to defend me, should the need arise."

"The military does breed a certain amount of confidence in a man, whether to his detriment or benefit, I am not sure." Leaning back on the carriage seat, he said, "You have certainly matured beautifully. Little did I know back then that you were to become a published author. If things keep progressing, you will be as famous as Jane Austen," he gently teased.

"Pooh, pooh. I am only a lamp compared to her bright sunshine. You, however, took several firsts at Cambridge, I understand."

"That is true, but that and my military service seem so insignificant. The calling I feel to enter the ministry has given new meaning to my life."

"I am glad to hear it."

At this point, the conversation was interrupted as the older

Virtue and Vanity   121

men returned to the carriage. The entire party was thankful to be returning home unmolested.

The next morning, Mr. and Mrs. Darcy arrived at Staley Hall with Maria. Sir Thomas handed the ladies out. Mr. Darcy stepped down and told Sir Thomas, "Your brief stop last night greatly allayed our concern, but now you must tell us all about it."

Mrs. Darcy said to Sarah, "For once we have a female observer. It is not often one of our own sex reports on these disturbances."

"Thankfully, there is little to report," Sarah demurred. She turned her head away quickly and covered her mouth with a hankie as she coughed. "Please excuse me from too much talking, I seem to have developed a cold." After she coughed again, she added, "Colds are so unladylike, do you not agree?"

Elizabeth Darcy chuckled, "I will agree that a cold is something a lovely young woman, such as yourself, should not have to endure." With a smile she continued, "I shall tell Andrew that he must use his knowledge of science and botany to find a solution to the problem of colds."

The group headed into the parlor of Staley Hall and Sir Thomas urged Sarah to describe the events of the prior evening. With a slightly raspy voice, Sarah told the tale, particularly emphasizing Sir Thomas' and the Reverend and Paul Westbrook's roles. By the time she finished embellishing her story, all three men looked liked gallant heroes who had fought down a vicious mob--without injuring anyone, of course, since that would have been an unsuitable type of story for a proper lady to tell.

Maria clapped her hands, "How brave they are."

Thomas laughed loudly, "I am afraid our novel writer has added her own special touch to the story. Sarah, my dear, you made it so exciting, I almost wish it had happened as you say. Instead, I must confess, it just took a bit of reasoning with a few of the men known to me. They, inturn, influenced the others. These men simply want to make sure someone will listen to their grievances and try to make changes."

Sarah smiled demurely, "Is that not what I said?"

The entire group chuckled. Maria said, "Since the rioters

have settled down, may we continue with our plans for the ball next week?"

Elizabeth responded, "I do not know if that would be wise."

Maria quickly turned to Mr. Darcy, "Father, please. It will be a wonderful diversion."

He finally replied, "Indeed, we do not want an atmosphere of martial law. With the militia arriving tomorrow in Derbyshire, I think we can safely assume common law is reinstated. My concerns are alleviated, but the burden of a ball falls most heavily on your mother."

All eyes in the room turned to Mrs. Darcy, as she reparteed to Mr. Darcy, "You certainly have learned how to avoid being unpopular with your children." Turning to Maria, she said, "Yes. Yes, Maria. The princess shall have her ball."

"Thank you, mother," Maria said as she hugged her mother's neck. "May Sarah and I be excused to discuss the ball?"

At Elizabeth's nod, Maria and Sarah walked up to the latter's sitting room. Sarah tried not to sniffle.

As they settled into their seats, Maria began, "I suppose you are wondering about Mr. Johnson."

Sarah nodded, as she stifled a sneeze.

"Well, I have not had any opportunity to tell him to desist, but I am resolved that is the proper course of action. Do you think a letter would be appropriate?"

"Has he proposed?"

"No, but he has hinted."

"It is difficult to refuse an unvoiced petition by letter."

"In any case, it will be difficult to forestall his affections." Maria said hopefully, "Perhaps, if I avoid him, he will lose interest."

"That certainly would be the most graceful way for this problem to resolve itself."

After a moment's silence, Maria said brightly, "It seems to me that I need to decide who I should marry. I mean, now I know who I do not wish to marry. . . ."

"Maria," Sarah chided. "I think you are confused about the role our sex plays in the courtship procedure."

"No. No. No. I do not mean to propose; but, I have decided upon the man and I am going to use every resource of en-

Virtue and Vanity 123

couragement to fix him upon me."

"Do go on. This sounds like a good plot for my next novel."

"Perhaps it will be," Maria answered seriously. "With my simple-mindedness and foolishness, I need a man with wisdom and intelligence. Of course, he will need an eye and soul of appreciation for my beauty." With a bright smile she added, "With my beauty and his intelligence, we will go far."

"Who do you have in mind to play this brilliant, yet reluctant Romeo?"

"I am not going to tell you now, lest you think me foolish."

Chapter Nineteen

The day of the ball dawned sunny and bright. Sarah looked forward to it now that her cold was better. She had a nagging cough, which was becoming less frequent but still sounded severe.

Anna came bouncing into Sarah's room as soon as she was out of bed. Full of questions about the ball, she listened to every word her cousin spoke, dreaming of the day when she would be old enough to attend the festivities.

"Oh, Sarah, please teach me a dance."

As Sarah dressed she said, "My dear one, since you have done so much to cultivate your mind, I think it is time to begin learning the simplicity of a basic English country dance."

Sarah then began showing her the steps to a quadrille. Anna was so enthralled with watching her mentor's steps that soon Sarah said, "The motion of the feet is but half the art of dancing; the other lies in the movement of the body, arms and head. This time, do not watch my feet."

Anna soon jumped up to imitate her beloved governess. She tripped in the middle of her movement and fell down laughing. Sarah scooped up her charge and carried the giggling girl downstairs to breakfast. The twosome entered the room in high spirits.

When Sarah and Anna had settled into their seats at the table, Georgiana inquired, "What is the cause of your good spirits?"

"Oh, mother, Sarah has been showing me some dance steps," Anna replied.

Georgiana then asked Sarah, "Are you going to attend the ball tonight?"

"Whatever gave you the idea I would not?" was Sarah's reply.

"Both your cold and your age."

"My cold is almost gone, despite my occasional ugly cough; and, why should my age matter?"

Virtue and Vanity 125

"You may find, as I did, a tendency in English society, absent from our French acquaintances, to have your age of six and twenty speculated about. At your age, I was suddenly made aware that I was about to become an 'old maid' with my next birthday of seven and twenty."

"I hope not. While I am not opposed to matrimony, I also do not long for it. I do wish to meet my old friends at Pemberley."

With a sweet voice, Georgiana replied, "Good. Rest assured, we are not playing matchmaker. Good people always seem to find each other despite well-intentioned helpers."

During the carriage ride to Pemberley that evening, Sarah was thankful her aunt and uncle were so kindly disposed towards her. They truly loved her and kept her best interests at heart.

As she was handed down from the carriage by Mr. Darcy, Maria came running and excitedly exclaimed, "Guess what, Sarah? Yes, I know, you will never guess. John has returned to Pemberley today and is getting ready for the ball."

"This is wonderful; how long have you known?"

Maria looked at her father, who said happily, "We knew he would be here sometime this week, but he could not forecast the day."

Maria added, "He is between merchant marine ships and waiting for a new command."

As Maria and Sarah walked towards the portal of Pemberley, Sarah mused at how grand, yet welcoming, Pemberley always seemed to her. The twelve foot high, ornately carved entrance doors were wide open with light suffusing out. The sweet fragrance of banquet food and pleasant perfume mixed with orchestral music delighted her senses. Maria softly chattered on about another special man attending the ball as they joined the line behind Lady Staley.

Mrs. Elizabeth Darcy greeted her sister-in-law, Lady Staley, at the door with a hug and said as she pulled away, "Your elegant presence at the ball shall surely bless it. To have the ambassador and his wife here will help to divert us from the usual local topics of discussion."

Smiling in return, Georgiana quietly said, "I never envisioned my presence would help encourage conversation. Remember how terribly shy I used to be?"

Elizabeth patted her arm, "I daresay you have blossomed into a lovely, graceful woman since your marriage to Thomas. I hope you find the country air bracing for the nerves and favorable to the complexion. It is so good to have you at home again."

"At one time, I thought I could never leave my home, but I am quite happy at Staley Hall. With our sojourn in France, homecoming is all the sweeter."

"If you are so disposed, please play the pianoforte or harp for us sometime this evening."

"It will be a pleasure."

Lady Staley moved on and the hostess focused on Sarah. "How delightful to see the daughter of my dearest sister." Elizabeth then moved to hug her niece as she said, "Your face, and especially your gentle and amiable spirit, always give me a pleasant reminder of the love your mother and I shared."

Releasing her, Elizabeth continued, "No doubt you have heard the good news about John?" Pointing to the young men standing at the base of the stairs, she said, "I am sure you will want to greet both Andrew and John."

Sarah headed to where the Darcy sons were. They were engaged in light-hearted banter, but as they saw her approach, John stepped forward and swept her off her feet, exclaiming, "My dear cousin. I have not seen you since I left Paris three years ago." Putting her down, he inquired, "How is my special nurse?"

"John, you make too much of my assistance, I. . ." quickly she covered her mouth as a spasm of cough took hold.

Andrew stepped forward and gently asked, "Are you all right?"

"Yes, thank you," she said with a touch of hoarseness remaining. "I am recovering from a cold." The solicitude in Andrew's manner touched her.

Andrew took her hand and started walking as John fell in on her other side. Her elder cousin said, "I am so glad you have returned to Derbyshire. I look forward to the renewal of our friendship in person." He gently squeezed her hand and then let go during the last sentence and continued, "As I was telling John, I hope they cannot find a command for him for some time, as I wish him

Virtue and Vanity 127

to stay here."

"And I also," was her reply.

As the trio walked to the refreshment stand, John said, "Andrew tells me you have had a second novel published."

Sarah nodded yes, and John said, "Congratulations. I must read it--perhaps on my next sea voyage."

"Are the Darcy brothers like all other men? Do they disapprove of women writers?"

"Of course not," John said.

She glanced at Andrew and noticed he seemed embarrassed at the question.

Sarah thought, *Surely Andrew does not object to my writing. . . or does he? If he does, he never said so in any of his letters.*

Arriving at the table, John served a glass of punch to Sarah, "My quiet brother here is about to address the Royal Society with a paper on something in regards to Derbyshire flora."

She turned to Andrew and said, "Congratulations. What is it about?"

"There are several new species to be reported."

"I have heard you are about to publish a scientific book. I must have a copy of it when it becomes available."

"You shall, indeed. However, it is more of a booklet than a book and I am afraid it only contains what many would consider dry botannical descriptions."

"Still, that seems much more substantial and important than fiction."

"I would not be so sure," was his amiable reply.

At this point, the Earl and Countess Westbrook dressed in their finery, along with Sarah's sister Laura, were announced. The tall and slender Countess (formerly Caroline Bingley) and Laura approached the threesome. As they came near, the Countess loudly said, "Mr. John Darcy! It is good to see you again. Whenever you are in London, you must visit us."

John bowed smoothly and said, "I have been gone so long, I am unaware of your current situation. Are you now residing in London?"

"No, not yet; however, we hope to move from this detestable locale, with its mobs, into the permanent finery of London society."

John glanced at Laura inquiringly, and the Countess continued, "My niece, Laura, has decided, for reasons incomprehensible to me, against moving to London with us."

Laura said, "Mr. and Mrs. Darcy have said I may stay here at Pemberley as long as I wish."

The Countess continued, "Why you would decide to hide your beauty here in rural seclusion is beyond me." Raising her eyebrows haughtily, she continued, "I cannot understand why you did not find a husband during our seasons in London; perhaps you set your sights too high."

"Auntie, I simply followed your advice on who was an appropriate beau," Laura answered with a mischievous smile.

"Well," the Countess harrumphed, "despite your teasing, I do hope you will not stay secluded here for long. You are always welcome to live with us in London."

With this, the Countess moved away and Sarah's heart sank. Her beautiful sister was obviously going to implement her lifelong plan of capturing Andrew, since she seemingly could not capture anyone of higher rank. Laura's move to Pemberley could hardly be interpreted as anything else. Why this disquieted her heart so much, Sarah was at a loss to understand. After all, since her disfigurement with smallpox, Andrew seemed to treat her as a dear friend, but nothing more. Perhaps it was the reminder of his botanical work which brought back the fondness she had for him as a child. Certainly, a man like Andrew deserved to be loved for himself and not sought after merely because of his potential wealth.

Mr. Paul Westbrook and Maria approached the foursome. Andrew stepped forward and eagerly shook his long-time friend's hand and said, "Paul, it is good to see you. This is a night of homecomings. I heard of your recent return from the regiment and your gallant action at the Westbrook estate. I have been remiss in not calling on you before tonight."

"The fault is equally mine. Our friendship is so old that it may be easily taken for granted."

"We must rectify the situation and spend some time together. I understand you have surrendered your commission."

"Yes, it is true. I feel a calling to enter the ministry, as my

Virtue and Vanity 129

father has done."

"I daresay yours is a good decision."

John then interrupted to shake Mr. Westbrook's hand and said, "I hear you too have avoided marriage." With a big grin John playfully asked, "Do you have anyone in mind?"

"No. How about yourself? Andrew told me stories about your stay in France. Have you gone to see Mademoiselle Magdelan at the exiled French court in Dorset?"

"The thought has crossed my mind," John said cavalierly.

Sarah watched her sister's face during the exchange between John and Paul and noticed both surprise and then furrowed eyebrows. By the time Paul turned his attention to Sarah and Laura, Laura's face had returned to a look of ease.

John then bowed gracefully to Laura, "If you have truly forgiven me, and if I find grace in your eyes, I would like to beg of you the first two dances."

"John Darcy, of course I will dance with you. Your impudence livens the atmosphere. All is forgotten," with a flirt of her fan she added, "Mercy is bestowed easily to handsome men."

Paul and Andrew then fell in step together and walked away. Maria nudged Sarah and said in a low voice, "Is he not wonderful?"

Sarah thought she should be cautious until her cousin clarified whom she meant. She supposed Maria intended Paul Westbrook, but she might be matchmaking Andrew with her.

Maria saw her reserve and continued, "I mean Mr. Paul Westbrook, of course. His gallantry, his ease of manner and amiability are all that any woman would desire."

"Is this the special man you mentioned?"

"Yes."

"Do you have any proof of his returning your esteem?"

"He has asked me for the first two dances."

"I wonder if you gave him a chance to ask anyone else," Sarah said with a slight smile.

Maria playfully responded, "Your skepticism will not dampen my spirits tonight."

Mr. and Mrs. Darcy stood at the head of the line and Mr. Darcy said, "Our honored guests this evening are the recently returned English Ambassador to France and his talented wife, Sir Thomas and Lady Staley. We have had four years of peace with our old adversary under their skillful diplomacy. I am truly prejudiced in their favor. Welcome them back as they lead off the first dance."

Sarah was pleased at their handsome appearance--Sir Thomas in his impressive red ambassador's suit and Lady Georgiana in her most elegant cream-colored ball gown. *A couple truly made for each other*, she thought. John and Laura were next, with Paul and Maria following. She began to back up and sit down at a table. She looked around and observed Andrew standing, talking to his father. There appeared to be far more ladies here this evening, so Sarah resigned herself to being an observer. She felt tired and realized she was not completely recovered from her cold. She was still glad to have come to Pemberley. The atmosphere seemed friendlier to her than the extreme formality of the embassy in Paris.

After the first dances were over, Sarah watched her sister walk to Andrew and ask him for the dance! Andrew appeared reluctant, but soon he escorted Laura onto the dance floor. Maria came and sat beside Sarah. "Is he not a wonderful dancer?"

"Yes, of course," Sarah answered absently.

At this point, Mr. Johnson came to the table and bowed. He then sat next to Maria and turned to her, "May I have the next dance with you?"

Maria stammered, "I do not feel very well at this moment. I should like to rest for a while."

"Then later?"

"No. I do not think so."

He paused for a minute with eyebrows furrowed and then inquired in a gentle voice, "Are you avoiding me? Do you wish to tell me anything?"

"I am sorry, Mr. Johnson. I do not wish to dance with you this evening or any other."

"May I ask why?"

"I do not wish to hurt your feelings further."

"Nay, you cannot."

"I daresay many of the women will find you reasonably gallant and handsome. You are. . . you are. . . you cannot help it that you are not of high enough rank for me."

Virtue and Vanity 131

In a disappointed, yet steady voice, he said, "I understand. You do not wish to condescend to being seen with me." With this, he stood, "A gentleman farmer should not aspire to the pinnacles of Pemberley, eh?" He bowed stiffly and strode away.

"Maria, how could you be so unkind?" Sarah whispered.

Looking a bit surprised, Maria answered, "Well, I would not expect his pressing my position. Honesty is the best policy where there is no hope. Do you not agree?"

At a loss for a proper reply, Sarah mumbled as the third dance finished, "I will get us some refreshment."

Sarah stood and proceeded on her self-appointed errand when a large drop of falling wax narrowly missed her, causing her to lean back and begin to fall. A hand caught her and held her steady as the voice of Andrew said, "Falling wax is one of the hazards of an evening ball."

She turned to look at him and sincerely hoped again she was not blushing as she said, "I was just getting some refreshment for Maria and myself."

"Allow me. Please sit down, I will bring it in a moment."

As Sarah rejoined Maria and explained, she noticed Maria's eyes were following Andrew with a peculiar gleam. *Is Maria plotting something?* she wondered. *Did she arrange for Andrew to be there to rescue me?* Shaking her head at the impossibility of timing such an incident, she nonetheless felt uneasy as she saw the glow in Maria's eyes. Even if Maria was matchmaking, it would be for naught, now that the beautiful Laura was making her move to fix Andrew's attention. *How could anyone resist Laura?*

Andrew returned with beverages and sat down next to Sarah. "Do you find Derbyshire dull after living in the city of lights?"

"Not at all. I prefer the north of England over any other place."

"Good. Would you find it in your heart to have the next dance with me?"

"Yes," was her happy reply.

"Excellent."

Sarah enjoyed the dance as much as any in her life. Andrew was quiet during the minuet, allowing her to observe him as never before. *A handsome young man*, she thought to herself. The presence of his hand when they touched and the frequent glances made her heart whisper that Andrew might be falling in love with her. Her mind quickly rejoined that this was only her imagination. As she mused, she felt that it was a shame there were so many obstacles between the two of them. He was probably just being kind in performing as host to their party. Perhaps, his father had urged him to dance with her, to make everyone feel welcome. The latter thought intruded frequently when she watched him ask several other here-to-fore unengaged ladies during the evening.

Finally, the dancing was brought to a stop and the banquet served. Sarah was seated between Andrew and Maria. She noticed that Mr. Paul Westbrook was on the other side of Maria.

After the first course, Mr. Darcy stood and addressed the assembly, "I have been asked to relate some riddles tonight. Is there desire for the same?"

The large seated group murmured favorably and several men said, "Here, here," at once.

As the approbation calmed down, Sir Thomas asked, "And what shall be the prize for the person answering the most correctly?"

"I do not know," was Mr. Darcy's thoughtful reply. "What would you suggest?"

Sir Thomas replied, "I have one in mind, but perhaps we can name the prize later, depending on the difficulty of the riddles."

"Here, here," the group continued.

Mr. Darcy began, "What is it you will break if you even name it?"

Maria piped up, "Mother's valuable vase." The group laughed. Mr. Darcy shook his head, indicating no.

When the room quieted down, Mr. Paul Westbrook ventured, "Silence, of course."

Mr. Darcy smiled as the group applauded. "The next one is. If you feed it, it will live. If you give it water, it will die."

"Father, you make these much too difficult," Maria complained.

"Are you guessing your father?" Sir Thomas asked as the group laughed again.

Maria remained quiet with a smile.

"Is it fire?" Andrew asked.

Virtue and Vanity   133

"Correct," was his father's reply.

"Tell me the following. . . The man who made it didn't use it, the man who bought it didn't want it, the man who got it didn't know it."

The group murmured over this one with several incorrect guesses. Finally, Elizabeth ventured, "Can it be a 'coffin'?"

As Mr. Darcy nodded affirmatively, the group again applauded. Several members amicably murmured "favoritism" to Elizabeth as she batted at them with her closed fan.

Regaining their attention, Mr. Darcy continued, "One final riddle as a tie breaker to the three correct guessers. What is it–the more you take away, the larger it becomes?"

The entire assembly was perplexed.

Mr. Paul Westbrook finally asked, "Is it a 'hole'?"

"Mr. Paul Westbrook, you have given the correct answer," Mr. Darcy announced. Applause went up from the group before Mr. Darcy continued, "Sir Thomas, what would you name as the prize for our wise clergyman-to-be?"

"My lady has suggested the country scene painting by Gainsborough, which is hanging over the mantel."

Everyone took a moment thinking about the implication of the prize from Lady Staley's life, and then the group roared with approval and clapped their hands. As the applause died down, Mr. Paul Westbrook bowed and said, "I am honored with such a celebrated painting. If I take a curacy away from Derbyshire, it will serve to remind me of many excellent friends here."

The festivities continued until 2 A.M. when a very tired Sarah asked Sir Thomas, "When are we to return to Staley Hall?"

"We are going to stay at Pemberley tonight and leave after breakfast. Ask Mrs. Reynolds where you are to sleep."

"Good," was Sarah's tired response as she headed to find Mrs. Reynolds.

Chapter Twenty

During the late morning breakfast, the members of the Darcy and Staley families appeared not quite awake. Maria's eyes instantly flashed a meaningful look at Sarah when a servant proclaimed, "Mr. Paul Westbrook."

The former army officer walked into the room and announced, "The painting is safe at the rectory."

Maria stood up, walked over to him and curtsied. He bowed smoothly as he kissed her hand. Maria said, "Thank you for your return call. Shall we walk in the south gardens?"

"I shall be honored. The day is as beautiful as my companion."

Sarah was pleased to see Maria leave the breakfast room with her hand secured in Paul Westbrook's arm.

She was taken by surprise when Andrew's voice behind her said, "Good morning, Sarah."

She turned and saw Andrew smiling. He continued, "If you are finished with your breakfast, perhaps you will take a turn with me in the garden?"

"I shall be happy to do so," was her honest reply.

A hundred yards from the steps of Pemberley, they walked through an archway of ivy into a nursery of seedling stock that covered nearly an acre. The blanket of greenery was interrupted only by bright colored patches of flowers.

"Andrew, I do not remember seeing this," Sarah said delightedly.

"Of course, I have been working on this since you have been in Paris. Mr. Taylor, whom you see slowly coming towards us, is an invaluable assistant. As we walk this path you will see apple trees, peach trees and plum trees." Mr. Taylor approached and greeted them. "Is this the Miss Sarah Bingley I have heard about?"

He nodded. "Mr. Taylor is an old friend of my grandfather. They were in the same regiment. He lived here for years with my

Virtue and Vanity

135

grandfather and returned a few years ago to be welcomed by my father. He wishes to live near the servants' quarters, but he is counted as a family friend."

"Thank you, Andrew," said the elderly man who had a trowel in his dirt-covered hand.

Mr. Taylor eyed her and said, "This is much the way Andrew's grandfather kept the nursery." He then proceeded to give a tour of the seedling arbor.

"Mr. Andrew is the director of the garden."

"Please don't downplay your loving care and practical expertise in cultivating the greenery."

"Aye, but your knowledge of new species has expanded my experience. Mr. Andrew is one of the finest botanists in the country."

As they turned the corner, they saw a small girl with dark-colored hair, perhaps ten years of age, amongst a bed of beautiful pink roses. She was clipping flowers and placing them in her bag.

Sarah thought the little girl might be in for a reprimand, but the girl came up to Sarah and handed her a rose before darting off.

"Andrew, tell me about the girl."

"That's the daughter of Mrs. Lundy, who has been quite ill. She comes to our garden to pick roses and sells them in the village to raise money for her family."

"I am glad to see you allow her in."

"Allow her in?" chuckled Andrew. "Why old Taylor often shows her the best flowers to take."

The tour of the garden encompassed several hours, with Andrew and Sarah discussing all of the species present. They finally came to a four-foot wide wooden bench in the nursery, which was shaded by an arch of ivy. Mr. Taylor left them.

In the weeks to follow, Sarah's mind and soul often returned to the hour which ensued. She and Andrew spoke amiably about the nursery and the neighborhood and she shared her thoughts about returning from Paris. The light perfume wafting from the roses made time pass all the more pleasantly. Before they arose, she glanced at the wooden arm of the bench and noticed the name "Sarah" carved into the wood. *Could this be her name or some other*

Sarah? She knew of no other women in the parish with her name. *Did Andrew secretly guide her to see it?* In later rumination, she realized the carving was quite old, perhaps dating before her small-pox. In any case, the pleasant connotation associated with such a discovery often returned to her, though she frequently tried to discount its symbolic importance.

As they stood, Andrew said, "The afternoon is fine and I would like some exercise. Would you consider walking back to Staley Hall and allow me to be your escort?"

Sarah's heart filled with tenderness as she looked at her handsome companion and said, "I would like to very much. Let us return to tell those at Pemberley and be off."

As the twosome returned from Pemberley and passed the garden nursery, Andrew pointed out one of his favorite spots by the lake. "See the bench there. . . under the chestnut tree? I like to sort botanical specimens there. It also gives a very good view of the nearby hill and its top, Becker's Point."

"Your tone of voice makes the trail sound special."

"It is. I remember at age nine seeing Thomas and Georgiana descend from Becker's Point after their long separation. I ran from here into the hall to tell everyone about it."

"I see," Sarah replied. She was pleased at Andrew's happy countenance; so much so, that she began wondering if his conversation and outing possessed deeper meaning, perhaps romance. She tried to push away such pleasant thoughts and felt chagrined at having them. *Andrew is only a friend. I will only frustrate myself if I allow any further ideas to develop.*

The climb of a half mile to Becker's Point was filled with ruminations about her relationship with her sister and with Andrew. Andrew was quiet until the ascent was finished.

They looked upon the southern valley of Pemberley where Andrew pointed out many of the landmarks. Turning north towards Staley Hall, Sarah helped him identify several features he was uncertain about. The breeze was mild and refreshing.

Sarah could see Staley Hall about a half mile away. The clean, whitewashed tenants' cottages and the short bridge as the trail crossed the small stream at the base of the hill were in view. Andrew interrupted her gaze by saying, "I wish I could stay up

Virtue and Vanity   137

here forever."

"So do I. This spot is so peaceful," she sighed. "I think being able to see home makes it a very comfortable place as well."

"Perhaps that is part of the enchantment of this spot." He took his handkerchief and dusted a spot on the large, flat rock. "Shall we sit and enjoy the view for awhile?"

"That sounds delightful."

They enjoyed a companionable silence as they looked out over the two estates. The softness of the shaded area and a fresher breeze began to lighten the sultry air. Sarah said, "From up here one gets a better perspective of the beautiful addition your trees have been to the area."

"It does seem like the trees have proliferated profusely, but then, you must remember that my grandfather began the tradition."

"Yes. What beauty it adds to both our homes."

"This is such a wonderful day," cried Sarah and without thinking she added, "It is a pity that you and I were not lovers, to enjoy it thus alone together!"

Sarah instantly realized the import of her innocent statement and hastily added, "I did not mean it the way it sounded. . . I was thinking of a scene in my current novel."

She thought she detected Andrew regaining composure as he answered with levity, "I make no pretensions to the character of a lover; but if you allow me to converse with you like a friend, that will do as well."

Playfully she replied, "Oh, the very worst substitute possible; for the conversation of lovers is all complaisance, whereas I find friends meaning to ask something I do not wish to tell, or to tell something I do not wish to hear."

Even in jest, she could not believe her utterance. A character in her current composition made such a statement. Was her make-believe world of fiction overshadowing reality?

She wondered if Andrew was going to say anything else, but he remained quiet. After a minute, he continued, "I suppose we should descend." And so they did. As they were going past the last outcropping of rock at the base of the hill, two large men, with black hoods covering their heads, accosted them.

138 Ted and Marilyn Bader

"We seek donations."

"Tis a funny way to request donations," Andrew reparteed as he moved in front of Sarah.

"Give us your purse and we might let you go."

"Here it is," Andrew replied throwing it at their feet.

"An arrogant, uppity fellow," the shorter man growled and proceeded to assault Andrew. Andrew pushed him back. The other advanced. Fisticuffs went back and forth. Andrew knocked down the smaller of the men and the man was slow to rise. Unfortunately, the larger man kicked Andrew in the leg and then held and pummelled him as he sank to the ground.

Meanwhile, Sarah began slowly retreating. She had placed twenty feet between herself and the robbers.

"Hey, she's escaping," the knocked down bandit observed as he was getting to his feet. . She turned to run and then. . . blackness.

The next thing she knew, she was flat on the ground with her face in the grass. She sneezed and turned over to sit up. Upon doing so, she felt a throbbing in her head and noticed the twilight of the closing gloam. How long had she been there? Perhaps an hour or more. As she slowly stood up, she remembered she had been with Andrew.

"Andrew," she exclaimed, "are you all right?"

Silence greeted her. Both nausea and terror gripped her.

She started to stumble towards Staley Hall and soon discovered his body, face-up.

She knelt, holding her breath for fear that he was dead. She could feel a pulse, but he was unresponsive to her gentle shaking. She noticed one of his legs not having a normal angle to it–probably badly broken. "My hero!" she exclaimed.

What to do? I must get help. She began walking to Staley Hall as fast as possible in the twilight and trying not to stumble. She made it to the door of the Hand's cottage. After knocking, the door opened and she fell into Mr. and Mrs. Hand's arms.

"Miss Bingley," they exclaimed.

"Andrew is badly hurt," she quickly said.

"Where is he?" Mr. Hand asked.

"He is back on the trail to Pemberley, just across the bridge.

Virtue and Vanity

139

We were robbed." Then it was black again.

The next thing Sarah knew was a light touch on her hand. She immediately withdrew it, fearing some animal was nibbling on it. Then, she opened her eyes to discover she was in her own bedroom at Staley Hall with Anna at her side.

"I was waiting for you to open you eyes," the young girl quietly said. "Now it's my turn to play nurse." Scooting towards the door, she turned and said, "Mother told me to come get her whenever you awakened."

Anna scurried out of the room and returned with Lady Staley.

"How are you feeling?" her mistress asked.

"A little foggy." She then sat up and asked, "How did I get here?"

"The men brought you here last night."

Waking entirely with a jolt of alarm she asked, "Last night? How is Andrew?"

She noted a momentary grimace on Lady Staley's face before it became hopeful. "The surgeon said he has been severely injured. His leg is broken and was set. We hope for better news this afternoon when Mr. Barnes returns to see his patient."

"I must get up," Sarah said. Lady Staley and Anna went to support her. Pushing their hands away, Sarah said, "I shall be fine." She took a few steps without their support.

"Do you have a headache?"

"Not at all. . . where is Andrew? May I see him?" she asked as she leaned against her writing desk.

"You must be feeling well to ask multiple questions," Lady Staley said. "We had a bed moved into the small downstairs parlor for him. With his broken leg, the first floor seemed a most reasonable place for him to convalesce."

"Then let us go see him."

Chapter Twenty-One

Quietly they stepped into Andrew's darkened room. Sarah asked to have the lone candle brought closer so she could see how badly he was injured. An audible gasp escaped her lips as the light fell onto the bruised and swollen face. She could not restrain her hand from reaching out and gently caressing the side of his face that looked least injured. "Oh, Andrew," she whispered, "what have they done to you?"

Anna tugged on Sarah's sleeve, bringing her back to reality. "Will cousin Andrew be all right?" the young girl sobbed, with tears streaking down her face.

Georgiana placed a loving arm around Anna, and answered, giving Sarah a moment to compose herself. "The surgeon, Mr. Barnes, says he will be fine; but, he must stay in bed for several weeks"

"What can I do to help?" Anna asked as her gaze returned to Sarah.

"We certainly can pray for him."

"Of course, but what can I do for him?"

Sarah smiled at the child's eagerness to serve. "It is very difficult for an active man to stay abed while his body heals itself. So, when he awakens, we will be needed to keep him entertained. Perhaps you can find some books he might enjoy having us read to him or think up some stories we can share with him."

Anna smiled and bounced out of the room, "Mother, please have someone call me the moment he awakes!"

As Georgiana and Sarah watched Anna leave the room, they noticed Edgar standing outside the door. "You may come in if you would like," said Lady Staley.

Edgar came in, but was careful to stay several feet away from the bed. After several moments of quiet thought, he asked, "Sarah, whatever happened? If there were only two ruffians, could he not have fought them off?"

Virtue and Vanity

141

"Perhaps he could have; but, I believe he was most concerned for my safety and seeing that I was given a way of escape."

"If Cousin John and I were there, this would not have happened. We would have taught those thieves a lesson they'd never forget."

"Edgar, your Cousin Andrew was very brave." Sarah said with feeling. "He tried to reason with those horrible men and when that failed, he took their punishment upon himself. I know, that had it not been for me, he would somehow have been able to slip through their grasp."

The young boy looked chagrined for having obviously upset Sarah and said, rather condescendingly, "I suppose he did have to let you get safely away. If only I had been there with him instead of you."

Sarah smiled shakily at the lad, "I'm sure your assistance would have made all the difference."

Georgiana said, "Now, young man. Why don't you help me escort Sarah back to her room. She needs the rest."

"Indeed, no," said Sarah. Blushing slightly, she said, "I will rest much better if you would allow me to sit here and watch over Andrew. I promise to call for assistance if I become overly tired."

After studying Sarah for a moment, Georgiana acquiesced. "Be sure to keep your promise though. We will need you to help nurse him back to health and you can only do that if you take care of yourself as well."

Sarah smiled. "Thank you." Turning to Edgar she asked, "Would you be kind enough to retrieve the book I am reading and my embroidery basket from my room?"

Edgar ran to do as he was bid. Georgiana said, "I will have a light meal brought in for you." Then, with an exaggerated stern, matronly tone, she added,." If you are not well enough to eat, then I will have to insist you return to your room."

The day passed slowly as Sarah watched over Andrew, hoping for some indication that he would be all right. Anna came in and out of the room throughout the day and brought books and pictures that she thought Andrew would enjoy when he awakened.

The surgeon came again. He emphasized the need to keep Andrew quiet and make sure he did not thrash about in the bed lest he further damage the broken leg. After giving Sarah some suggestions for his care, he left her to continue her vigil in solitude.

Late that afternoon the Darcys arrived. Sarah slipped out of the room, allowing them some privacy with their son. She went upstairs to refresh herself and then knelt by her bed and prayed earnestly for the healing of her friend.

Soon, Edgar and Anna came to her door. "Mother asked us to see if you feel up to joining them for tea," Anna said.

Puffing his chest out a bit, Edgar said, "I shall be glad to assist you if you are still a bit tired."

Sarah smiled and took Edgar's proffered arm. "What will you two be doing while we have tea?"

"Cook has promised to let me help make biscuits," Anna said excitedly.

"I shall be their official taster," Edgar added.

The children greeted Mr. and Mrs. Darcy before excusing themselves to the kitchen.

Sarah settled herself onto the couch beside Elizabeth. "I am so sorry Andrew is injured. . . perhaps if I had not been there. . . ."

Elizabeth took her hand. "My dear, it is certainly not your fault that he was accosted."

"Indeed not," said Mr. Darcy as he stood and began to pace. "We shall have to do something about these highwaymen. It seems there is no safe place to travel anymore." Taking his seat once again, he softened his voice, "Perhaps if you could tell us what happened. . . give us some clue as to the attackers' identities."

"I am afraid I cannot tell you much. . . it all happened so fast," Sarah said. With gentle prompting, her novelist's mind recalled more details than she thought possible.

"Do you think any of this will help you find those terrible ruffians?" Sarah asked.

Mr. Darcy said with earnestness, "If this information does not allow us to catch them, I believe it will put us close enough on their heels that they will leave the area."

"I hope so," Sarah said. "Now, if you'll excuse me, I would like to sit with Andrew again. Certainly one of us should be there when he wakes up."

Virtue and Vanity   143

Mr. Darcy nodded his approval. "We are so pleased you are feeling better today and appreciate your keeping an eye on him. His mother and I will be in shortly to relieve you. I shall need to return to Pemberley later this afternoon and pass along the information you've given us regarding the bandits."

Elizabeth smiled, "I will, of course, stay here tonight and help watch over Andrew. I hope, Sarah, that you will be able to rest well tonight. I fear your nursing skills will be sorely needed for the next several weeks."

Sarah replied. "I shall, if you will promise to call me if he awakens?"

"Of course, my dear."

The next morning Sarah was beginning to fear Andrew would never wake up, but if he did, she wanted to be there to care for him. She took her meals at his bedside and sat working on her embroidery between meals; although, an observer might have found her paying much more attention to the sleeping Andrew than to her stitchery project. Elizabeth spent much of her day in the sick room--watching both Andrew and Sarah's response to him.

Late that afternoon they heard a carriage arriving. Sarah cringed a bit as she heard Laura's voice bubbling greetings. She acted like she had come to attend a ball, not to visit a very sick man. Elizabeth Darcy joined her husband in the hallway. Laura bounced into the room. "Andrew, I have come to cheer you. . . ." She stopped as she took in his bruised face. Her voice dropped to a fearful whisper, "Sarah, I had no idea he was so badly injured."

"His face will heal," Sarah replied with a sigh. "It is his broken leg and the blow to the back of his head that are of real concern."

Laura turned toward the bed once again and noted the unusual bulging of the blanket from the huge splint which protected the broken leg. With tears in her eyes, she turned and hurried from the room, "Poor Andrew. He will probably never dance again."

John and Maria quietly came to stand beside their brother's bed and simply gazed at him as though willing him to awaken. After a long moment, Maria looked to Sarah and implored, "He is

144 Ted and Marilyn Bader

going to be all right, isn't he?"

Sarah patiently explained the doctor's opinion to them and then said, "We will know more when he awakens."

Putting a reassuring arm around Maria, John said, "With Sarah as a nurse, I am sure he'll recover quickly. I know from experience what a great nurse she is."

The next day Sarah was reading by Andrew's bedside. An uneasiness stirred her and she placed the book in her lap and just sat watching her patient. His eyes blinked and he moaned. Sarah rushed to his side and grasped his hand. "Oh, Andrew, please wake up."

After several more blinks, Andrew's eyes remained open. He looked up at Sarah and then slowly glanced around the room.

Sarah quickly gave him some sips of water from the bedside stand. With a slight smile he said, "I see I am a houseguest."

Before she realized what she was doing, she bent over and gave him a brief hug.

"I shall visit more often if I can awaken to this kind of treatment," he jested.

With cheeks ablaze, Sarah pulled herself away. Smiling, she said, "I am so glad you are awake that even your teasing will not bother me today. Is there anything I can get you?"

"Some more water, please." Gratefully, he took several sips. Pointing to the bulging sheet, he said, "I take it my leg is broken?"

"Yes. I have some medication for the pain, if you'd like."

"I think I'd rather visit with you for awhile before I take something that will likely make me sleepy again. I'll let you know when I need the medicine."

After helping him settle comfortably, Sarah instructed, "Now lay still. I need to tell your mother and the Staleys that you are awake. They will want to send word to your father at once."

"My awakening from a nap is not usually cause for such excitement. I take it I have been here for some hours?"

"Two days. We will talk more of it later," she said as she rushed to spread the good news.

A messenger was immediately sent to Pemberley. Sir Thomas, Georgiana and Elizabeth Darcy quickly came to Andrew's room

Virtue and Vanity   145

to see for themselves how he was faring. Anna and Edgar barely glimpsed Andrew, who winked at them, before Sarah shooed the children out of the room.

"I suspect the rest of his family will be coming soon," Sarah said, "so we had better let Andrew rest for awhile."

That afternoon Sarah left the sickroom, allowing Mr. and Mrs. Darcy to visit privately with their son. Mr. Hand, the foreman, approached her in the hallway and asked, "Miss Sarah, may I be so bold as to ask a word with you?"

She smiled, "Of course you may, Mr. Hand. I was just going to take a turn around the garden. Perhaps you will escort me?"

"It will be my privilege, indeed, Miss Sarah," he said as he offered his arm.

"It feels good to be outside on such a lovely day," Sarah said as they stepped into the garden. Turning to her companion with an encouraging smile, she added, "But I am sure you wanted to discuss something more important than the weather."

"Yes, Miss. As steward of our Methodist class I have been asked to inquire that if in addition to your Sunday School class teaching you might consider filling in for Grannie Williams on Wednesday nights while she is ill."

"Perhaps I could. I only know Grannie Williams by appearance, though. What function does she serve in your group?"

"For many years she has been our class leader," Mr. Hand answered somewhat hesitantly.

Sarah gasped and pulled them to a stop. "Your class leader? Surely this is not a job for a woman. . . and if it were, I certainly do not feel like a spiritual leader."

Mr. Hand smiled, "My dear wife said you would have such a reaction; but, she also said we could depend upon you to be fair. You do not need to give your answer now, just pray about it and, if it is convenient, visit with Grannie and ask her if you are qualified."

"Surely there is someone else you could enlist."

"We could think of no one we would rather have teach in Grannie's place. It would, of course, just be until she is well enough to return."

Sarah softened visibly, "Being a temporary leader would be

146 Ted and Marilyn Bader

a different situation than a regular teacher," she mused. "However, teaching men and women much older than myself seems out of the question."

"Pardon my boldness, Miss, but you have done a fine job teaching men and women of all ages how to read and write."

"But I have not the audacity to try and teach spiritual truths to those who certainly know far more than I."

Mr. Hand smiled as they returned to the entrance of the house, "Just pray about it, Miss. If you would like to visit with Grannie Williams, I'll be happy to see you safely there."

"I will consider it," Sarah promised. "Perhaps if I visit her I could discover someone else in the class who would make a good leader. You may schedule a visit when it is convenient, but mind you, that does not mean I am obliged to be your class leader."

"Aye, Miss. I do not take that to be your meaning at all," he said seriously, without hiding a broad smile.

As Sarah removed her wrap in the hallway, she overhead Andrew replying to his father, "I am sorry to hear Grannie Williams is so ill, but perhaps now the Methodist class will be forced to get a male teacher, as would be proper. You would never see such a thing in our church as a woman having the presumption to teach men about the scriptures."

"I daresay," Mr. Darcy replied, "the Methodists have been most helpful to the poor in England. Perhaps we need to be a little more tolerant of them in this area."

"I don't think so, Father," Andrew said. "This is one area I am sure our Anglican leaders have right."

Sarah quickly sat down in the hall chair. *Indeed*, she thought, *they are probably right, women should not be religious teachers; but, is it better to have no teacher at all?* With a sigh she wandered toward her room, where she spent the next hour in prayer. "Lord," she asked, "is this your plan for me? You know I do not want to do it, but I am not sure if my reluctance is because it truly is wrong or because I don't want Andrew to think unkindly of me. Please help me to be open with you about my feelings and to listen to your voice as you direct me. When I visit Grannie Williams show me what is right."

When she returned to the sick room, she immediately noticed a vase of lovely, multicolored roses. Andrew smiled at her,

Virtue and Vanity

"Anna thought I might enjoy having some of 'my flowers' as she calls them."

"They are indeed beautiful, especially the white ones."

"Indeed, I have many beautiful things to look at while I recover," he said.

Sarah turned to find him gazing at her. To cover her surprise, she said, "Perhaps you could see better if we open the drapes. Do you think your eyes can tolerate a bit more light?"

"I hope so. More light would be cheery. Why don't you open the drapes on the north side first and we'll open the others after my eyes adjust?"

"You are a very wise patient," she said as she went to move the room-darkening material. "You'll notice we positioned your bed so you could see into the garden."

Andrew said something so quietly that Sarah could not hear. She decided it might be best to not inquire about it.

Soon the room was full of light each day. The Staley children enjoyed hunting for interesting plant specimens to show Andrew. He would then spend time teaching them about different plants. They were amazed that by looking at just a leaf Andrew could describe the whole plant. Edgar especially enjoyed learning about plants that were edible (should he ever be stranded while on some noble quest).

Days passed quickly now as Andrew continued to heal. Sarah spent many hours reading aloud to him. She was surprised the first time he asked her to read something she had written, since she believed him to be opposed to women writers. Perhaps he was more opposed to women being published than to women writing. She began with a few of her shorter poems and, before she knew it, she was reading her first novel to him.

"You have a wonderful way of describing things," he said. "It almost seems as though I'm part of each story."

Sarah hoped he didn't notice her chagrin, for in a sense, it finally dawned on her that he was a part of all her stories. Every hero she wrote about incorporated some of Andrew's fine qualities and every villain was given at least one trait that could not be found in Andrew (deceit, dishonesty, cruelty). Until Sarah began to read the stories aloud to him, she had not realized that he was the source for much of her ideal of manhood. "Oh, Lord," she prayed silently, "don't let him recognize himself in my stories. He must not know my foolish desires. He is intended for my sister, Laura."

Virtue and Vanity 149

Chapter Twenty-Two

Three days later, Sarah and Lady Georgiana were sitting in the parlor of Staley Hall. Anna was sitting between them and trying to learn a new fill stitch as she was embroidering.

Maria was ushered into the room. Sarah noted the lack of usual gaiety on her visitor's countenance as she entered the room. After the customary greetings, Sarah asked, "Is anything bothering you?"

Maria looked at the floor.

"We can talk in private if you wish."

"No. . . no. . . I would like my aunt to hear this also."

Georgiana turned to Anna, "Please go up to your room or outside to play so we can talk with your cousin."

After Anna left, Maria began to explain. "I have been distressed since Mr. Paul Westbrook's visit three days ago. As you know, he followed the usual custom of calling the day after the ball and we took a turn in the south garden."

"Our conversation was pleasant. I do not recall our words exactly, but he seemed to make an encouraging remark, something like, 'I enjoy our times together,' and then I replied, 'Why, Mr. Westbrook, I enjoy being with you. Indeed, you may court me, if you like.'"

"He became very quiet for a long time whilst we were walking back. At the end of the walk, he made a few observations about the beautiful garden and then begged to leave. I watched with an uncomfortable feeling as he walked away."

Sarah noticed tears began to form in Maria's eyes, as her cousin continued, "This morning I received a note from him. Since you have been my counselor, Sarah, please read it."

Sarah took the note and read:

Dear Miss Darcy,
I am sensible of the honor of your interest. Your

150   **Ted and Marilyn Bader**

friendship is valuable to me, so I must speak the truth in kindness.

My objections to beginning a courtship are several-fold. First, the roles are somehow reversed and I should be the one who is seeking a greater intimacy. This may be old-fashioned and traditional, yet I cannot avoid it. Second, hearing your disdain of the social level of Mr. Johnson is troublesome. Even though I am adopted by worthy parents, my birth is of much lower origin than even Mr. Johnson's. I should think that irksome to you.

Finally, my call to the ministry involves the sense of servanthood. Love demands service. As our Lord hath said, "If any man desire to be first, the same shall be last of all, and servant of all. . . . Even as the Son of man came not to be ministered unto, but to minister, and to give his life a ransom for many." Any woman who would be my wife would need to understand the gentle humility of service to others. Growing up in your exalted position, I am uncertain as to whether you can wait on yourself, let alone attend others.

Please forgive me for my bluntness. However, as one of my acquaintances has said, "Honesty is the best policy where there is no hope."

No one has a greater desire for your lifelong happiness than this correspondent.

Your devoted friend,
Paul Westbrook

After reading the note, Sarah handed it to Georgiana. Maria then sat down and asked, "What shall I do?"

"What do you wish to do?"

"I wish he would change his mind about me and begin the courtship."

With gentle tenderness, Sarah asked, "What about his objection about initiating the courtship?"

Maria waved her hand, "Oh, that. . . I think he will get

Virtue and Vanity   151

used to the idea. Probably after a few months he will think it was his idea all along."

"What of his low birth? How do you feel about it?"

"I had no fondness at all for Mr. Johnson. His social position was a convenient excuse for the refusal. Mr. Westbrook, on the other hand, was adopted by quality parents. I think he could be reassured on his qualifications along that line."

Sarah felt compassion for her visitor as she softly asked, "Have you ever fixed your own hair?"

"Why should the 'pampered princess of Pemberley' fix her own hair?"

"Have you ever prepared a meal?"

"No. Why should that matter? Ladies are not required to do those things. What does he mean by servanthood? Does he actually expect me to become a servant to please him? I know I need to yield to my husband, but is this carrying it too far?"

"It might not be a bad idea," Georgiana spoke her thoughts aloud after she finished reading the letter. "I mean, the part about your becoming a servant for awhile."

"Whatever do you mean?" Maria asked incredulously.

"Certainly you should take a good look at what it would mean to be a clergyman's wife before you spend time pining over such a position. I would urge you to discuss this with your similarly positioned Aunt Kitty." Georgiana continued gently, "If you are to become a rector's wife, it means a life of service to those who need help. In poorer parishes you may not always have a maid to help fix your hair or prepare the meal."

Maria replied thoughtfully, "I think I am beginning to understand."

Her aunt continued, "Those activities represent practical examples of a deeper theological mystery involved in the ministry."

"I have struggled over the past few days with the vanity of my life," Maria replied. "What do I have to show for my life? Nothing."

The trio was quiet for a minute.

Maria spoke slowly as she pulled at a button on her dress, "If I become a servant for awhile, I must do it without reference to Mr. Westbrook. I doubt he will ever seriously consider me again. I must do it for my own soul."

Sarah asked, "Where can you be a servant?"

Maria appeared perplexed.

Georgiana said, "Obviously, you must not do it at Pemberley or its near environs, because if you are known as Miss Maria Darcy, you would not be treated the same as any other servant. Indeed, you would probably not be allowed to serve others."

"What do you suggest?" Maria asked.

Sarah replied tentatively, "I know a wonderful old couple, Mr. and Mrs. Busby, who run a roadside inn in Yorkshire. Mrs. Busby used to be the assistant housekeeper for my parent's house."

"What is she like?" Maria asked eagerly.

"A more jolly woman you will never know. However, her kindness is not weakness, as she knows how to keep order in her household. I have seen her chase a few servants with her spatula to make her point."

Maria looked at Georgiana, "Will you help me explain this decision to my parents? Your influence on my father is second only to my mother's."

"Certainly. However, first we must ask Mrs. Busby's opinion and then think about how long you are to be in service."

Chapter Twenty-Three

Sarah stood in front of Granny Williams' small, rustic-looking cottage with mixed feelings. Would the elderly woman beg her to take the class? Would she be dogmatic and authoritative? Or, would she be weak, ill and confused? She almost walked away. Finally, she timidly knocked as though fearful of being answered.

A woman about ten years older than Sarah opened the door and said, "Are you Sarah Bingley?"

"Yes."

"My mother has been waiting for you. Please come in. I must leave now to return to my own family."

Sarah entered to see a small and elderly looking Granny Williams in a rocking chair in front of the fireplace. As the door closed behind the retreating woman, Sarah remained motionless as she grew accustomed to the atmosphere of the cottage. The strange stillness was broken only by an occasional crackle from the fire. Sarah continued to stand for a minute and felt the "thickness" of the cottage air; not the physical air but the emotional feeling present; or, was it a spiritual sensation which caressed her soul? The sensation was not unpleasant, but, nonetheless it produced a serious response. The only time Sarah could recall a similar feeling was a few instances in the parish church.

"Come and sit, my child," her hostess said as she pointed to a chair across from her and in front of the fireplace fender.

Sarah did as requested, expecting further conversation. The old woman looked into the fireplace and said nothing for a long time. At first Sarah was impatient and thought to volunteer a statement but refrained, not wanting to appear impertinent or even rude.

Granny Williams finally spoke, "How do you feel about teaching the class?"

Surprised by the direct question, Sarah was freed to confess her misgivings. "Ma'am, I am so young to lead those who are older than me."

Her hostess did not respond except by beginning to rock her chair slowly. Sarah felt her excuse weak, so she added, "Is it right to offend men by teaching them?"

Granny Williams tweaked a weak smile and helped Sarah, "Do you think it is wrong?"

"I am not sure. I have not devoted any time to consider it. My friend, Mr. Andrew Darcy, clearly believes it to be wrong."

"Why?"

"I am uncertai. Perhaps because it has been traditional in the church," her voice trailed off. Sarah then asked, "What do you think?"

"I thought as much, or should I say, as little about it as you have before being asked to lead the class." Granny Williams paused for a few seconds and then said, "The principle founder of the Methodist church, John Wesley, who I would remind you remained an Anglican priest until his death, struggled with this issue. However, when he saw the Lord using women as wonderfully or even better in the Lord's work than men, he asked, 'Who am I to stand against the Lord Almighty?'"

With this she lapsed into silence and Sarah realized her hostess could only speak in short spurts and the last statement had taken much effort.

"Come here, my daughter; let me see you better."

Sarah moved and knelt before her ill-appearing and pale hostess.

"Do you feel a prompting to lead this class?" Sarah gazed at her and observed that the old woman suddenly appeared younger (or was it a glow?) as she returned Sarah's look. "Of course you do, or you wouldn't be here. . . however, I see fear. I hope to recover from this illness, but if not, eternal glory awaits. Lord willing, your involvement would be temporary."

They sat in silence another minute before her hostess asked, "What are you afraid of, my dear?"

Sarah put her head into the woman's lap and tears began welling up. "I am anxious about what others think. Nay, I fear that one person in particular will disapprove. I am afraid I am putting others before . . . ."

"You mean before God."

Virtue and Vanity

"Yes, yes."

"My child, the Lord understands. If it is meant to be, the people in your life will respond. Deeper help and understanding will only come after obedience." The old woman began praying and Sarah now recognized the feeling in the cabin. What could it be other than "holiness"? She wept and then felt a burden lift. Peace and joy filled her heart.

Sarah came to the cottage unconsciously seeking help and had found it. The path she should follow was now clear. She felt like dancing. The room seemed filled with sunshine. Her reverie was interrupted.

"Daughter, will you help me into bed?"

Sarah did so and kissed Granny on the cheek as she pulled the worn green quilt up over her hostess, who seemed to have fallen instantly asleep.

Chapter Twenty-Four

As Sarah walked to the Hand cottage on a Wednesday night, she again felt doubts about her decision to lead the Methodist class. It was not because the Methodists had any differences in Christian belief from her Anglican raising, save, perhaps, a more heartfelt approach or, as some would put it, emotional display.

The impertinence of leading those older than herself had lost its effect after months of literacy teaching to children and adults in Sunday School. Similarly, her reticence to teach Christian ideas to a class containing men would probably also fade.

No, the struggles over the latter issue had resulted in her not taking time to ascertain what usually transpired in a class. This deficiency now loomed ahead of her. .

As she knocked at the familiar door, where she taught Sunday School, her realization of being ill-prepared produced a reluctance to enter.

The door opened and Mrs. Hand smiled and ushered her in. A cheery fire was blazing in the fireplace. Four men and Mr. Hand were present, along with six women of diverse ages. Three of the men were sitting with their wives with the remaining women to the left and the one unmarried man sitting to the right.

The cottage atmosphere and smiling faces immediately told Sarah she was welcome and this helped to lessen her apprehension. As she sat on her usual stool for her Sunday class, she began, "I must honestly tell you I feel unqualified to lead this class. I have little knowledge of how you conduct your meetings. Am I not supposed to have a ticket to enter?

The class laughed as Mr. Hand rose, "Miss Sarah, I have no doubt the parson will issue you a ticket showing you are in good standing. We will forego that requirement tonight. I am the steward of the class and my responsibility each meeting is to collect a penny from everyone for the Methodist relief fund for the poor. As you know, my reading is better but not yet good enough to read

Virtue and Vanity

the Bible out loud. Our class session is simple since we are simple people. We read the scripture, listen to testimonies and then pray together."

The group nodded while Mr. Hand sat and the unmarried older man with white hair and a bushy white beard (who Sarah later learned was a widower) stood and said, "We don't need any of that high class, high church palaver they serve down at the parish church. Much of it I don't understand anyway."

"We know that, Sam," Mr. Hand rejoined.

Sarah ventured, "I am glad you are not expecting a theologian or minister, since I am neither. I can read a passage of scripture, however, and will be happy to do so. Is there a request for a particular passage?"

"Please read the story of the lost sheep," one of the young men requested.

Sarah read, "And he (Jesus) spake this parable unto them, saying, What man of you, having an hundred sheep, if he lose one of them, doth not leave the ninety and nine in the wilderness, and go after that which is lost, until he finds it? And when he hath found *it*, he layeth *it* on his shoulders, rejoicing. And when he cometh home, he calleth together *his* friends and neighbours, saying unto them, Rejoice with me; for I have found my sheep which was lost. I say unto you, that likewise joy shall be in heaven over one sinner that repenteth, more than over ninety and nine just persons, which need no repentance." (Luke 15:3-7)

"Aye, that be my story," one of the younger men stood again.

"I used to drink gin til I blacked out. I weren't no good to nobody. The gin ate my house and my hope; if it had not been for the good people in this room and the mercy of God searching for me, I would be in perdition now."

Quiet "amens" were said in the room as the younger man went on, "I don't want no gin. But I hate the cruel and mean life at the mine. I am glad the Methodist parson is trying to help the men and children who work in the mine."

"We need to pray for the parson. We don't want no strike. The mine might close, or worse, we might be dragged off to jail." The serious testimony of the young miner caused a lingering stillness as he sat down. The statements evoked pity and compassion in

Sarah. She would have liked to right all their wrongs and heal their hurts.

"We need to pray for Granny," Mrs. Hand requested.

Sarah's unspoken reaction to her hostess' remark was that Granny probably didn't need as much prayer as others did, but looking from face to face, she saw a heartfelt love in the group for their elderly leader.

The next morning Sarah returned to Andrew's sick room. He had now recovered from the acute sickness associated with his injuries and seemed much more his cheerful self.

"Have the apples started blossoming yet?" was his first inquiry.

"I do not think so," was Sarah's reply.

"I have never thanked you for the wonderful roses and fruit trees you gave Mr. and Mrs. Hand upon their wedding. They have already been planted and cared for by all."

"It is a pleasure to accept gratitude from a lovely woman such as yourself."

Sarah was a little surprised at the departure from the language of friendship into the realm of admiration.

"Have the black and blue marks on my face faded?"

"Yes, they have."

"Good. Unfortunately, I am finally to be moved back to Pemberley tomorrow. I shall miss our times together."

"So will I," Sarah replied.

"May I ask you to accept something tomorrow?"

"Whatever do you mean?" Sarah playfully responded, "Why are you being secretive?"

"No, I have not the items present that I desire. No, it will have to wait."

As Sarah was relieved by Georgiana, she was too busy with Anna and Edgar to think much about Andrew. However, that night she allowed herself to guess what Andrew might give her. Since she had mentioned her gratitude for the roses and trees given to the Hands, perhaps he had a new or exotic plant. She could not think of anything else as she finally drifted off to sleep.

Virtue and Vanity   159

Chapter Twenty-Five

The next morning, Sarah entered the parlor where Andrew was lying. It could certainly no longer be called a sickroom. Sarah was surprised at the transformation of the room into bright colors. The blinds were open with golden sunshine suffusing the room. Roses were everywhere. She was filled with delight as she looked from the white bouquet to others of yellow and pink.

"Oh, Andrew, you shouldn't have! Are these for me?"

"Of course."

She went over to where he was lying and spontaneously placed a friendly kiss on his cheek. "Thank you."

"I could do no less for my wonderful nurse."

Sarah turned to sniff one of the white roses near his bed as he continued, "I hope you will not mind me saying that the happiness of my whole life depends on your esteem. Nothing short of your entire affection will be so desirable. With truth, I declare that I prefer you to all women. . . will you consider marrying me?"

Sarah was stunned as she turned to her old friend whose face was all brightness. She was speechless from her surprise. She felt a surge of pleasure and happiness, which immediately evaporated as the implications of such an offer began to take hold.

He continued, "I have always felt a strong regard for you; you are very special to me. I hope our friendship will grow to another level."

She sat down.

With uncertainty, Andrew quietly spoke again, "I see this was unexpected. I had hoped your feelings mirrored mine. I am not trifling with you. Please do not tax your amiability by searching for studied phrases of acceptance or denial."

She looked away.

In a halting voice she stammered, "I am fond of you. . . this is too good. . . I hoped, but never expected. . . I cannot." With that she began to sob quietly.

With restrained alarm, Andrew asked, "What is the matter? I have no desire to hurt you."

Sarah cried a while and felt Andrew was looking at her. Of course, he needed an explanation.

"I am sensible of the honor you bestow upon me . . .," she began. "Do you not know you are intended for someone else?"

"Nonsense. I know of no one else."

Sarah thought Andrew was so kind and it was just like him not to have noticed Laura's coquetry.

He continued, "You must have some other reason than to fancy another woman."

"Would you know the other reasons? Even if they might offend?"

"Honesty may hurt in the beginning, but it is surely best for understanding later."

"Would it irritate you to see me, a woman, continue to write and publish? Could you bear to have your wife teach the lowly Methodist class–a woman leader?"

Andrew said nothing as his countenance became serious.

"Could you ignore the scar on my forehead?"

His face reflected grief and disappointment as he replied, "Words fail me now. Perhaps the future will change your heart. I can only hope to gracefully remain your friend."

She felt faint and knew she must soon bid him adieu. She continued, "I have no desire to distress you. I value your friendship; however, we must part for a while to gain control of our feelings before seeing each other again."

She quickly stepped out of the room before he could reply, and as soon as she was safely out of Andrew's hearing, Sarah burst into tears.

Sarah was hopeless of happiness as she bitterly said to herself, "If only things had been different." Once again Laura stood in the way. If only she had not wished to be a writer or if the scar had never formed! She was fond of Andrew, and if these objections were not present, she could imagine herself quite capable of growing in love towards him. But, alas, this could never be.

A few hours later, after Andrew was carried out of the house, Georgiana knocked at Sarah's door, came in and walked softly to a

Virtue and Vanity

161

chair by her bed. Her visitor remained quiet. Sarah said softly, "I need your help. You are like a mother to me."

Lady Staley looked encouragingly.

"You can probably guess that Andrew proposed to me. I did not expect it, nor could I accept it."

Her aunt became very attentive, but remained silent.

"The objections are too many. He is intended for someone else."

Georgiana's eyebrows moved upward with surprise as she replied, "As one who has held Andrew as a newborn baby, I am surprised to learn he is matched to someone else. I understand his parents are quite opposed to that sort of thing."

"I am not certain how official it is, but it has always seemed to me that my older sister was intended for Andrew."

"I see."

"And, then, of course, Andrew is opposed to female authors and I doubt he would want me to continue writing."

"Has he said so?"

"Not in so many words, though once I overheard his friends laugh at the idea and he did not contradict them."

Georgiana was silent again. "I do not know what to think about you and Andrew. You are two of the dearest people I know. Andrew is a worthy man who is very capable of the right kind of love. Things are not always what they seem. Still, only you can know your own feelings. Your heart would have to be clear towards him. You should marry only with affection."

Georgiana paused for a minute and then asked, "May I tell Sir Thomas what has happened?"

"Certainly. It will help explain my countenance for the next few weeks as I try to quiet my heart."

The following evening, after dinner, and with the children in bed, Sarah returned to the parlor of Staley Hall where Sir Thomas read the *Times* and Lady Staley pursued her embroidery nearby.

She sat down and remained silent. Sir Thomas put his paper aside and looked at the fire. He picked up his pipe and began to tamp tobacco into it.

Sarah volunteered to Sir Thomas, "I suppose you want to talk to me about what happened yesterday."

"My dear Sarah, I would not think of intruding into your feelings."

"Still, I would like a man's point of view about Andrew."

"It sounds as though you are uncertain about him."

"I must confess I am."

Thomas winked at Georgiana as he said, "The guiding principle in selecting a partner for marriage is to choose a person of good and reliable character."

"What do you think about Andrew?"

"He is a good man. He has always done what he said he would do."

"Do you think he would force me to stop teaching the Methodist classes?"

"Did he say you should?"

"No; however, I overheard him say once that he disapproves of women leading religious groups."

The sweet aroma of pipe tobacco filled the room. Sir Thomas did not respond. After a few minutes, Sarah answered her own question, "I know you approve of the Methodists. I daresay you would tell me to ask Andrew directly what he thinks."

Sir Thomas smiled.

"What about his disapprobation of authoresses?"

"You may have misjudged him on that point." Sir Thomas drew on his pipe, but said nothing more.

Sarah waited a long minute before asking, "What makes you say that?"

"It never occurred to me to tell you that Andrew was responsible for getting your first poem published. He went to London for that purpose and presented it to a friend from college. After that, your writings were accepted on their own merit."

Sarah was thrilled. She hoped she could hide her reaction. She was glad that Sir Thomas and Lady Georgiana were often silent in the evening. This time the peacefulness was particularly charming to her.

When she retired to her room, she settled into a chair to muse. *So, he enjoys my writings!* She felt relieved as a barrier between herself and Andrew lifted. On such a basis, their friendship could be advanced. Now, she would have to make amends with him. No

Virtue and Vanity 163

wonder he looked perplexed when she leveled that charge at him.

Over the next week, Sarah pondered how she would contact Andrew, if at all. She started and crumpled a dozen letters to him. More importantly, he was rising in her esteem. As such, she felt humbled that she had ever concluded Andrew disliked her writings.

As for her involvement with the Methodists, though she was nominally their teacher, she learned more than she taught. While she could easily return full-time to the Anglican church, she did not wish to abandon teaching merely to please a friend or prospective suitor. In any case, what was Laura's role in all of this?

Chapter Twenty-Six

A week later, Lady Staley and Sarah entered the magnificent hall of Pemberley. Sarah had received a letter from Mrs. Busby, who stated that a six-month term of service seemed appropriate. With this response, Maria joined Lady Staley and Sarah in the parlor. They sat down after warm greetings from Mr. and Mrs. Darcy.

Maria began tentatively, "I have asked Aunt Georgiana and Miss Bingley to help me make a request." She paused and looked at Georgiana, who silently nodded encouragement. Maria continued, "I would like to ask permission to enter service under Mrs. Busby in Yorkshire."

"What?!" her parents gasped at once.

After a moment passed, Mr. Darcy composed himself and queried, "May I ask why?"

Maria stood, "Oh, Father, my life has become so vain. I have little understanding of what it means to serve myself, let alone others. My life has been that of a pampered princess. If I am to become a mistress of an English estate, I should at least understand what the servants do."

Mrs. Darcy sighed, "Is that all? Then why not watch our servants?"

"Oh, Mother, it would not be the same. The servants would still treat me as the princess of the house. I want to do it on my own."

"They would let you do all the work you wanted to. Mrs. Reynolds would see to it," Elizabeth said.

"Only to the point that I seemed tired or until some social obligation came up. Then I would resume my elevated station."

In a shaky voice, Mrs. Darcy said, "You mentioned a name and place, but I was so taken aback I did not pay attention. Where is it you wish to do this service?"

Maria replied, "Sarah has asked a woman who runs a roadside inn in Yorkshire."

"A roadside inn?" Elizabeth quietly gasped.

Virtue and Vanity

165

Maria looked towards Sarah.

Sarah asked, "Do you remember Mrs. Busby, the assistant housekeeper for my parents? On several occasions she came to Pemberley to help Mrs. Reynolds with big events."

The elder Darcys slowly nodded with faint recollection on their faces.

"She now runs a respectable inn. She is an extremely reliable and kind woman. She has agreed to take Maria for a period of six months."

A long pause ensued and then Mr. Darcy looked at his sister, Georgiana, and asked, "Are you also a conspirator in this matter?"

"Yes. You know in your heart that Maria needs the maturity that would come from an activity such as this." With a slight smile, she continued, "I remember you telling about the times you worked in the fields as a young man and that it helped you to be a better master."

Mrs. Darcy interrupted, "But it is different for a woman." Grasping Mr. Darcy's hand as though for support, she said, "My baby. . . I mean Maria, may be exposed to all sorts of dangers. Service is not befitting a lady."

Georgiana moved to sit beside Elizabeth and grasped her other hand, "My dear sister, I have heard my brother speak with pride about your non-genteel activities--such as you walking miles alone to Netherfield with muddy shoes and your refusing to send your babies out to a nursemaid. . . ."

"That is quite different," Mrs. Darcy replied with a low tone, pulling both her hands free.

"Perhaps, not," Mr. Darcy ventured. He gently stroked Elizabeth's back as he looked to Maria and said, "I can see the wisdom in your request and I am inclined to permit it."

As Elizabeth stiffened, he quickly added, "However, your mother must concur. She may veto my permission."

All looked to Mrs. Darcy, who replied playfully, "Well, I must say, my dear husband is quite permissive with his children." She now looked at Maria, "Perhaps someday, Maria, you will have your own daughter and comprehend how difficult it is to let go of your offspring for what can only be termed an adventure in toil.

Please let me think about this overnight. I will search my mind for a method to discourage your scheme, but with so many in favor of your cause, the chances of my doing so seem doubtful."

Maria stood and went to hug her mother. As she pulled back from the embrace, Mrs. Darcy said, "I have always been unconventional. That my daughter is also should come as no surprise. I never knew how hard it was to be a mother to a daughter who scoffs at society's rules."

In the morning, Mr. and Mrs. Darcy met Maria in the parlor. Mrs. Elizabeth Darcy appeared weary as she said, "Is there not any way I can dissuade you from your intention?"

"No, Mamma, my mind is certain."

"My dear Maria, there are vulgarities and dangers in the commonplace world that you have never been exposed to. Hard work never hurt anyone, but I am very concerned about the type of people you will come in contact with." Seeing the eager hope on Maria's face, she took her hand and said, "With a reluctant heart, I will permit you to enter service under Mrs. Busby for six months. Please be assured that you may return sooner--at any time."

Mr. Darcy asked, "How are we to contact you without revealing your name?"

"I have already thought of that, Father," Maria bubbled. "So as to not arouse suspicions, I would like our correspondence to be received and sent through Miss Sarah Bingley, with her position noted as governess at Staley Hall. This should not create questions about my connections. My name will be Maria Harwood. Oh, and another thing. Father, I do not want you to come visiting me. Your presence might lead to the revelation of my true identity." Before he could reply, she continued, "And, I do not wish anyone outside the family to know. Please tell others I am traveling in Europe with an older friend."

Elizabeth hugged her and sighed, "It is obvious you have spent much time thinking about this. Our thoughts and prayers will be with you. With John leaving for his ship and your departure for Yorkshire, we have only Andrew remaining; and, of course, your cousin, Laura."

Virtue and Vanity   **167**

Chapter Twenty-Seven

A week passed. Sarah was sitting at the breakfast table of Staley Hall. She felt reasonably well, but coughed briefly several times during the meal. Finally, Sir Thomas asked, "How are you doing, Sarah?"

She tried to reply, but when she opened her mouth, her voice was labored and raspy. "As you can hear, my voice is worsening," she managed.

Sir Thomas stated, "Then we need to send for Mr. Hewett to see you. He has the best remedies."

Sarah nodded gratefully.

"You may also be excused from teaching Anna and Edgar until you have recovered."

Sarah replied in a staccato rhythm, "We can communicate by writing. . . I really feel. . . quite well except for. . . my . . . voice."

"As you wish," Sir Thomas replied, "but please let us know if you need a break from your teaching duties."

A servant entered and said, "A letter for Miss Bingley."

Sarah took the letter from Maria and retired to the parlor to read it.

My Dear Sarah,
My first week here at the Royal Pheasant Inn
has been quite eventful.
Mrs. Busby is everything you described her to be.
She is jolly, rotund, tireless and strong. If she does
not like what a servant is doing, or how a guest is
behaving, she will raise the spatula she always seems
to carry--shaking it to emphasize her point. Last night,
one salesman did not believe her prohibition of early
eating and reached for a biscuit. His hand was
promptly swatted and a look of respect came into
his eyes.
I have had the treatment I wanted and expected;

that is, I am treated no differently than the other servants.

When I arrived, my small trunk was taken to a third floor attic room, with a sloping roof. Little things, like where my clothes were to be put, have provided a challenge. Finally, it occurred to me that the few dresses that Mrs. Reynolds gave me could just hang on the pegs.

The next morning, Mrs. Busby woke me at 4:30 and told me to get ready. I did not know life even existed at that early hour of the morning. I tried to look in the small mirror to brush my hair and could not even seem to get my brush on the side I wanted it. I watched my maid fixing my hair the week before I came to Yorkshire and it all looked so easy in the mirror. I am afraid my hair was quite disheveled the first few days.

Apparently, the lowest servant in the household has to arise first and start the fires. Fortunately, Mrs. Busby was very patient with me as she demonstrated multiple times how to get the fire started. I never before appreciated the blazing fires that were always present at Pemberley upon my arising in mid-morning. There is a peculiar smell to old ashes at 5:00 A.M. My hands are quite cold as the match is struck to begin the household activities.

The cook, Mrs. Fellows, begins boiling water for tea and coffee about half an hour after I light the fire. I supervise the steeping of the tea and obtain ingredients and dishes for her. She has no idea who I am and is often snappish and demanding.

Needless to say, my late nights are over. Early rising clearly demands early retirement. I have never been so exhausted, yet slept so well, in my life.

One of the maids, Jenny Williams, is about my age and has befriended me. She is quite handsome but has very little education. She is kind and has shown me many things. I think she is suspicious of my background

Virtue and Vanity 169

since my language and lack of housekeeping knowledge
have almost betrayed me at times. My story of being
the destitute daughter and orphan of a gentleman-
city dweller named Mr. Harwood seems to satisfy
most inquiries.

You may show this letter to Uncle Thomas and
Aunt Georgiana. I have enclosed a separate letter to
Mother and Father.

Sincerely,
Maria Harwood

Sarah penned the following reply:

My Dear Maria,

Your first letter was full of news. I am having a
vicarious experience listening to your challenges
and admire your determination to empty yourself
and discover the meaning of servanthood.

My voice is suffering. Some days it is clear and other
days it is raspy and inconstant. At least letter writing
is always possible.

Yes, your adventures may provide the plot for
another novel in the future, but only with your review
and approval.

Love,
Sarah

A second letter was received three weeks later:

My Dear Sarah,

I find little time and energy to write letters. Most
of the servants cannot read or write and I do not
wish to demonstrate my ability.

After three months here, the novelty of the occupation
has worn off. Getting up early is drudgery and helping
irascible guests and servants above my pretended
station is taxing.

I sometimes feel like the pigs that must be fed twice

a day with the scraps from the inn's table, as I have taken only one complete bath since my arrival. I look (and smell) much more like a servant.

Jenny shows me around the place. Last week, we watched the milk maids obtain milk. Modesty prevents a description of the activity, but sometimes the milk maids squirt each other when the foreman is not around.

Observing Mrs. Fellows cook has been an education. I am the cook's assistant and I have learned a lot about fixing hearty meals. These may not be the delicate dishes of my parents house but one's appetite is certainly aroused by the savory flavors and hard work of the day.

I am sorry my letters are so infrequent and short.

Your next inquiry is anticipated. No, I am not ready to return home. I have much of the Darcy stubbornness and would be embarrassed to return early. I am determined to finish the six months. Then no one, including Mr. Paul Westbrook, will ever be able to say I have no understanding of an English household. All my life, it seems I have learned such useless things--how to dance, pour tea, do needlework. At last I am learning something of use-- how to take care of myself and a household. I take great pride in my small accomplishments.

Sincerely,
Maria Harwood

Chapter Twenty-Eight

A few days later, Anna came into Sarah's room at Staley Hall and relayed a request from Lady Staley for Sarah to come down to the parlor.

Entering the downstairs room, she saw Mrs. Darcy sitting across the room from Georgiana. Her aunt, Elizabeth Darcy, was evidently agitated as she stood and said, "I suppose you are wondering at my visit. . . I must confess my enormous curiosity and concern over Maria."

Georgiana asked, "What has happened?"

"Oh, nothing special. We have received essentially the same information that you have had from Maria. Nonetheless, I am worried about her." Looking intently at Sarah, she continued, "How can my baby, er, my daughter be surviving in a world apart from Pemberley?"

Sarah replied, "I think she is probably doing as well as can be expected. She is under the shadow of Mrs. Busby's wings and under the constant care of Providence."

Her aunt replied, waving her hand as though in dismissal, "I know those truths in my head." Pulling her hands towards her chest, she continued, "However, in my heart, I yearn to see her. . ."

Georgiana interrupted, "Dear sister, you promised not to visit her during her service."

"I did not," Elizabeth snapped. "I am sorry, I did not mean to sound harsh." With a mischievous smile she said, "Truly, I did not. She specifically asked her father not to visit her."

She leaned forward in her chair and continued somewhat breathlessly, "Sarah, will you accompany me and show the way as I visit my daughter? I plan to go incognito, so she will not notice me."

"Incognito?" Sarah queried.

"Yes," Elizabeth said smiling brightly. "I plan to go in disguise." At this, she pulled out a brown wig and placed it over her head.

Sarah's smile turned into laughter when her aunt pulled out a rounded artificial nose and place it over her own natural one.

Elizabeth asked in an innocent tone, "Do you think she will recognize me?"

"Only if you speak," Georgiana said mirthfully.

"As you know, I quite enjoy mimicking other people." With a low, shaky voice she continued, "I will simply talk like this when it is necessary to speak."

The plan was soon settled. Elizabeth would return in the morning and they would use a new carriage. The driver and footmen would be men Maria would not recognize. Sarah was to show the way and do all the talking. Mrs. Darcy offered another wig for Sarah's use and the group laughed as she put it on her head.

The next day, the carriage from Pemberley arrived at Staley Hall with the dawn. Quickly, the two spies were off.

As they settled in their seats, Elizabeth asked, "Are you sure we can reach this inn before nightfall?"

"With such an early start, we should be able to," was Sarah's reply. She continued, "Pardon my curiosity, but does Mr. Darcy know of this mission?"

"Oh, dear me, no! He would have restrained me if he had known. I told him I was taking you to visit my relatives and let him assume that meant my relations in Hertfordshire."

After several hours, the driver, Mr. Riggs, stopped the coach and came back and asked, "Would my ladies like to stop soon for breakfast?"

"Yes, we would. Can you find an open meadow?"

"I will do my best."

The carriage went on for another ten minutes and the coach stopped again. This time the driver had a little concern in his voice as he said, "This is a meadow with a pleasant vista. However, my lady, I am concerned that we may be followed."

"What do you mean?" Elizabeth asked.

"Well, it may only be my imagination. There have been so many tales of highwaymen recently. . . but I seem to keep glimps-

Virtue and Vanity 173

ing a man on a horse who appears to be trying to stay out of sight."

"How many are there?"

"I have only seen one, but he could be the scout for more. One can never be too cautious about highwaymen."

"What do you recommend?"

"I think it will be reasonably safe to stop for a short visit here. The footman and I will keep our pistols at the ready." Seeing the concern on his passengers faces he said, "I am willing to continue on if you feel that to be the wisest course of action. There have not been any recent reports of villainous activity on this road."

"What do you think, Sarah?" Elizabeth asked.

"I would like to at least stretch my legs for a few minutes and then we might eat while we continue on."

The two women were assisted out by the driver. The second time they circled the coach, Sarah saw a black figure on a horse come galloping up the road towards them. They rushed back to the carriage door as the footman and driver pulled out their pistols.

The face of the black-coated rider was hidden by a dark scarf. At a distance of twenty yards, his horse came to an abrupt halt. He then turned and rode away in the direction from whence he had come.

"Drive on, Mr. Riggs," was Elizabeth's command as they climbed back in the carriage. Leaning back in her seat as the coach briskly started, Elizabeth sighed, "What does this mean?"

"Perhaps, it is only someone following from Pemberley."

"No, I am quite sure Mr. Darcy does not suspect my coming in this direction. He has never sent an escort before."

"And, if he were an escort, would he not show his face?"

"I agree," her aunt said. "Fortunately, if he is a highwayman, he appears to be alone and our weapons seem to have scared him off."

For the remainder of the trip, they took only the briefest of stops. Sarah periodically turned around to look out the back of the carriage and fancied she saw the dark figure several times. At dusk, it was with relief for both passengers when the carriage arrived in front of the Royal Pheasant Inn. Both ladies had put on their wigs on and Elizabeth had just placed her facial accoutrements on. Before getting out, Elizabeth asked, "How do I look?"

Trying to restrain a laugh, Sarah replied, "Everything is in order. You do not look like the Mistress of Pemberley."

Mrs. Busby met them at the door. "Good evening, ladies. Welcome to the Royal Pheasant." She curtseyed to Mrs. Darcy and then also to Sarah. She stared for a moment at Sarah, who dropped her head. "How long will you plan to stay?"

Mrs. Darcy replied, "One night."

"We are fortunate to be able to offer you our finest room." In a soft, conspiratorial voice she added, "And, you need not worry. The mattresses were recently aired and fresh linens put on this morning."

"Wonderful. Sar. . . I mean, a friend told me I need not bring my own linens to your establishment, but could trust you to provide a clean room."

"I am pleased to hear our reputation has spread. We do try to keep things in proper order." Leading them towards the main room of the inn, Mrs. Busby continued, "Now, would you like tea served while we finish preparing your quarters?"

Both of the visitors nodded affirmatively as they followed their hostess towards a sitting area in the large room. They were seated across from each other on two large sofas. Jenny brought the tea service. While Elizabeth was distracted by the arrival of the refreshments, Mrs. Busby came over and whispered into Sarah's ear, "You cannot fool me, Miss Sarah Bingley."

Sarah turned toward the innkeeper and smiled, saying quietly, "It is so good to see you again. Please keep my secret."

"Of course, my dear. I am sure you have a good reason for your disguise."

Indicating Elizabeth, Sarah said more loudly, "And this is Mrs. Elizabeth. . . Wilson."

Mrs. Busby smiled and softly said, "Have no fears, Mum. The party you are interested in is out back beating the rugs." Leaning in closer and pouring the tea, she whispered, "Do you wish me to tell Maria anything?"

"No. No. . ." Elizabeth gasped. "Please do not tell her anything about us."

"As you wish, but Miss Bingley had better stay out of sight or Maria will easily recognize her."

Virtue and Vanity 175

"There is one thing, Mrs. Busby. Have your man be on the lookout for a black coated horseman who may arrive later. We think we have been followed since we entered Yorkshire."

"Yes, my lady." Mrs. Busby winked at Sarah and returned to the kitchen.

Jenny came in a few minutes to inquire about the service. Mrs. Darcy asked, "Are you Jenny?"

"Yes, Ma'am."

"Do you like it around here?"

"Mrs. Busby treats us well. We work hard, but we have no great wants."

"Is there anyone else your age?"

"Yes, Ma'am. A girl named Maria."

"What is she like?"

"A lovely orphan girl, she is."

Mrs. Darcy's facial expression clearly encouraged Jenny to continue, "I have helped her begin her service here. Lord, she did not know how to do anything, but she is a fast learner and educated. She is helping me to learn how to read and write." Glancing guiltily toward the kitchen, Jenny asked, "Is that all Madam wishes to know?"

"Yes, thank you very much."

As Elizabeth finished her cup of tea, Sarah noticed her aunt's nose was beginning to droop. It was all Sarah could do to prevent herself from laughing. Sarah pointed to her own nose to give a hint to her aunt, who immediately readjusted her nasal appendage.

Mrs. Busby came to show them to their rooms and asked, "I presume you will be wanting your supper in your room," she then lowered her voice, "I think you would be recognized if you stay down here."

"Indeed," was Elizabeth's consenting reply as she looked cross-eyed at her nose.

Upon entering their second floor room, Sarah followed her aunt to the window at the back. Looking down, she saw Maria, with hair pulled back and covered with a scarf. She watched as the slender body repeated swinging the long-handled beater at the rug, creating clouds of dust.

"I never thought I would see my daughter work that hard,"

176   **Ted and Marilyn Bader**

Elizabeth sighed after watching awhile. "Not that I think it is wrong; it is just something I did not think she would ever want to do."

"Does it help to observe her?" Sarah asked.

"Yes. Seeing Maria, the inn, and meeting Mrs. Busby will help to calm my imagination and dissolve my anxiety." Elizabeth sat down and began again, "I suppose I am becoming an old worrywart. I cannot help being concerned about the futures of my children. . .wondering if they will marry or not."

Sarah remained silent. A thought of Andrew as the unwary prey of Laura flitted through her mind.

"John gallivants all around the world on merchant ships." Elizabeth paused, "Did you know he is leaving soon to command another ship?"

"No. I did not." Sarah entertained a brief, depressing vision of Andrew being continuously pursued, since John would not be there to distract Laura from her intent. She forced her thoughts back to what Elizabeth was saying.

"Oh, and when John does leave, Andrew plans to go to London to finish his work at the Royal Society and do other things--I am not sure what his full intentions are." Elizabeth smiled, a somewhat melancholy expression, "That means Mr. Darcy and I would be alone, were it not for your sister, Laura. We have not been truly alone since our honeymoon and in some ways I look forward to it, but it will certainly require a lot of adjustment in my daily routines and I will miss all the children dearly."

Sarah quickly shook off thoughts of what else Andrew might be doing in London--surely not looking for a an academic position or a home for himself and Laura--it could not have progressed to that stage without Elizabeth knowing. . . or, could it? Trying to divert Elizabeth's attention away from her own children and sadness a bit, Sarah asked, "How is Laura doing?"

Elizabeth paused for a moment and said more cheerfully, "Your sister is much improved since leaving your Aunt Caroline. Her vanity and restlessness seem to have lessened. She is content to be at Pemberley and to practice her dancing and drawing."

As Elizabeth turned back to the window, Sarah's mind returned to her rumination that Elizabeth could have been her mother-in-law! What a disappointment! Elizabeth would have been the

Virtue and Vanity 177

best of all possible mothers-in-law. The feeling resurfaced that she had made a mistake in refusing Andrew and that her chance for marital happiness had passed her by.

A noise in the hall below interrupted Sarah's musing. Mealtime in the inn was beginning.

Sarah went to the door and opened it partway, with Elizabeth close behind her, and peered out. She closed the door, pressed her back against it, and said, "I think we could safely watch the supper by standing against the wall of the balcony. The servants will be so busy taking care of the patrons that they will not look towards the balcony as long as we are quiet."

"Let us do so," her aunt replied as they walked stealthily onto the balcony. Five men were seated at the table. One was an army officer in his bright red top, while the remainder were dressed in dark overcoats that all seemed to match. Except for the officer, they did not appear to be gentlemen. In fact, they acted surly during the meal and placed many demands on the servants. Maria and Jenny performed their duty of serving the food.

Elizabeth whispered, "It galls me to see such low-life rant at Maria."

Suddenly, one of the men stood, and grabbed Maria to accost her. All the men stood and Mrs. Busby was about to whack the offender with her ladle, when she was grabbed by both arms and restrained by two of the rude foursome. The first man also grabbed Jenny by the arm and pulled her toward the table.

The fourth man, evidently the leader, was very fat and began to chuckle. The officer had stepped back into the shadows. Alarmed, Elizabeth commanded, "Go at once to fetch Mr. Riggs. Tell him to bring his pistol. Maria is in danger!"

Sarah began to hurry along the balcony when she heard the fat man say, "My sweet little ones. How would you like to find out what real men are like?" He put his hands on the table after beckoning Maria to be brought forward.

A bright glint of steel flashed and a sharp thud brought a sword onto the table, a hairbreadth away from the fat man's hand.

Pulling it back, a young officer emerged and said, "I am Captain James Gray. If you do not let these women go, the next move of my blade will separate your hand and arm."

The fat man turned and chuckled, "But, sir, there are four of us and one of you."

"All the better. When I end up skewering you, no one can say it was not fair." The captain pulled out a pistol with his other hand and aimed it at the two men across the table restraining Mrs. Busby. "Now, which of you wants to die first?"

The two men released Mrs. Busby's arms and she quickly retreated behind them.

The captain turned slightly to the fat man, but before saying anything, two loud cracks and thuds were heard across the table. He glanced toward the sound. Mrs. Busby held a heavy pitcher in each hand as she stood over the two outlaws now prostrate at her feet.

Maria kicked her captor in the shins as Jenny jumped on his back and clawed his face. He fell, moaning, to the ground, trying to shake her off.

The captain, who had been holding the fat man at bay with his sword now turned back to directly face him and said, "Now, do you wish a sword, so we can say you were armed?" With a sly smile he added, "Though, it would be a pity to mess up the floor with your innards for these hard working women to clean up."

"I am your prisoner, Sir," was the scowling, uneasy reply of the fat man as he raised his arms.

Mrs. Busby said to Jenny, "Go and fetch the constable."

Sarah was only part way down the steps from the balcony when the scene had resolved itself. She turned around and stepped quietly back to Elizabeth. They watched as the Captain tied the hands of the four highwaymen and the constable took the villains away.

Mrs. Busby, Maria and Jenny then expressed their gratitude to the Captain by serving him a repast fit for a king. At one point in the meal, while Maria was serving him, the Captain looked at her intently and said, "You look familiar to me. Do I know you?"

"It is unlikely, Sir."

"What is your name?"

"Maria."

"Your surname?"

"Harwood," she answered with a shaky voice.

Virtue and Vanity 179

"The Christian name seems familiar, but not Harwood."

After this exchange, Maria allowed Jenny a much greater presence in front of the officer than herself. This was not difficult to accomplish, as Jenny was clearly enamored with the handsome junior officer. He seemed to enjoy Jenny's continual hovering-- many gentlemen had respectfully described her as "a handsome young woman" and "pleasing to the eye."

After the evening activities were over, Sarah and Mrs. Darcy finally retreated to their room.

Sarah mused aloud, "I wonder if those were the highwaymen who were following us."

"Possibly. Though the rogue following us seemed taller than any here tonight. . . but, that may be due to the fact that we were looking down on them this evening."

Elizabeth sat down and continued, "Now, I am both vexed and anxious. How can I leave Maria in this dangerous situation? Yet, how can I ask her to return home?"

Sarah remained thoughtful and quiet.

A soft knocking was heard at the door. Sarah arose and let Mrs. Busby in. The innkeeper curtseyed and said, "I am so sorry, my lady, about the lateness of your supper. I suppose you saw the commotion in the dining room?"

"Yes."

"This is the first time in my seven years as proprietor of this inn that anything like this has ever happened. Captain Gray said he would arrange for an officer and gentleman to dine here every night for the next few months to help scare away any felons in the future."

"Do you think the highwayman who followed us was part of the gang?"

Mrs. Busby smiled broadly, "No, Ma'am. Your spy is none other than Mr. Reynolds. I spotted him outside a few minutes ago."

Elizabeth produced her first relaxed smile of the day as Mrs. Busby said, "Your supper will be here any minute."

Jenny brought the meal and the two ladies partook of more food than expected. With the meal finished, they were soon in bed with all light extinguished.

Elizabeth asked, "What do you think I should do about

Maria?"

After a pause, Sarah said, "I think you need to let her go. The Almighty cares more about Maria than you or I ever could."

After a further pause, Elizabeth said, "I now understand the feeling my father had in letting me marry Mr. Darcy. Sarah, you are a wonderful niece, your beauty of mind and wisdom go far beyond your age."

"Thank you. I love you, Aunt Elizabeth."

"And I love you. I appreciate your being with me through this trial of a mother's love. Good night."

Chapter Twenty-Nine

The next morning, Mr. Riggs assisted Elizabeth and Sarah into their waiting carriage. As Mr. Riggs closed the door, Mrs. Darcy said, "Do ask that fellow across the street to come and talk with us."

"Yes, Ma'am."

The tall, black-cloaked man came over to the carriage but kept his face turned away, and with an obviously altered voice said, "Your driver said my lady wished to see me."

"You no longer need secrecy, Mr. Reynolds."

Sheepishly, Mr. Reynolds turned toward Elizabeth. "How did you know?"

"Mrs. Busby spotted you yesterday." With a kind voice, she asked, "Will you not join us in the carriage on the way back to Pemberley?"

"Thank the Lord," the elderly servant said. "I was dreading riding all that way on horseback again. I almost froze to death last night sleeping in the livery."

Once he was seated, Mrs. Darcy continued, "Now, tell us Mr. Reynolds, who sent you to spy on us. Was it Mr. Darcy?"

"No, Ma'am. Mrs. Reynolds sent me to follow your carriage. I do not believe Mr. Darcy knows anything about your adventure."

"Good. And please, see to it that he does not learn anything about it when we arrive home. I feel foolish for coming."

Mr. Reynolds nodded, "You may depend on me; but, Mr. Darcy would understand that a mother needs to know her child is safe and well-cared for."

"Yes, he sometimes seems to understand my thoughts even before I do." Here the carriage took off and Elizabeth finished, "At least I do not think Maria discovered our presence while we were here. She has such a desire to prove herself that she would be quite upset with me."

182   Ted and Marilyn Bader

That evening, after supper, Elizabeth was working on an intricate embroidery piece, while Mr. Darcy was reading the *Times*. Sarah sat quietly working on a poem, having agreed to spend the night at Pemberley before returning home. Laura had excused herself to bathe before bed.

From behind his paper, Mr. Darcy innocently inquired, "Elizabeth, how was your visit with Maria?"

Elizabeth answered absentmindedly, "Fine," and then became very quiet. After a moment she asked, "Who told you? Mr. Reynolds promised not to."

He lowered the paper and smiled tenderly at his wife, "No one needed to tell me of your true destination."

"How did you find out?"

"My dear Lizzy, for the week prior to your departure, you spoke of nothing else except Maria and your concern for her welfare. The cover of your visiting relatives in Hertfordshire was rather transparent--especially to anyone who loves you and understands your mother's heart. I was tempted to ask to go along. . . a father worries about his daughter, too, you know."

Elizabeth smiled at him, "Sometimes I forget what a tender heart you have. I should have told you where I was going so you wouldn't have to worry about us, too."

"With the disappearance of Mr. Reynolds, I knew that you were being looked after, so I didn't worry about you and Sarah overly much, but I hope you know I would like you to share all your concerns with me." He glanced at Sarah. "Miss Sarah, perhaps you will tell me how my daughter is faring."

"She looks very tired, but she also looks happy. The proprietor seems to be quite pleased with her work."

"Does the inn seem a safe, respectable place as we were told."

Elizabeth and Sarah glanced at one another, then Sarah said, "It has a very good reputation. The rooms are quite clean and the meals are tasty. There was an incident when we were there. . . ."

"What kind of incident?" Mr. Darcy asked as he jumped up and began to pace. "Did this incident involve Maria?"

Lizzy set aside her needlework and went to her husband. Grasping his arm she explained, "Maria is fine. She has many people watching out for her welfare."

He drew her into his arms and said, "Thank God. I should have known you would not have come home without her if she were in any real danger."

Sarah slipped out of the room as Elizabeth settled into the lap of her longtime beau and began to give him details about their adventure.

Chapter Thirty

At the next mid-week Methodist class, as Sarah finished reading aloud the final scriptural verse, "They that wait upon the Lord shall renew their strength; they shall mount up with wings as eagles; they shall run, and not be weary; and they shall walk, and not faint." She looked up and, to her surprise, she saw Andrew Darcy sitting behind Mr. and Mrs. Hand. She tried not to stare. As the class progressed, she noted that his countenance revealed close evaluation of the proceeding. At one point, his eyebrows were furrowed and his face was perplexed while she responded briefly to a question. She was determined to talk to him after the closing prayer, but when the heads were raised at the end of the meeting, Andrew was no longer present.

That night and the next day, she tried not to think about Andrew's visit, but it kept leaping to the forefront of her thoughts. *Why had he come to the Methodist class?*

She soon forgot about Andrew's visit the next day as she received the following letter from Maria:

My Dear Sarah,

It has now been four months since I began my service here in Yorkshire.

I must tell you about an important incident yesterday. I was washing the kitchen floor on my hands and knees. A wood splinter thrust itself into my calloused hand. It was a small one, which I quickly removed, but the vexation of it and the coarse appearance of my hands caused me to start crying. I am afraid my tears mixed with the soapy water on the floor.

An enormous sense of unworthiness fell upon my soul. I did not deserve to be born a Darcy; how easily could I have been assigned washing floors for the rest of my life. Sorrow for my past foolishness

Virtue and Vanity

185

filled my heart. In the midst of my brokeness, a desire
to do something more substantial with my life began to form, and with it a deep seated peace
started to envelope my heart. The drudgery of my
service lifted as I realized all service, no matter how
menial, is done to the King of Kings. My tears of
sorrow changed to tears of joy.

Uncertain about the future, my heart opened
to Providence for direction.

I heard someone march into the kitchen with the
sound of boots. The sound stopped in front of cook,
who evidently pointed to me. The boot steps then
proceeded over to me. My hair was all around my
face and, because of my tears, I did not wish to
look up, assuming it was one of the workmen.

The visitor got down on his hands and knees on
the wet floor and asked, "Does an unworthy suitor
have any hope with you?"

I looked up and I saw the handsome and anxious
face of Mr. Paul Westbrook. I am afraid I burst
out with renewed sobbing and moved forward
enough to place my head against his strong shoulder
as we sat on the floor.

Mr. Westbrook, nay, I can now call him Paul, told me
about how his friend Captain James Gray rode to
Derbyshire to tell him about this young servant
woman who looked very much like Miss Maria Darcy.
Once Paul extracted the story of my service from
Mr. Reynolds, he immediately visited Yorkshire.

Mrs. Busby came in. Paul stood and pulled me up.
Once he introduced himself as a friend of Captain
James Gray, Mrs. Busby could not do enough for him.
She told me I should change clothes and spend the
rest of the day with the "tall, handsome man
from Derbyshire."

I will not give you a long story, but suffice it to
say, that Paul is now on his way back to Pemberley
to ask permission of Father to court me. He wanted

186

Ted and Marilyn Bader

me to accompany him, but I told him my time of promised service was not done; though Mrs. Busby will not let me stay any longer if Father's response is favorable.

The word is out now. The cook treats me with great respect. Jenny is thrilled and wishes to treat me like a lady, though I will not allow it. I have asked her to visit me at Pemberley and this has given her great pleasure as we talk about what I shall show her.

Tell Thomas and Georgiana that their years of gentle patience and advice to me may actually bear fruit.

I thank you, Cousin Sarah, for your suggestion of Mrs. Busby. While I would not recommend entering service for every young lady, it has been good for the "pampered princess of Pemberley."

Sincerely,
Maria

Sarah was delighted to show the letters to Sir Thomas and Georgiana and to watch their faces fill with joy.

"Fitzwilliam and Elizabeth must have received the news last night," a delighted Georgiana said as she continued. "We should receive a message at any moment. . . ."

Sir Thomas said thoughtfully, "I am pleased at Maria's change from frivolity to maturity."

His wife replied, "Let us visit Pemberley at once."

And so they did. The Staleys and Sarah arrived at Pemberley to find Mr. Paul Westbrook was already there talking solemnly with Mr. and Mrs. Darcy. It was obvious to the group arriving that Mr. Westbrook had been accepted as they saw Mrs. Darcy embrace the young man and Mr. Darcy pat him on the back; the threesome were all smiling. Mr. Darcy noted the Staley's arrival and called them and Sarah over to congratulate the young man who had captured their daughter's heart. The groom-to-be soon excused himself from the impromptu celebration as Andrew came in and said, "Well, Paul, it seems I am to travel to Yorkshire to escort my sister

Virtue and Vanity 187

home. Would you care to join me?"

"Indeed," the young man said. "I trusted enough in a positive response to my request that I came prepared to accompany you." Turning to the group in general, he excused himself.

Andrew chuckled and said, "I have never seen anyone so eager to go to Yorkshire." Then he followed his friend out of the room.

Chapter Thirty-One

The following week during the Methodist class, Sarah again noted Andrew in attendance. She was not quite sure when he arrived, but it was sometime after the class started.

When a class activity allowed, she tried to look at him out of the corner of her eye. His expression was changed this week. He appeared to be listening intently to everything said. He appeared relaxed and even smiled several times during the hour.

Sarah scanned the cottage meeting area after the final prayer to find Andrew. He had slipped out again. Mr. Hand came up to her, placed a note in her hands and said, "Mr. Andrew Darcy said to give this to you."

She waited until she was back in her bedroom at Staley Hall before opening the note. She hardly knew what to expect.

Dear Sarah,
You are an excellent leader for a worthy cause.
Andrew

She sat down and tears streaked down her cheeks. Drying her eyes, she looked at the note again. *Oh, Andrew,* she thought. *I have misjudged you. I thought you were so against women directing such a group that you would not look at the situation fairly. If only I'd known this sooner. . . .*

Her undeception about Andrew gave her remorse and hope at the same time. Remorse, since she had unjustly accused him of not honoring women writers and thought him unable or unwilling to change any prejudice he might have against women class leaders. Here was a man of outstanding character! The best of all men!

Hope then began to wash away the remorse. Hope that they could renew their friendship and, perhaps, even more.

Sleep deserted her, but happiness did not. She recalled Andrew's proposal and envisioned the warm look he gave her, felt the touch of his hand. *What a wonder that such a man would honor*

Virtue and Vanity

189

me with a proposal and that I foolishly turned him down; however, at the time, I thought there were good reasons.

In her mind, the first two reasons had now been dismissed. She had misjudged him. Andrew certainly was not against women writers, and he had shown an openness to new ideas in attending the Methodist class meetings to see what kind of leadership Sarah had to offer. But, the third reason seemed hopeless. Laura had stated that Andrew was intended for her. Sarah could never compete with her beautiful sister, nor did she wish further enmity..

Yet, as she tossed and turned, a feeling began to grow in her that Laura was no longer a factor in Andrew's life. She could not explain why.

Perhaps Laura has turned her attentions elsewhere.

Her heart then whispered that she must contact Andrew since she had asked for a period of separation after his rejected proposal. He had honored her request. Now, it seemed clear to her that it was her move. But, how was she to do it? Should she write? If so, what could she say? She now felt the uncertainty that men must feel when they need to initiate contact with the other sex. The feminine role of acceptance or refusal now seemed more of a privilege than previously. The heroines in her novels always handled these situations easily; whereas, in reality she felt perplexed.

She soon realized that this problem did not need to be solved before morning. Peace enveloped her heart as she fell asleep.

Chapter Thirty-Two

The following night, the inhabitants of Staley Hall were awakened after midnight by a couple acting mysteriously.

Sir Thomas Staley reached the door almost as soon as his servant turned to announce the visitors.

"Mr. John Darcy and a lady, sir."

"Show them in," replied Sir Thomas.

A hooded woman entered behind John and lifted the hood off of her head, while John stepped forward to shake hands. "Thank you, Uncle Thomas. I apologize for the late hour." Turning to his traveling companion, he continued, "You, of course, need no introduction to Laura Bingley, or, I should say, Mrs. John Darcy."

"You never cease to surprise me, John." Pausing but a moment to regain his composure, he said, "Come, let us sit in the parlor."

By this time, Georgiana and Sarah were standing in the parlor and greeted the couple.

John said, "We are come from Gretna Green as a married couple."

Sarah noticed Laura was looking down at the floor--an unusual posture of humility for her sister. Sarah went over to her and sincerely exclaimed, "Oh, I am so happy for you."

Her sister's face brightened and they embraced for the first time in many years. They pulled apart and Laura said, "Will you forgive me for not inviting you to the ceremony?"

"You have my blessing, of course. I had no clue as to your attachment to John. I thought. . . ."

Laura put her finger to her sister's lips and said, "Do not say it. I have always admired John, even if I said otherwise."

The group sat down as John said, "I suppose you are wondering as to our late night visit. Laura and I are on our way to Liverpool to catch a ship for passage to Canada."

"Are you not going to Pemberley first?" Georgiana asked.

"No, Father would only try to talk us out of the voyage. I

Virtue and Vanity 191

am tired of his fixing problems for me. I have vengeful minded pursuers and other problems to forsake." Scooting forward to the edge of his seat, he earnestly continued, "Uncle Thomas and Aunt Georgiana, I want your promise that you will not tell my parents about our situation until we safely leave the shore."

Georgiana looked anxiously at Thomas. Her husband said in his most diplomatic tone of voice, "Surely, John, you do not wish to deprive your mother and father the opportunity of a farewell?"

"It is not that. Given enough time, my father seems to be able to convince me of any position. My mind is set. I wish a clean start and the adventure of a new land."

Thomas was quiet for a moment and then ventured in a tone of negotiation, "Your father may never forgive me, but I will offer you a twelve hour headstart before I inform Pemberley Hall."

John replied, "If you must let them know after twelve hours, then you may do so. Please try to discourage Father from coming to Liverpool. Tell him and Mother we shall write regularly."

"I will promise only the twelve hour interval. Now, is there anything you need for your journey? The resources of Staley Hall are at your disposal."

"No, thank you, Uncle Thomas. We have enough money for a good start in Canada and it is better to travel light."

Sarah turned to Laura and said, "Is there anything I can give you?"

Laura looked a little sheepish and ventured, "Could I have a copy of your two books? I will treasure them because they come from you."

Forcing back tears, Sarah arose and went up to her room and brought the requested books back to Laura, who was now standing with the others at the door.

"You must promise to write me," enjoined Sarah, "since I shall not know where to write you."

Laura embraced her sister once more, "I will write you."

Sarah felt empty as she saw her sister and new brother-in-law leave by carriage in the darkness.

The implications of this sudden news did not strike her fully until she attempted to return to sleep in her own bed.

She might not ever see her sister again! Sailing to Canada was not like moving to a distant county in England where everything was within two to three days journey. Laura was the only living relative in her immediate family. Sarah rejoiced at the softened attitude of her sister and now had a multitude of things she wished to express to Laura.

Furthermore, this shed a new light on Andrew Darcy. She had been mistaken as to the intended link between her sister and him. Sarah grieved that she had so summarily dismissed him. How she must have vexed him with her objections. Would he ever reconsider? Her heart was growing in esteem and desire for him. However, she warned herself that she would probably never marry. Andrew would be her only and last suitor. At least they could be friends; but, what if he were to marry someone else? She could not bear the thought. She knew the jealousy evoked by such thinking was immature, but this did not help it disappear.

With such struggles, Sarah tossed and turned until near dawn when she fell into an exhausted sleep.

When Sarah entered the dining room for breakfast at 10 o'clock the following morning, she saw only the Staley children. She asked the servant, "Where are Sir Thomas and Lady Staley?"

"They have already gone to Pemberley Hall to discuss the events of last night. They said to have their fastest carriage ready for a trip to Liverpool as soon as they returned after 12 o'clock. Apparently, there was a communication that Sir Thomas could only give to Mr. Darcy at that time."

After breakfast, she went upstairs to pack a small bag and to put on a dress for the carriage ride. At the expected time, Sir Thomas and Lady Georgiana arrived hastily in their older carriage. The couple stepped down.

"Oh, Sir, may I go with you to Liverpool?"

"Certainly. Mrs. Stokes may watch the children."

Sir Thomas helped Sarah and Lady Georgiana into the waiting carriage.

The second carriage took off with a jolt. Sir Thomas looked at Sarah and said, "Mr. Darcy was angry at us, as expected, for waiting the twelve hours to tell them about John and Laura."

Virtue and Vanity

Georgiana rejoined, "However, he softened once he heard the entire story. He has no greater respect for anyone than Sir Thomas."

Thomas continued, "They plan to follow us as soon as possible."

After a few moments, Georgiana said, "I believe Andrew is coming with my brother and sister-in-law. Do you think you can face him?"

"There is no one to blame for his disapprobation but myself. I will have to see if we can rebuild our friendship."

Arriving at the Liverpool docks, eight hours later, Sir Thomas was soon able to ascertain the frigate *Euterpe*, bound for Canada.

Directing the carriage to the pier, Sir Thomas spotted a ship's mate and stepped out of the carriage. "Hello. Are you from the *Euterpe*?"

The man replied in a heavy french accent, "I be the first mate."

Thomas switched to French and asked, "When will she leave?"

"In two hours with the high tide."

"Where are the passengers?"

"In Stoneleigh Inn over by the church spire."

Entering the inn, Sarah spotted her sister and ran ahead of the Staleys. Laura stood and embraced Sarah. The elder sister then said, "I have thought much since last night--how horrid I have been to you. Can you ever forgive my meanness and arrogance?"

"Yes, yes, yes," sobbed Sarah as they held each other tightly. After a few moments, Sarah pulled back and said, "I have not always been the sister I could have been."

"Nonsense, no one ever had a better sister. Besides, you are the only one that remembers our childhood at Bingley Hall and how much our mother and father loved us."

The sisters then sat down and shared as they never had before. During their talk, Sarah overheard Sir Thomas getting all the necessary facts of where Mr. and Mrs. John Darcy were planning to settle and how they could be contacted.

An hour after their arrival, the door to the inn opened and Mr. and Mrs. Darcy entered, with Andrew following. Andrew spot-

194 Ted and Marilyn Bader

ted them first and dashed over to John. John stood and they embraced. Elizabeth, not caring about her dignity, ran lightly to Laura and embraced her.

Before much could be said, the ship's mate entered and yelled, "All aboard the *Euterpe*."

Sarah was glad she could follow behind Andrew and John as they proceeded to the ship. She could hear them talking. Andrew said, "England shall be deprived of her best swordsman."

"That is one reason I am leaving. The dragoon is after me again for a duel. If I refuse him, my honor is in question. . . ."

Andrew interrupted, "And, if you fight him, you will surely win and become guilty of murder." Andrew was quiet for a few moments and then said, "I hope you are not angry at me for being born five minutes earlier and becoming heir to Pemberley."

"Not at all, my good brother. I have wanderlust and could ill abide staying in one established place and taking care of it. The Almighty ordained our birth order in the most propitious manner."

"Nonetheless, my good man, I would feel more comfortable with your staying in England so you could brighten my life periodically. . . ."

"And fight your duels?" John interrupted.

"But, of course, no one would threaten Pemberley if it was under John Darcy's protection."

"Now, you, brother, need to get married."

"I doubt if anyone will have me."

"Nonsense. I am sure there would be ladies in waiting if you would only start searching."

"I do not have the heart, at least for now. I plan to leave for Ireland in the near future to visit an old friend and think about my future."

Sarah winced. At a time when she felt she could become Andrew's wife, he had lost interest. It was all her own fault. Furthermore, he was planning to leave!

"Seriously, my brother, please visit me in Canada. I do not know if I shall ever return to England."

"Lord willing, when you have established yourself, I shall do my best to come. I have heard there are many new plant species

Virtue and Vanity 195

being discovered in Canada."

Elizabeth approached and interrupted, "Is there any way I can dissuade you from this trip?"

"No, Mother, once my mind is made up, it will not be changed."

"Unfortunately, you sound just like your mother."

Mr. Darcy stepped up, "I have always been proud of you, son."

"Despite my difficulties?"

"Despite your difficulties. You are always welcome to return. If you need anything, feel free to ask for it."

"Thank you, Father. A son could not ask for more."

John and Laura walked onto the ship amid shouts of blessings from their family. As the Darcys and Staleys returned to stay at the inn for the night, Sarah could not help but notice that Andrew avoided her.

Chapter Thirty-Three

The next day the Darcys, Staleys and Sarah returned to Derbyshire. The following morning Sarah awoke with a longing to speak to Andrew. She had dreamed of never seeing him again and felt it was due to her indecision. *Well, life is not a dream!* she thought.

She must tell him what was in her heart. Perhaps he would only wish to renew their friendship. In any case, she must let him know how she had grievously misjudged him and allowed Laura to come between them.

Caught between a longing for friendship and desire for marriage, she concluded that she must throw protocol and caution to the wind and visit Andrew before he left Pemberley.

When she asked Georgiana to accompany her to Pemberley, Georgiana smiled with a knowing expression about the purpose of her visit.

During the carriage ride, Lady Staley said, "I hope Andrew is still home. I heard he was preparing for another trip."

"Then you have guessed my intent," Sarah replied.

"I do hope you make amends with Andrew. He is the most worthy of young men."

As Sarah turned to look out the carriage window, she said softly. "I hope it is not too late."

The carriage arrived in front of the steps. It being a fine, sunshine-filled day, Elizabeth came out to greet them.

Sarah nervously asked if Andrew were still home and Elizabeth smiled and pointed towards the lake.

Sarah spotted Andrew down by his favorite tree next to the lake. He was sitting at a bench with his back to her and a small table in front of him. As she approached, she noted colorful flowers and leaves lying flat as for botanical study. Her quiet approach did not alert him to her presence until she stood behind him. Startled, he turned and stood to look at her.

"Sarah, your presence is a pleasant surprise."

Virtue and Vanity   197

"May I sit down?"

"Of course."

"What are you studying now?"

He gently lifted a small flower and held it up to her. "There is this one flower that looks very much like a wild primrose, but which is not in any of my guides. I wonder if it is a new species." Sighing, he continued, "I have difficulty with classifying some flowers like I have difficulty understanding people."

He looked away.

"Oh, Andrew, do not be hard on yourself. I have a confession to make. . . I misjudged you when I told you that you did not like authoresses. Little did I know you saw to the publication of my first poem. I want to thank you for the love you showed without my knowing it."

Andrew sat down next to her.

She looked out on the lake. "Your recent note assured me of your constancy. . . ."

Andrew turned his head with a look of surprise and hope. He sat back and was quiet for a moment. Sarah eagerly awaited his next statement.

"Sarah, you know there has never been anyone else in my heart."

"I am afraid that first my scar and then my pride has wasted much time between us. . . ."

He moved closer to her, placed his hands on her face, brushed back her hair to reveal her left temple and leaned over to kiss the scar.

Tears filled her eyes.

"It seems that many things have changed since we were children." He tenderly lifted her head until her eyes met his. Glancing away, he slowly began, "Perhaps hope has made me interpret things in the wrong way. . . ."

Cautiously, she raised a hand and turned his face back to hers. "I think your heart has always seen things clearly."

Andrew gazed into her eyes for a long moment, before finding the confidence to proceed. "I lay my heart open before you once again. Will you complete my happiness and marry me?"

Tears freely ran down her cheeks now, as with a shaky smile, she whispered, "Yes, yes, yes."

Her tears were quickly wiped away as Andrew embraced her. Their lips met in a tender kiss, full of restrained passion. Both were unaware of the passage of time as they sat on the bench lovingly sharing their hopes and dreams for the future, and brushing away regrets of the past.

Epilogue

Andrew and Sarah were married in a double ceremony with Paul and Maria at Pemberley. A finer day of celebration has never been recorded in the history of the estate.

Granny Williams soon recovered to resume leadership of the Methodist class. After another year, one of Sarah's pupils was able to teach literacy at the Sunday School class. It is the best kind of teaching that renders a teacher no longer necessary.

Sarah's participation in the Methodist classes and Andrew's approval gained them widespread esteem among the working class of the area. While general political unrest existed among the lower classes in the mid-nineteenth century throughout England, this section of Derbyshire experienced little of it.

As happily married couples tend to live long, Elizabeth and Fitzwilliam lived well into their seventies, thus not relinquishing Pemberley to Andrew and Sarah until they were in middle age. Prior to that time, the young couple was very content in the roomy cottage the Darcys had built for them near Andrew's favorite spot by Pemberley Lake. From their letters to each other during Andrew's botannical expeditions, Sarah and Andrew's love for each other continued to grow. And why not? Their parents had provided such excellent examples.

As of this writing, we have been unable to discover, from the Pemberley archives, if Mr. and Mrs. Andrew Darcy had any children. Nor have we learned further history about Mr. and Mrs. John Darcy. Maria, however, continued as a graceful companion to her husband, Mr. Paul Westbrook. Quality always rises and it took a shorter than usual time for Mr. Westbrook to become a bishop in the Anglican church.

Maria was a key part in her husband's success. When they visited smaller and poorer parishes, where the help of servants was minimal or absent, she was known to tie her hair back, and start helping with chores. The natural manner in which she engaged in such unusual servanthood caused many a hard-pressed pastor's wife to fall in love with this bishop's wife; confiding their stresses and anxieties to Mrs. Westbrook then provided them natural relief.

The authors wish to thank the Pemberley Estate directors for their cooperation in providing access to their archives.

"Imagination is everything." -- Jane Austen.

Ted and Marilyn Bader

Historical Notes

Chapter One

Virtue and Vanity, the continuing story of *Desire and Duty*, is written to stand by itself. However, readers told us they enjoyed the appended historical notes and so we will continue a set for this volume. Readers may wish to peruse the historical notes of the previous story for a more complete understanding of English aristocratic society in the early 1800's.

The British Embassy in Paris is still at 39, rue du Faubourg-Saint-Honore. It was acquired by the British government in 1814 from Pauline Borghese, sister of Napolean.

In the spring of 1830, the French army embarked on an expedition to punish the Algerians. To the British, the extent of the preparations suggested more than a temporary operation and London pressed for a promise that France was not planning conquest and the establishment of a French colony. The French remained vague and the British government was annoyed, and its sympathies with the Bourbon regime, which it had helped to found only a decade earlier, noticeably cooled. (Pinkney, 16)

In retrospect, the invasion was an effort by the current French monarch, Charles X, to raise popular support for his sagging monarchy before dissolving the uncooperative deputy chamber and calling for an unprecedented third election in one year. The French had not savored a military victory since the bitter taste of Waterloo in 1815.

Chapter Two

A *guinea* was an odd sort of historical British coinage equal to the old pound plus a shilling (or 21 shillings total). It was the proper currency to pay an artist, lawyer or physician.

Chapter Three

Sarah's bout with smallpox is borrowed from an episode in Fanny Burney's *Camilla*. It is difficult for the modern reader to appreciate the terror that smallpox represented in eighteenth and nineteenth century Europe and America.

Smallpox epidemics regularly swept through cities and villages producing mortality rates of 10 - 35% in those afflicted; in survivors, single or multiple facial scars were an often sequalae. Of interest, it is thought that the portraits of Queen Elizabeth I, where her face is literally painted white, represents the heavy use of makeup to cover smallpox scars.

In the mid-eighteenth century, *variolation* was introduced whereby a needle and thread were passed through an active pustule and then used to probe the skin of a non-infected person. The disease produced was usually much milder and resulted in lifetime immunity. However, variolation still caused a 1 - 2% mortality which lead to vociferous opposition.

Edward Jenner's treatise in 1798 stated his observation that milk maids who had contracted cowpox never suffered from smallpox. Thus, vaccination with cowpox material began to be widely practiced over the next century since there was no mortality associated with it.

Strength of constitution, as in Sarah's case, from the previous practice of variolation, would have still been thought important prior to vaccination.

More than 110,000 cases of smallpox were reported in the USA for the year 1929 and none at all since 1949. Aggressive international cooperation in vaccination during the mid-twentieth century led to the WHO Global Commission declaring on December 9, 1979 that smallpox had been eradicated entirely from all nations (White, 868).

Marriage among first cousins was both legal and even promoted among Western society until near the end of the nineteenth century.

Chapter Four

That it might not be to a woman's advantage to exhibit a "head and a heart" was a topic of feminine debate in nineteenth century literature.

Americans unfamiliar with the aristocratic social scale should understand a marquis was one step below a duke, which in turn was only a step below a prince.

Chapter Six

Many of the 1830 social customs of Paris were gleaned from the famous American author, James Fenimore Cooper, who stayed extensively in Paris from 1828-1829. The story about the process of matchmaking and advertisement are taken directly from his travel book (Cooper, *France*, 306).

The turned around social custom of those new in town sending cards to the established French socialites may seem strange to Americans, but Cooper discusses this extensively (Cooper, *France*, 76).

The story of the Marquis is taken from Moliere's seventeenth century play, *Les Precious Provencials*.

Chapter Eight

Hand fans were an important ladies accessory from the 16th century until World War I with the peak of production in the 19th century. The non-verbal language using the fan was extensive and a few of the signals are listed in this chapter. The *eventail* (hand fan) museum in Paris is an enjoyable way to spend 1 - 2 hours. It is small and hard to find, but worth the effort.

Chapter Nine

The *Jardin des Tuileries* is a 63 acre park in central Paris, laid out in the year 1564 adjacent to the new Tuileries palace being built. The name *Tuileries* derives from the kilns for the manufacture of tiles, or *tuiles*, which occupied the site before the palace was built. The garden has been a popular place for strolling and promenading for more than two centuries. However, walking on the grass was traditionally reserved for royalty. The ban continues today, so one does not see anyone walking on the grass as we do in American parks.

In 1830, Paris was behind London in having piped water to homes–few, if any Parisians had indoor plumbing as evidenced by lack of plumbing even to the palace! In contrast, most apart-

204 Ted and Marilyn Bader

ments and homes in London had indoor piped water (Willms, 222), but operational toilets with return to the sewer were yet to be invented thirty years later. However, Paris was the first major city in the world to install gas lighting in 1829, while London was to take another 5 - 10 years to do so.

The *Monitor* was the official government newspaper and on the fateful day of July 26, 1830 it listed the King's plan to dissolve the upcoming deputy congress and censorship of the press.

Chapter Ten

The historical events concerning Charles X are accurately portrayed in this chapter. The interested reader may wish to refer to David Pinkney's detailed account–*The French Revolution of 1830*.

The Palace of St. Cloud is no longer standing as it was razed by fire in 1870, deliberately set by the Prussians during the Franco-Prussian war. The Grand Cascade waterfalls, however, are still functional.

The charter of 1814 formed the post-Napoleanic agreement between France and the Allied Powers as to how the new French government should function. Unfortunately, parts of it were vague, which led to an inevitable difference in interpretation and subsequent rift between the monarchy and deputy congress.

Charles X and family were allowed to emigrate to Great Britain and form exile in Castle Lulworth in the county of Dorset. A return to France by way of a counter-revolution never materialized beyond written plans.

Chapter Eleven

Mr. James Woodforde writes in *The Diary of a Country Parson* (late eighteenth century) about the common remedy for epileptic seizures being *Assafoetida* drops.

Chapter Seventeen

While it is difficult for modern Americans to appreciate, in 1830's England and America only a small percentage of adults could read and write.

Virtue and Vanity

205

The Methodists were among the first to promote Sunday School in the eighteenth century, an effort which was principally a literacy class rather than religious teaching. Even in the 1830's, this was still true.

Methodism was a strong social-religious force at the time of this story, particularly in northern England where Staley Hall is set. As much as 12% of the population of the northern counties were affiliated with them.

While the authors are not Methodist, they share, with the famous French historian, Elie Halevy (see *History of the English People in 1815*) admiration for their social contributions which are often overlooked.

Chapter Eighteen

Social unrest was great in England from the rise of industrialism through the mid-nineteenth century when worker's unions gained legal acceptance.

Control of land was a key issue. Many previous lands, which were considered available for community use and planting, were being privatized with the resulting in reduction of the lower class' already tenuous income. We have tried to show a typical scene of worker unrest. In the early 1830's, window smashing took place at Derby; houses were burnt at Nottingham, and the Duke of Newcastle's Castle was destroyed by fire. (Wearmouth, *Working Class*, 43-44)

Chapter Nineteen

All of the riddles given by Mr. Darcy in this chapter would have been known in 1835. They are derived from Archer Taylor's *English Riddles from Oral Tradition*.

Chapter Twenty-One

Methodists were the first major religious group in England to allow women to teach men and women together. However, their founder, a conservative Anglican priest, John Wesley, did not come to the position easily since this view differed from the Anglican church of the time. However, given the two to one ratio of women to men in the movement and his observation that women leaders,

Ted and Marilyn Bader

when needed on an exceptional basis, brought as good or even better spiritual results as men, he began to allow the practice–but not without grief from his critics. The Methodists were also the first major social group in history to call for universal suffrage (i.e. the right to vote) for all adults, including women. It is true there were a few women voting rights advocates before Methodism, but numerically these latter groups were quite small compared to the hundreds of thousands of Methodists.

In 1739, women were appointed to be the leaders of classes at Bristol. "It might be claimed that emancipation of womanhood began with him [Wesley]." (Wearmouth, *Common People*, 223)

Chapter Twenty-Four

The reader is presented with a typical Methodist class session. Classes consisted of fewer than twenty adults. Classes were subdivisions of a larger society and ultimately one conference. Many later nineteenth century political groups (e.g. Marxists) recognized and patterned their group's structure after the ingenuous Methodist organization.

It is difficult for the modern reader to appreciate the challenges of the social disruption that the production of cheap gin caused in eighteenth and early nineteenth century Britain. Accurate statistics for consumption in the eighteenth century were not kept, but some historians have said that eighteenth century England was the most inebriated country in the history of the world.

Coffee and tea were aggressively promoted in the early nineteenth century as alochol substitutes. There were only eight coffee houses in London in 1805, but more than 800 by the start of Queen Victoria's reign.

Sometimes the local Methodist parson was the only literate man living among the lower industrial class and it often fell to the local pastor to represent the worker's grievances.

The industrial management was backed by the controlling triumvirate of aristocracy, government and state church, which were comprised essentially of the same small number of wealthy individuals.

This social arrangement also explains why most of the early nineteenth century writers (i.e. well to do), wrote in contemptible

Virtue and Vanity

terms about the Methodists, since the latter group was seen as a supporter of both the poor and unions (and thus, a real threat to the ruling aristocracy).

Given that only a few landowners could vote, the British government was not sympathetic to the worker's plight of six day work, sixteen hour days and child labor (often down to age 3 - 5, if they were physically able). Unions were outlawed and attempts to improve conditions jailed many a worker and Methodist pastor.

"The typical miner was drunken, dissolute, and brutalized, tyrannized over by his employers and their underlings. The majority had never received any education whatever. To these people the Methodist class leader or preacher brought the Bible and the Methodist Hymn Book. They were eventually taught to read and reflect. There came to them a desire for learning and for improvement which had to be gratified. They sent their children to the Sunday School, and not content with that, they often accompanied them. Men who had grown up and had children to go to school, have been sitting side by side on a form learning the very rudiments of reading and writing. The miner not only went to school, he took to going to Chapel, and, finding it necessary to appear decent there, he got new clothes and became what is termed respectable." (Wearmouth, *Working Class*, 226)

The aristocratic government was perplexed by these brave Methodist pastors. On one hand they wanted to brand them revolutionaries and ban them; but, learning of their strong loyalty oaths to the king, found no basis to legally persecute them. Eventually, in the latter half of the nineteenth century, unions were legalized and role of the pastors working in unions faded away.

Because of their hard work to improve the conditions of the poor, prison reform and health care (the Methodists were the first to open free health clinics in England), the famous French historian, Halevy, credits the Methodists with preventing the gruesome French revolution from being duplicated in England (see discussion in *Desire and Duty*).

In Cooper's notes on England, which range from 1828-1836, he fully expects that a dramatic revolution would also occur in England due to the great unrest and social injustice (from the viewpoint of an American democrat).

208 Ted and Marilyn Bader

Two quotes from British newspapers in 1831 and 1834:

"distress and starvation now existing among great numbers of the working classes are due to the land being held in the hands of a few, instead of being cultivated for the benefit of the community at large."

"high rents, high tithes, high tolls, high usury (interest rate), high profits and low wages amongst working people are the cause of their poverty." (Wearmouth, *Working Class*, 168)

Works Cited

Cooper, James Fenimore. *Gleanings in Europe: France.* State University of New York Press: Albany, 1981.

Cooper, James Fenimore. *Gleanings in Europe: England.* State Univeristy of New York Press: Albany, 1979.

Halevy, Elie. *A History of the English People in 1815.* Routledge and Kegan Paul Ltd: London, 1987.

Pinkney, David. *The French Revolution of 1830.* Princeton University Press: New Jersey, 1972.

Taylor, Archer. *English Riddles from Oral Tradition.* Octagon Books: New York, 1977.

Wearmouth, Robert. *Methodism and the Common People of the Eighteenth Century.* Epworth Press: London, 1945.

Wearmouth, Robert. *Methodism and the Working-Class Movements in England: 1800-1850.* Augustus Kelley Publishers: Clifton, 1972.

Willms, Johannes. *Paris: Capital of Europe.* Holmes and Meier: New York, 1997.

Woodforde, James. *The Diary of a Country Parson.* Folio Society: London, 1992.

210 Ted and Marilyn Bader

If you enjoyed this story, you will also want to read:
. . .the award winning:
Desire and Duty:
a sequel to Jane Austen's Pride and Prejudice
By: Ted and Marilyn Bader
ISBN #0-9654299-0-3, Hardcover

. . .a reprint of the first ever Jane Austen sequel
Old Friends and New Fancies
An Imaginary Sequel to the Novels of Jane Austen
(originally published in 1913)
By: Sybil G. Brinton
ISBN #0-9654299-1-1, Hardcover

. . .the first in the **Jane Austen Library Series**
(books Jane Austen read and commented on)
Self-Control:
A Novel
(originally published in 1810)
(Jane Austen said she wanted to write a close imitation
of this story)
By: Mary Brunton
ISBN #0-9654299-3-8

Further books in the **Jane Austen Library Series**
will be published beginning in 2001

For information on any of the above titles, contact
your local bookseller or:
Revive Publishing
1790 Dudley Street
Denver, CO 80215 USA
800-541-0558
www.RevivePublishing.com
Contact the authors through the above address or via email
at: Bader_TandM@msn.com